CW00530390

**About**

Susie Murphy is an Irish h.
historical fiction so much that she often wishes she had been
born two hundred years ago. Still, she remains grateful for many
aspects of the modern age, including women's suffrage, electric
showers and pizza. A Class Entwined is her second published
novel.

ISBN-13: 978-1-915770-02-8

**www.susiemurphywrites.com**

Join the Susie Murphy Readers' Club
for updates and free stories:

**https://bit.ly/susie-murphy-readers-club**

# A Class Entwined

## A Matter of Class, Book Two

**Susie Murphy**

**Also by Susie Murphy**

A Class Apart
A Class Forsaken
A Class Coveted
A Class Reunited
A Class Inherited

*To my husband, Bob,*
*for being my rock in wild storms, and for always waiting patiently*
*while I took 'two more minutes' to finish up what I was writing*
*before dinner. (Sorry for all the times dinner went cold.)*

# CHAPTER 1

'Oh, help me, help, I'm going to fall!'

'No, you're not,' Cormac said, doing his best not to wince; the girl's shrill voice was piercing enough to cause earache. 'Just be calm. He won't throw you.'

He tugged gently on the lead rope and continued to guide the horse around the paddock, while Cecily clung to the pommel of her sidesaddle like she expected her mount to buck at any moment. A more mild-mannered horse Cormac had never encountered, so he harboured no concern in that respect, but convincing his student of the same was proving impossible.

'What if a hare runs out in front of us? Or Papa goes shooting pheasants nearby? Or a bee stings him? Oh, oh, I'm so frightened! Please, Cormac, let me down.'

He reiterated his reassurances but refused to give in to her plea. She would never learn if she did not keep trying. And it was past time she did learn. At sixteen, she was woefully uneducated in the art of riding a horse, despite having grown up on an estate which boasted one of the finest studs in the country. But then, she was only a daughter and hence of no great consequence to Lord Strathroy, who had three sons – more than enough offspring to secure the future of Willowmere Estate and Stud.

It was no surprise that Cecily existed so far beneath her father's notice for, aside from being a girl, she was also the most timid creature Cormac had ever encountered. One of the kitchen maids had told him that the young lady seldom ventured out of doors for fear of catching a cold, was afraid of sewing in case she pricked herself, and never once expressed a moment's interest in getting on a horse. That was, the maid had added slyly, until the stable master had hired a new stable hand.

Within a week of gaining his position at Willowmere, Cormac had been informed that the daughter of the house finally wished to learn how to ride and that the task must fall to him to teach her. He had embraced the challenge at first but soon came to loathe the time of day when she arrived at the stables with a simpering smile. The sessions invariably contained much squealing and cowering on her part and sorely tested the limits of his patience. It was repugnant to him who had once known the most fiery female spirit on horseback.

He tightened his grip around the rope until his nails dug into his palm. It was the eleventh time he had thought of Bridget since Cecily's lesson had begun. He tried his hardest to block her out but she always found ways to slip through his defences.

Oakleigh and the events that had transpired there were in the past, he had to remind himself. Now he was a stable hand on a new estate with a new family to serve and a different path to tread, however much he might wish it be otherwise.

Following his banishment from Oakleigh and a period of deep melancholy which he would rather not recall, he had crossed Carlow's south-western border into Kilkenny and reached Willowmere Estate, where, upon his enquiry into any vacant posts in the stables, John Corbett's character reference had played a vital role. His former stable master's glowing account of his diligence and reliability had been sufficient to earn him a trial which had converted to a full position after just two days. He had swiftly gained a reputation for being an adept carpenter as well, and he and his father's tool chest had been put to work on more than one occasion already. He had even met Lord Strathroy when the gentleman had visited the stables to appraise his livestock and believed he had left his employer with a strong impression of his competence.

While he did not suppose he would ever be happy again, he could at least tolerate his new life at Willowmere.

If only Cecily would stop her yammering.

He was about to coax the horse from a walk to a slow trot when, above Cecily's bleats of panic, he heard someone shouting. He turned and saw Lord Strathroy himself striding across the field towards the paddock, waving his arms and bellowing something unintelligible. His noisy approach merely startled Cormac but it gave Cecily a severe shock. With a whimper, she lost her balance and started to slide out of her sidesaddle. He saw it happening and was there in time to catch her. He eased her feet to the ground, which was muddy with recent rain, and she beamed up at him within the circle of his arms.

'Oh, thank you,' she said breathily.

He tried to release her but she kept a tight grip on his shoulders, as though she did not quite trust herself to stand without support.

By this point, Lord Strathroy had reached the paddock's fence. 'Get your hands off her,' he growled.

'Let go, miss,' Cormac said sternly and she loosened her hold with obvious reluctance.

'Cecily,' Lord Strathroy said in chilling tones, 'go back up to the house at once.'

'But Papa, we are not finished—'

His forbidding look quelled her. She gave a frightened squeak and, after a bashful glance up at Cormac, disappeared through the gate in the paddock fence, her boot squelching as it got stuck in a puddle of mud. She peeked one more time over her shoulder and then ran back across the field towards the big house, the long skirts of her riding habit bunched in her fist.

Lord Strathroy stalked into the paddock. Cormac patted the horse's neck and waited for the gentleman to speak. He clutched a piece of paper that had been scrunched into a ball and his features were twisted into an ugly snarl.

'How long did you think you would last?'

Cormac stared. 'M'lord?'

'I am disgusted that one so vile as you has lived three weeks under my protection. Well, no more. You are gone, blackguard, and immediately so.'

Cormac had no response to this incredible defamation. What on earth was he talking about?

'You have nothing to say to defend yourself. That all but confirms that the charges against you are true.'

'M'lord, I haven't said anything 'cause I don't understand you. What charges d'you mean?'

Lord Strathroy brandished the crumpled page at him. 'Deceit. Disloyalty. Dishonour. You are a scoundrel of the highest order.'

'I don't—'

'Does the name *Garrett Lambourne* signify anything to you?'

Cormac's blood ran cold.

'I discern that it does. Further proof, though I had no need of it. How you managed to procure a character, I cannot imagine. Its author must have been coerced into writing it. You shall leave my property at once and never show your face here again. I have Stafford on his way to run you off if necessary.'

'Whatever that letter says, I swear 'tisn't—'

'Do not even attempt to refute its contents,' Lord Strathroy retorted. 'I wholly believe Mr Lambourne's words and count them far higher than those of an ignorant stable hand.'

4

Cormac reached out. 'May I see what crimes I'm supposed to have committed?'

Lord Strathroy laughed without any trace of humour. 'And now you pretend you can read! It would be comical if it was not so repulsive.'

Cormac dropped his hand to his side. 'What does he say?'

Lord Strathroy smoothed out the letter with a flourish. 'That he feels it is his obligation to contact landowners both within the county of Carlow and beyond. It is possible a fellow named Cormac McGovern may come seeking work in the stables but he is not to be trusted for he took advantage of an heiress during his previous employment and had to be expelled from the estate. No young lady is safe in his presence.'

Cormac felt heat rise in his cheeks. 'That's outrageous!'

'Do you deny there was inappropriate conduct between you and the heiress?'

He tried to school his features into bland denial but the lord was not fooled. He went purple with rage.

'To think you have been in Cecily's company these past weeks! What have you done to her? Have you ruined her prospects?' He advanced towards Cormac, eyes bulging at the idea that his daughter's only value as marriage fodder might have been spoiled.

Cormac took a step back. 'I didn't touch her! I'd never—'

'I don't believe you. You had her in your arms just there, and I saw the way she looked at you. Did you defile her?'

Without waiting for an answer, he swung his fist out. Cormac ducked and instinct made him push at his attacker. Lord Strathroy stumbled and regained his balance by grabbing onto the paddock fence.

'And now an assault on my own person,' he said in vindictive triumph. 'Get out of my sight, you miscreant, and never set foot on Strathroy property again.'

Cormac realised that any further effort to argue his case would be useless. There was no convincing the gentleman that he was no danger to his daughter. Apart from the fact that he only viewed Cecily as a source of annoyance, the truth was that there could never be anyone for him but Bridget. However, he had no way of explaining that and, what was more, he could see Lord Strathroy's agent, Mr Stafford, sprinting towards them from the big house and carrying a long, rifle-shaped object against his chest.

'I'll get my things,' he said, resigned to the loss of his employment.

'You shall not. Turn around and be gone this instant.'

'You can't—'

'I damn well can. We shall burn your belongings and hope that your brief spell here will soon be forgotten.'

Mr Stafford came up to the paddock gate, panting. It was indeed a rifle he held. 'My lord?' he said, looking like he was itching to level it at the criminal before him.

Cormac thought of the precious possessions they expected him to leave behind: his father's tool chest, John Corbett's character reference. Where could he go without those? 'Please, if I could just have one minute to get—'

'Stafford,' said Lord Strathroy and the agent handed him the rifle over the fence.

Cormac spun and fled, his humiliation superseded by his fear. Not fully acquainted yet with the terrain around Willowmere, he just opted for the nearest route that would take him far away from Lord Strathroy and his rifle – a copse at the end of the field behind the stables – and hurtled towards it, a warning shot ringing in his ears.

He had nothing but the clothes on his back. He was done for.

# CHAPTER 2

Cormac made for the distant tree line, dashing over the field as fast as he could, and crashed into the undergrowth with his heart pounding and his breath coming in shuddering gasps. Though he didn't think they would follow him, he kept pushing forwards, slapping wayward branches out of his way and imagining that each one bore the face of the fiend known as Garrett Lambourne.

The lengths that gentleman had gone to in order to ruin him were unfathomable. Not content with ensuring Cormac's separation from Bridget and his permanent exile from his home, now he had taken steps to prevent Cormac from making any kind of new life for himself. Garrett was a person of far-reaching influence; no doubt a copy of that wretched letter had been sent to every establishment with a stables within a hundred miles of Oakleigh. Anyone who received it would be on high alert for a stranger seeking work. Cormac could lie about his name but the letter would raise enough suspicion to deter any employer from taking the chance. Garrett had obliterated Cormac's entire livelihood as a stable hand with a ruthless stroke of his pen.

A carpenter without tools was no temptation either. Cormac blazed with rage and distress that the last things belonging to his father were also to be destroyed. In the three years since Jack McGovern's death, Cormac had cherished that tool chest and preserved every implement in its best condition, keeping handles polished, metal clean and blades sharp. He could still recall in perfect detail his father's agile hands, wielding the hammer or the chisel or the saw and showing him how to use each one. Now he pictured them being tossed into a fire, the wood of the chest blackening and disintegrating, and let out an inarticulate scream of grief. Somewhere above him, a startled bird emitted an answering shriek and flapped away through the branches.

When he broke out of the other side of the trees, he found a small lake before him, gentle swells lapping against a reedy shoreline. He knew he should not linger but he stopped to slake his thirst; his throat and lungs burned after the mad sprint for cover. He squatted among the reeds at the water's verge and gulped greedy handfuls of the cold, clear water. Wiping his mouth on his sleeve, he tried to take his bearings but the sky was still overcast following the earlier rain, the unending bank of cloud hanging low and oppressive.

In any case, at that moment he was less concerned with the compass points than with the feeling of despair that was building inside him. It grew and grew, like a colossal wave racing for the seashore, then reared up and crashed over him with enormous force. The weight of it bore him down and he hunched at the edge of the lake, his head heavy in his hands. Mere weeks ago, he had had a mother, three sisters, a nephew, and a girl who loved him. He had had a position of employment, a social standing in his own small way, and a home. Since then, the whole lot had been stripped away, leaving him naked and lost in the world. The desolation he felt was unlike anything he had ever experienced. It was devastation with the complete absence of hope.

When he dragged himself to his feet again, it was not by an impetus to go in any specific direction but by the dim recollection that he didn't have permission to remain where he was. He meandered along the periphery of the lake and up a gorse-covered incline beyond it, without any of the drive that had propelled him forwards through the copse. He had no way of telling precisely when he would pass over Willowmere's borders but he supposed that if the big house was behind him then he could not go far wrong. The rain returned, a light drizzle which spat into his face, and prompted the vague thought that Cecily would be relieved she had gone indoors before the inclement weather could induce an attack of pneumonia.

The rest of the day, and the night which followed, passed by in a haze. He fell into a dreamlike state where nothing was real except for the notion of keeping his body moving. He crossed fields, streams, lanes and woods but took no notice of the landscape around him; so long as the ground supported him, he did not care whether it was wet or dry, soft or hard. Exhaustion threatened to take him over but he kept going mechanically, one painful step after another. It wasn't until the morning of the next day, when he tripped over a tree root and fell sprawling to the ground, that he considered taking a rest. Then the tiredness washed over him so powerfully that he just lay where he had fallen and allowed sleep to pull him into oblivion.

When he awoke, it was nearing dusk, the sun a low, orange orb in a sky clear of cloud. He sat up stiffly. He was in a large meadow where a scattering of cows grazed in the distance. The wide-spreading canopy of a horse chestnut towered above him; several sore spots along his back informed him that he had been lying on a bed of fallen conkers. Though the rain had stopped, his clothes felt damp and chilly against his skin.

A ravenous growl alerted him to his empty, aching stomach; it had been almost two days since he had eaten. Hopelessness may have dulled his spirit but it had not abated the demands of his body. He regarded the cows with closer attention. Cows meant a farm, and a farm meant people, and people meant food.

He struggled to his feet and, to gain a more elevated view of the landscape, clambered awkwardly into the branches of the tree, many of them bare as their leaves had begun to drop for the winter. Sure enough, a thin plume of smoke coiled skywards on the horizon beyond the grazing animals. His gnawing insides clenched with relief. He jumped back down to the ground, numb limbs quivering upon impact, and set off across the meadow. The cows turned their heads lazily as he passed. He tried to ignore his frozen extremities and chattering teeth – if he was cold now in October, he did not care to imagine what December might feel like.

After crossing two more fields, he distinguished a cluster of farm buildings through the twilight. It was not a large homestead – just the main house, from which the chimney smoke issued, and a number of sheds nearby – but its swept yard and clean windows spoke of a proud proprietor. As he approached, a broad-shouldered woman emerged from the front door of the farmhouse. She strode over to one of the sheds, opened it, and shooed a brood of flapping hens inside. Shutting the shed door against the gathering night, she turned to go back to the house.

Taking a deep breath for courage, Cormac called, ''Scuse me,' and stepped forwards into the yard.

She started and squinted into the gloom. Suspicion and distaste coloured her features. Did he look that much like a beggar already?

'Go away,' she said. 'We don't want any trouble here.'

He did not know what he should say. Though he came from a humble background, his family had never been so poor that he had been forced to beg. This was a new and altogether degrading experience for him.

'Please,' he said. 'I need something to eat, that's all.'

'We don't feed tramps.' She started hurrying towards the house.

'Then just give me some directions,' he said loudly.

She stopped and looked back, curiosity getting the better of her. 'Where to?'

'Dublin,' he replied without hesitation.

There was nothing for him in the countryside. If he stayed here, he would starve. He might have had a better chance of surviving if it were summer and the bushes and trees were laden with fruit. But the end of autumn was drawing near and whatever fruit had not already been taken by the birds was falling to the ground to rot. He needed to make his way to a place of civilisation which could offer the prospect of obtaining some kind of labour. Failing that, at least he could scrounge through rubbish for food or – he desperately hoped it would not come to it – steal.

The woman snorted and folded her brawny arms. 'Don't be foolish. 'Tis several days' walk and you've got no food.'

'I'm going to try,' he said, wondering how far he had wandered in his dazed state. Just his luck to have strayed further from the city instead of nearer. 'Please can you tell me which way I should take?'

She stared at him, assessing his scruffy appearance, his polite manners, and the determined set of his jaw. Then she tutted in irritation and, without a word, stalked back to the house and disappeared inside. He dithered – should he wait, or give up and leave?

His patience was rewarded when her stout form reappeared at the front door, silhouetted by candlelight. She carried a small sack in one hand and a folded blanket in the other, both of which she held out to him. He stumbled up to the doorstep and accepted them, feeling a mixture of shame and deepest gratitude.

'You guilted me into it,' she said with a frown. 'I'd never have peace of mind if I let you attempt a journey like that without giving you some kind of help. You'll find apples and some bread and cheese in the sack. The blanket isn't very thick but 'tis better than no blanket at all. You'll need it, 'tis going to freeze over the next night or two.'

Gaping at her generosity, he managed to stutter, 'Th-thank you.'

She nodded, still looking annoyed at herself. 'As for directions, 'tisn't complicated. Go across the land north-east from here. After about a mile, you'll come to an untilled field of weeds which belongs to the farmer next to us. He's too elderly to till it himself and too miserly to sell it to anyone else. Next to the field, you'll find a crossroads. The main road will start you along the route towards Dublin. Now, go before my husband comes home and sees what I've done.'

He stammered his thanks once more and hastened from the farmyard. Using the emerging stars to guide him in a north-easterly direction, he passed a pond, its surface like black glass, and climbed over a stile into another field. He wanted to keep going but, now that he had food in his grasp, his hunger overwhelmed him. Crouching in the shelter of a hedge, he wolfed down two wizened apples (looking like the last of the autumn crop) and some of the bread (fresh enough that it might have been baked that morning) before he remembered that he should ration his provisions to make them last as long as possible. Resolutely, he tied up the sack, though his stomach ached for more nourishment, and stood again.

The woman's forecast about the weather had been correct – the air was growing even colder as night fell fully. He wrapped the blanket around his shoulders, loose strands of material scratching the skin at the nape of his neck. Marching across the field at a quick pace, leg muscles straining after two extended spells of motion and inertia outdoors, he headed for the crossroads.

# CHAPTER 3

The tea tray rested on a low table by her knee, tea cup full and biscuits untouched. A fire blazed in the hearth and a soft blanket covered her lap but still she felt the November chill seep into her bones. With the passage of every second, the ticking of the pendulum clock on the wall beat loud and relentless in her ears, drowning out the sounds of the bustling Berkeley Square beyond the windows.

The drawing room door opened. Bridget did not turn her head but a figure stepped into her peripheral vision and stood there waiting until she dragged her gaze away from the fireplace. It was her new housemaid, Lizzie. The girl had bad skin, her forehead, nose and cheeks marred by a haphazard sprawl of pockmarks and pimples, but it was self-consciousness which made her face so red.

'Begging your pardon, mistress,' she said with an awkward curtsey. 'I can't help noticing you ain't had nuffin to eat nor drink.'

Bridget didn't speak for a while, counting the clock beats until the maid would fade from view.

'I was not hungry or thirsty,' she said at last when it became clear Lizzie was staying put.

'But you ain't had nuffin for breakfast neither. And hardly a scrap at dinner yesterday evening. You need to eat something.'

Although she tried to appreciate the maid's concern, she could only muster a sense of mild irritation. 'I shall eat when I feel like it.'

She waved languidly in dismissal but Lizzie stood her ground, clutching at the folds of her apron.

'The tea'll be cold by now. I'll fetch you a fresh cup. And if you ain't liking these biscuits, Muss-yoor Lévêque can make you something else. A bowl of broth? Anything you fancy, mistress, I can get it for you.'

'I am fine. I do not desire anything.' Though a lie in general terms, it was true for the purposes of this conversation. She genuinely had no appetite. Whenever she tried to force down even a morsel, it roiled in her stomach until it came back up again.

'But you must look after yourself, mistress.' Lizzie gulped, gathering her courage. 'You're wasting away.'

Bridget supposed that a proper mistress would remonstrate her servant for the effrontery of such a comment. However, she glanced down at her thin arms and knew the girl was right – and yet she could not stir herself to care. She no longer paid heed to any part of her existence. Her lady's maid dressed her and her butler announced dinner and her housemaid reminded her to retire to her bedchamber, and that was all. She had stopped weeping every night in the confines of her lonely bed because the effort of it had become too much. Now she just did nothing and thought of nothing. To think would be to face the grief and the guilt, and that would finish her.

'I do not want—' she said faintly, but Lizzie's nerve held out.

'I'm going to refill the tray,' she said, voice firm. 'Would you like anything in particular?'

Bridget had no energy to heave a sigh, but a tiny breath of exasperation escaped her. 'Some broth would be nice, thank you.'

She remained motionless after Lizzie departed from the room. Her correspondence also lay on the low table but she disregarded the two letters arrayed neatly side by side. By the writing styles of the addresses, she recognised one author as Miss Madeleine Wallace, her closest friend during the seven years she had spent in Dublin, and the other as her mother, now residing full time at Oakleigh. However, neither held any appeal, when she could only presume the former to contain a dramatic string of trivialities and the latter to be as cold as her bones.

She did not react when Lizzie scurried back into the room and set down the replenished tray, now bearing a bowl of steaming beef broth, but she blinked when the girl knelt beside her and lifted the spoon to her lips.

Lizzie gave her a lopsided smile. 'I'm determined to get you to eat, mistress, even if I have to feed you myself.'

Had Bridget not felt so numb, she would have cried at the despair and the shame of it all. But she just opened her mouth to accept the spoonful of broth and swallowed, like a child.

She made it through half the bowl before she refused to take any more. Still, Lizzie looked quite satisfied.

'The master'll be pleased,' she said, dropping the spoon back onto the tray.

Bridget's fingers twitched. 'He spoke to you about me?'

'He's worried about you, mistress. We all are.'

She shrugged. If Garrett was worried, it was probably about what society would think were his wife to be found starving in their own house. London would get weeks out of that bit of gossip.

Lizzie stood and picked up the tray with a hopeful expression. 'Now you've eaten something, would you feel equal to going for a stroll in the gardens across the way?'

Bridget looked away. 'Did *he* suggest that?'

'No, mistress, I did. I open the windows in here every morning but it ain't no match for the proper outdoors. It'd do you a world of good.'

'Perhaps another day.'

And she was left in solitude to stare at the fire, listen to the clock, and sense neither heat nor time.

The door opened again.

'I'm not hungry, Lizzie.'

'It's not Lizzie.'

Garrett came around into her line of sight and took the chair at the other side of the fireplace.

'Is this some sort of protest?'

She didn't reply.

'If it is, you will achieve nothing by it. You need to stop this absurd behaviour.'

Her stomach churned. She imagined the broth sloshing around inside it, masticated meat tossing in bile-coloured juices, and closed her eyes against the sickening image.

'Forget him, damn you!'

Her eyelids flew open. Garrett was sitting forward, hands clenched and jaw line rigid.

'He's *gone*. You cannot get him back, so wake up from this trance and let us move on with our lives. I am weary of living with a ghost.'

It was the first time he had alluded to Cormac since they had left Oakleigh, preferring on the whole to act as though the events of the summer had not occurred. His capacity to ignore reality's more disagreeable aspects was remarkable, given that he had married her, even though she was not a virgin, and then brought her from Dublin to London, despite the fact that the move was blatantly against her will. But it seemed there was a limit to his talent, and the skeleton in his drawing room was it.

'What would you have me do?'

'Your duty. Be my wife.'

She had fulfilled her wifely obligations a number of times after their wedding but not since their arrival in London, where they kept separate bedchambers. Was that all he sought?

'Very well. Tonight, if you wish it.'

His gaze hardened further. He detested this, having to ask for her cooperation in the matter. With his silky, jet-black hair and captivating hazel eyes, he had never had to solicit such attention in his life.

He folded his arms. 'If we must negotiate it thus, then so be it. I shall come to you.'

He stalked out of the room and she sank back into her chair, relieved to be alone again.

The relief did not last long. The broth still bothered her stomach and a surge of queasiness sent waves of heat over her, making her skin clammy and her head dizzy. She would need to lie down until it passed. She pushed the blanket off her lap, rose shakily to her feet, and went out into the hallway. Praying no one would come upon her in this state, she took the stairs one slow step at a time. Her legs wobbled and her insides pitched about, reminding her of the unpleasant sea crossing from Ireland.

She entered her bedchamber but, instead of dropping down onto the bed, she fell to her knees, dragged the chamber pot out from under it, and expelled the contents of her stomach. It came out in sour, watery spurts and she gasped in misery and disgust. The smell was horrible. She crawled away towards the bell pull on the wall. Lacking the strength to stand, she moaned and stretched up to tug on its tasselled end.

Lizzie came running. 'Oh, mistress!' she exclaimed. 'I'll remove it at once.'

She returned with a clean pot and a damp cloth which she pressed to Bridget's forehead. Bridget did not protest; it felt cool and soothing.

Lizzie coughed discreetly. 'Mistress?'

'Mmm?'

'Do you think you might be with child?'

Bridget gaped at her.

Lizzie coloured, the pimples on her face turning redder too. 'I remember what it was like for my mother when she was carrying my youngest brother. She was sick for months. You ain't as bad as her, but it might be a possibility, if...'

If Bridget had had relations with a man. She had.

Her breath hitched in her throat.

Two men, in fact.

Her heart raced. 'How can I tell how long it's been?'

'It's hard to know. Do you remember when you last had your courses?' Lizzie's blush deepened even more. This was far beyond her remit as a housemaid.

Bridget tried to recall the last time she had noticed the blood. Never in London, that was certain. They had spent a month in Dublin around the wedding but she had no recollection of seeing it then either. Could it be as far back as Oakleigh? If that was the case...

'Thank you for bringing this to my attention,' she said and took the maid's arm to struggle upright. 'Please keep it to yourself for now. I shall inform my husband once I am very sure.'

Lizzie nodded. 'Can I do anything else for you, mistress?'

She looked ready for the usual dismissal but Bridget said, 'Yes, I would like hot water for a bath. I feel grimy after sitting idle for so long. Lay out a fresh gown for me and have Monsieur Lévêque prepare something that will be easier for my stomach to tolerate. Some dry toast, perhaps, and a cup of very weak tea. Can you do that?'

'Of course!' The girl looked ecstatic as she bounded out of the bedchamber.

Bridget stumbled over to the bed and sat on the edge, cradling her still-flat belly. 'I'm sorry. I didn't know you were there and I neglected you. But I will get healthy again for your sake. I promise.'

She had thought her life was empty, that *she* was empty. Far from it. Hope flickered within her; perhaps all was not lost as she had believed. She could make enquiries, send out letters in an attempt to locate Cormac. Maybe, by a miracle as great as the one growing inside her, she would find him.

She had been standing on a precipice but now she scrambled back from the plunging darkness beyond. This baby would keep her alive.

# CHAPTER 4

'Get off my property!'

Cormac struggled into consciousness as something hard dug into his side. He looked around with blurry eyes and discerned a burly figure standing over him, brandishing a shovel.

'You heard me.' The man's voice was rough. 'Get out of here!'

Cormac clambered clumsily to his feet, his thin blanket slipping from his shoulders to the ground. He had been curled up on the man's doorstep, taking what little shelter he could from the freezing night. Now he gathered up the blanket and staggered away with the man's words ringing in his ears.

'Don't you come back here again!'

Out on the open street, the bitter wind cut into him. He would need to find another refuge or suffer through the remainder of the night exposed to the cold. He felt so exhausted at this late, dark hour that even the cobblestones looked inviting, but he wrapped his blanket around himself and lurched onwards.

Two streets over, he passed by a church with a welcoming porch but did not stop; he had learned the hard way that the porch was the territory of a belligerent crone with a crutch and a viciously-accurate swing. As he blew on his hands to warm them, he walked through a pool of light cast by a gas lamp. Upon his arrival to Dublin, he had stared in awe at the extraordinary

21

spectacle of street lighting – now he plodded beneath without an upwards glance.

Further on, he came upon a greengrocer's shop, silent and shuttered on the corner of the street. Though it was his first winter in the city, he had learned quickly that the alleys behind such establishments, where rubbish tended to accumulate, were popular scavenging grounds for the homeless. The competition for scraps was fierce but he deemed it unlikely that anyone would be there at this time of night; the rest of the city's impoverished denizens would have enough sense to be holed up somewhere out of the cold.

His mouth watered as he imagined what pickings he might find behind the shop if he was lucky, and he decided to put aside his search for shelter in the hope of abating his ever-present hunger. He crept around to the back of the building and entered the alleyway. With one disappointed glance, he saw that he was not the first to come here tonight – the waste from the shop was strewn all over the filthy alley, as though it had been flung about during a very thorough search.

Not to be deterred, he dropped to his knees and began his own hunt for food, rummaging through the piles of refuse with shaky hands. He yelped when his thumb scraped something sharp. Groping more carefully, he uncovered a broken length of wood, several nails jutting out of it at bent angles. It looked like part of a crate that had once held fruit or vegetable produce. Had any of its contents been thrown out with it?

He continued to fumble around, and his dubious reward for his patience was the discovery of three shrunken potatoes which had been trampled into the dirt, evidently dismissed by the previous forager as inedible. He had no such dignity left to him. He pried the potatoes from the grimy ground, gave them a cursory wipe with his fingers, and choked them down. It was better fare than nothing at all and he cast his gaze upwards with a mumbled prayer of thanks.

He gave the alley another appraising look. Here was as good a place to sleep as any, he supposed. Gathering mounds of the rubbish together, he fashioned a sort of nest against the back wall of the shop and huddled down into it with his blanket over him.

He had never felt less like a human being.

It was either December or January; he could not be certain because he had lost track of the days, each one dissolving miserably into the next. Had he heard the church bells ringing in the new year? He could not recall. He only knew that mere months had passed since he had left the Oakleigh Estate, and yet it seemed like it had happened a hundred years ago to somebody else.

He often called to mind his brief encounter with the woman on the farm for that had been the last occasion when he had witnessed any act of compassion. Dublin had proved to be an unforgiving place. Arriving on the cusp of winter, he had found the city inhospitable and bleak with not a soul willing to lend a helping hand.

It was laughable to expect that he might gain employment anywhere. His trek from the countryside had taken its toll; the weather had been harsh, his rations had depleted too quickly, and he had reached Dublin in a dreadful state, unkempt, dirty and malnourished. His desperate enquiries at mews behind grand townhouses had been fruitless – no stable master would consider him for an instant. Acquiring labour at the docklands was even less likely; though he was young and opportunities were available, the local men were always given precedence and an interloper like himself didn't stand a chance. So he endured destitution on the streets, scrounging for scraps and skulking on doorsteps, and strove to convince himself that remaining in the countryside would have been worse.

He tried not to think too much about his past life or the people he had known then. The loss of human companionship cut him bone deep now that not another sinner ever spoke to him, except to tell him to clear off. He sorely missed his friend Liam, and the stable master John Corbett, who had once confessed his hope of seeing Cormac become stable master himself at Oakleigh one day. What a fine future that would have been.

Even harder to bear were memories of his dear mother and his sisters. His older sister Mary entered his mind more often than any of the others, because he was now walking the streets she had previously walked herself. She, too, had come to Dublin with no position and no place to stay; she, too, had experienced the brunt of the pitiless city. But she had eventually obtained employment and lodgings at a baker's and, regardless of how badly they had treated her, that was still a stroke of luck he had yet to receive himself. She had also found brief happiness in the arms of an upper class gentleman, although he had turned out to be a blackguard who had subsequently abandoned her and Patrick, their newborn son. Recalling how the despair of that had ultimately brought about the sad end to her life, Cormac revised his earlier assessment; Mary's luck had been no better than his own. He tucked her back into the recesses of his mind, unwilling to remember any more.

Of Bridget he blocked out all thoughts.

The pale light of dawn came, accompanied by yet another voice telling him to beat it or the dog would be set on him. He pushed the rubbish aside and shuffled away.

His breath puffed out in clouds as he trudged along the quays, the stink of the River Liffey pungent in his nostrils. It was no better than himself, which shamed him, but there was no way to get clean, not in this city. He peered over the quay wall into the river's murky depths – a dip in there would leave him grimier than before. Mercifully, he did not have to rely on the Liffey for drinking water; fountains dotted around the city meant that at least his thirst, if not his hunger, could be alleviated with little trouble.

The wind gusted up the river, stinging his cheeks with the promise of snow. During his childhood at Oakleigh, a snowfall had always been a tremendous surprise and delight. Now he regarded the prospect with trepidation, given that he could not skip home to a solid roof and a warm fire.

As he wandered into the maze of cobbled streets beside the quays, he became aware of the cramps burgeoning in his stomach: the price of eating soiled, uncooked potatoes. With a groan, he slumped onto a step in front of a boarded-up doorway to wait for the pains to pass.

An intermittent squeak drew his attention to an old man in tattered garb traipsing up the street and towing a small wagon. He had a long beard matted with dirt, and a grubby sheet of canvas was stretched across the hidden contents in the wagon bed. Cormac's carpenter instincts compelled him to assess the condition of the wagon; one of the wheels wobbled perilously on its axle, and the front section of the wagon had a large crack down the middle – a violent jolt on the cobblestones could split it apart. Despite the man's evident homelessness, he had somehow acquired a variety of mysterious items to fill his laden wagon, making him an object of acute envy to those who had nothing. Two or three barefoot children shadowed him, their covetous eyes on the covered mound, but he was wise to them and shouted abuse over his shoulder to scare them off.

He steered the wagon carelessly past Cormac and the wheels ran over Cormac's toes.

'Ow!' he protested.

The old man turned back and waggled thick eyebrows at him. 'You got something to say to me, boy?'

His self-assurance gave Cormac the impression that this was a king of the Dublin streets and not someone to be crossed. In any case, he had no inclination to assault an elderly fellow, even if he looked like he could fight back tooth and nail.

'No,' he muttered.

The man scratched his nose. He wore frayed, fingerless gloves and his nails were black.

'You new?'

'New enough.'

'Seems maybe you could do with a bit of help.'

'You offering?'

The man hawked and spat a gobbet of phlegm on the ground. 'I don't give nothing without getting something back. What can you offer me?'

Cormac was about to slouch back against the doorway – he had nothing, after all – until his gaze landed on the wagon. The wheel was beyond his skill to repair but a flash of inspiration made him point at the front section.

'That's soon going to break apart. You've got too much weight on it. I can fix it for you.'

The old man's eyes lit up. 'Can you indeed?'

'Depends. If there's something under that canvas I can use as a hammer, then maybe I can.'

'A hammer's no good without nails,' the man scoffed.

'You worry about the hammer, I'll worry about the nails.'

The man considered him for a moment, then crouched down beside his wagon. He lifted up the edge of the canvas, squinted at Cormac to make sure he wasn't sneaking a look, and poked around inside. At length, he produced a rusted chunk of scrap iron with a flourish.

'How's this?'

Cormac recalled his father's polished, balanced hammer with a pang of longing. 'I'll manage.'

'So what about the nails? Going to produce them from your backside?'

'I'm going to get them now. Can I borrow the, uh, hammer?'

The old man looked outraged. 'You trying to steal from me, boy?'

Cormac shrugged. 'No, but you can come with me if you don't trust me.'

He tied his blanket around his waist and set off without looking back. After a short pause, he heard a sporadic squeak trailing after him. He was glad; it might prove worthwhile to be owed a favour from someone with clout on the merciless streets of Dublin. At the very least, the venture would distract him from his stomach cramps.

He found his way back to the greengrocer's, now busy with its first shoppers of the morning. Sidling into the alleyway, he discovered that no one had troubled to clear it up yet and he stooped to search through the scattered waste. He located the broken piece of crate with a triumphant grunt and unearthed another beside it, which he hadn't noticed in the dark. Half a dozen battered nails protruded from the two lengths of wood.

'You here again? I told you to beat it!'

The greengrocer's incensed exclamation was followed by his shout for his dog. Cormac snatched the wood and ran.

The old man had waited at the head of the alleyway, too cautious to bring his wagon into the tight space. Cormac jerked his head up the street and they put some distance between themselves and the angry greengrocer, halting on the next corner where a fishwife was yelling lustily to passersby, thrusting her hand out to the wares on display in her wheelbarrow. Cormac breathed in the salty smell of fresh fish greedily but she took one look at him and his companion and pushed her barrow away, nose wrinkling.

Shoving thoughts of a nourishing meal and a sated appetite out of his mind, he turned to the old man and said, 'Let me have that hammer now.'

Seeing that he was in earnest, the man handed over his precious lump of iron, albeit with a glare that warned against any contemplation of theft. Cormac knelt and first tackled the task of removing the nails from the wood. Most had been pulled halfway loose whenever the crate had been forced open but it still took a good deal of persuasion, a few whacks from the makeshift hammer and some skinned fingers before he could prise them all out. He hissed and cursed when his thumb scraped the rough, wooden surface and acquired two splinters. The man let out a callous chuckle but Cormac ignored him, determined to finish now that he had started.

He used the piece of iron to straighten out what nails he could, discarding one that was too crooked to be salvaged. Then he squatted in front of the wagon, got the man to hold one of the boards across the split section and banged a nail into place. It was a shoddy job, with none of the finesse he could have achieved with the right materials and tools, but, by the time he had finished, the two lengths of wood were attached to the wagon and the nails, though awry, were in no danger of falling out.

He stepped back from his handiwork and the old man pushed the wagon backwards and forwards, testing its mobility. He cast Cormac a pleased glance.

'Nice work, boy.' He pointed at the chunk of iron. 'Now give me that.'

Cormac handed it over and the man secreted it beneath the canvas again. When he straightened up, spine cracking in several places, his expression was pensive.

'You hungry?'

'D'you have any reason to believe I'm standing here with a full stomach?'

The man barked a laugh, hoarse and humourless. 'That I don't. But I been 'round long enough to know the best places to get food, don't you reckon?'

'I suppose you have.' Cormac leaned against the wall and folded his arms. His intuition told him that the more eager he appeared, the less forthcoming his companion would be.

The man sniffed. 'Seeing as you did me a good turn, I'll do you one. I know a place where they'll give you hot, tasty soup for free.'

'Sounds like a tall tale to me.'

The man rubbed his beard and a few crumbs of dirt drifted down onto his shabby coat. 'It's no tale. You head up past the castle and you'll find them. A nice-looking building with big double doors and a shiny plaque. No idea what it says, mind, but they're very generous to folks like us. You want to pay them a visit?'

'I might do, sometime.' Cormac itched to make for the place at once but strove to maintain his air of nonchalance. 'Thanks for the advice.'

'Thanks for fixing my wagon.' As the old man trudged away, accompanied by the ever-present squeak, he muttered, 'And we'll see if you're desperate enough to take the soup.'

Once he was gone from sight, Cormac turned and hastened in the other direction. He knew where Dublin Castle was, of course – he could not wander the city streets and fail to notice that impressive edifice, which managed to dwarf even Oakleigh in stature and grandeur. He searched the warren of lanes beyond it with an attentiveness to his surroundings which he lacked in his usual, aimless ramblings. It took some time to locate the place and he began to suspect the old man had deceived him, but eventually he found it tucked down a narrow street; it had a welcoming facade of scrubbed steps and a gleaming, bronze plaque which proclaimed it as the site for the 'Grace of God Mission Society'. Seeing this undeniable proof that the old man had been telling the truth, he had to restrain himself from running up the steps.

Despite the cold weather, the double doors were wide open in invitation. He edged inside and met a woman wearing a spotless apron.

'Do come in,' she greeted him warmly, betraying no acknowledgement of the smell that wafted in with him. 'You're hungry, no doubt. Would you like something to eat?'

'Yes, please,' he said, feeling his lips stretch into something like a smile.

'What lovely manners you have. Come along and I'll show you where you can get some soup.'

She guided him down a hall and into a large room filled with long tables and benches. A vast fireplace dominated one wall and threw out so much heat that it made him momentarily dizzy. Several ragged individuals sat at the benches, eating soup from big bowls; there were a couple of adults but most were children and youths. Two clergymen sat among them, reading to them from Bibles. The woman in the apron beckoned to one and he desisted from his preaching to come over to her.

'We have a new boy, Deacon,' she said. 'I'll go and fetch him a bowl of soup now.'

She bustled away as the deacon turned to Cormac.

'I'm Deacon Haybury,' he said and shook Cormac's hand, showing no distaste at the grime. 'You are very welcome here. Come sit.'

He led the way to a bench near the fireplace and Cormac dropped onto it gratefully, untying the blanket from his waist and relishing the thawing effects of the fire on his back. He couldn't understand why the place wasn't teeming with people – it was a paradise compared to the desolate streets outside.

The woman came back and set a spoon and a bowl of mouth-watering soup, thick with vegetables, in front of him.

'You eat your fill and there's more if you want it,' she said with a kindly touch of his arm and she departed again, presumably to resume her post at the front door.

Cormac seized the spoon, wondering how long Deacon Haybury would stay beside him. He wanted to guzzle the soup in a most indecorous way but really couldn't in the presence of a man of the cloth.

Unfortunately, the deacon settled himself on the bench beside him. 'What is your name?'

'Cormac,' he replied, resigned to taking a more reserved approach to his first proper meal in over two months.

'Just before you start to eat, Cormac, I wish to say first of all that the Grace of God Mission Society is delighted to accept you, and we are committed to looking after both your physical and spiritual health. But you must answer one question for me. Are you of the Catholic faith?'

Cormac dipped the spoon in the soup, loading it with hunks of carrot and turnip. 'I am.'

'To be very clear, we are more than willing to feed you, but we cannot allow you to remain here as a Catholic. However, if you convert to our beliefs then we shall welcome you into the fold as one of our own and you will never again have to worry about where your next meal will come from.'

Cormac's gaze snapped from his spoon to the deacon. 'What?'

The deacon looked both patient and regretful, as though this scene was not unfamiliar to him. 'Yes, we espouse the Protestant doctrine here and can only assist members of our own congregation. But converting is a straightforward process and your body and soul will be the better for it.'

The hunger pangs in Cormac's belly warred with his conscience but it was a short battle. The deacon might as well have asked him to relinquish one of his limbs.

With a longing glance, he let the spoon drop back into the soup with a splash.

'Don't make any hasty decisions,' Deacon Haybury advised. 'The streets are a frozen and barren wasteland. This institution can be your saving grace.'

'I can't,' Cormac said simply and grabbed his blanket.

He stalked from the room, marched past the woman in the apron without even looking at her, and emerged onto the steps to realise that the first few snowflakes had begun to fall. The icy air slapped his face, excruciating after the blazing fire he had left behind. He pulled his blanket tight around his shoulders and stamped away.

Rage burned inside him. The old man knew. He had to have known. A fine trick to play on the young, green, unsuspecting fool who had the naïveté to do him a kindness and expect some in return. Well, he had learned his lesson, and he would be giving the bastard a piece of his mind if he ever saw him again.

That happened only three or four days later. He was passing the fishwife's corner when he stumbled upon the old man, sprawled on the ground, eyes staring up to the sky. Whether it was as a result of age, cold or ill health, Cormac could not tell. However it had come about, the king was dead. He was now no more than food for the crows and pickings for the homeless whom he had lorded over.

His wagon lay on its side next to him, ransacked and abandoned. The canvas had been ripped away, revealing that he had been hoarding nothing but the most worthless detritus scavenged from the streets – the chunk of iron had probably been his most valuable possession and it was gone. Someone had swiped his coat but they had left the tattered, fingerless gloves. Cormac debated the morals behind thieving from a corpse, decided the man still owed him a good deed, and peeled the gloves off his rigid hands. He pulled them on and then patted him on the shoulder, his cruelty forgiven. There was no sense in harbouring animosity towards the dead.

At least he had the questionable luck to still be alive.

# CHAPTER 5

Bridget cast a nervous glance around the assemblage of ladies. They were gathered in small groups at round tables and their incessant chatter filled the air like an invisible swarm of bees. Footmen hovered about, ready to refill a glass or pick up a dropped handkerchief. Fragrant flowers decorated the tables and the weak, early spring sunshine fell in through long windows down one side of the room. She felt as discomfited as she had on the day of the debutantes ball at Dublin Castle, when she had been sixteen and bereft of any trace of sophistication or social ease. But she had promised herself she would make an effort to live again. And living in London meant going out in society.

She searched the crowd for the one face she would recognise and was relieved to espy that distinctive nose, a good deal larger than the average but borne by its owner with admirable aplomb. Lady Newby was the wife of a close acquaintance of Garrett's; he had orchestrated the introduction once Bridget had shown she was endeavouring to lift the fog of gloom that shrouded her. Her new friend had vowed to facilitate her immersion into the most privileged London circles, and this included securing her an invitation to a charity event organised by the Ladies of Compassion Association.

Lady Newby was sitting near the long windows with two other companions. She spotted Bridget and gave an enthusiastic wave. Plucking up her courage, Bridget weaved her way among the tables to join them.

'Mrs Lambourne, I am so glad you could come! Do sit down. This is Lady Radcliffe and Miss Caulfield.'

Bridget took the empty chair between the two ladies she did not know. Lady Radcliffe, dressed in the height of fashion, was a beauty and comported herself with the confidence of one who knew it. Miss Caulfield, on the other hand, had mousy features and her clothes, while by no means shabby, were decidedly less fashionable. She cast Bridget a timid smile and then dropped her gaze as Lady Radcliffe leaned forward, intent on interrogating the new addition to their group. She had soon elicited the salient information needed to establish Bridget's credentials, including her childhood at Oakleigh (a rustic upbringing but not unsalvageable), her coming out in Dublin (a crucial step up in the world), and her recent marriage to the heir to the viscountcy of Wyndham (an estimable match which merited a high level of respect).

'And you are not long in London, Lucy has told us. How do you like it? You doubtless find it a marked improvement from the quaintness of Irish society!' Lady Radcliffe's laugh tinkled like the chime of a bell.

Aware of Ireland's inferior status in the eyes of the English aristocracy, Bridget had prepared herself to encounter such blatant denigration of her country.

'We arrived in October,' she said with extreme civility, 'but I have not had much opportunity yet to enjoy the delights of the city. I have been rather poorly these past months and am only lately back to good health.'

Although the curve of her belly was still neat enough to be concealed beneath her full skirts, the ladies added the necessary facts together – a new bride, a sea crossing, a prolonged illness – to make the correct assumption that she must be with child, and they required no further explanation.

'Do not fret, you have not missed a great deal.' Lady Radcliffe spoke with the earnestness of one assuring another that the death of a beloved relative had not occurred. 'Many of us are just returning to the city after having spent the winter on our country estates. But the season will begin soon and I declare I will do my utmost as always to make it a memorable one.'

Lady Newby grinned at Bridget. 'An invitation to a party at the Radcliffe residence is considered the most coveted prize in the social calendar.'

Lady Radcliffe affected a modest expression. 'I merely endeavour to promote the entertainment of my guests. And, of course, to secure a husband for Alice.'

Miss Caulfield went pink at this. 'Oh, I—no, Cassandra—that is—'

'Come now, dearest,' said Lady Radcliffe, pressing a quelling hand over her friend's. 'You are out three seasons already. You cannot hide in the corner of the ballroom forever. For a suitor to offer for you, he must be able to *see* you.'

Miss Caulfield looked around in desperation. 'I wonder when the speaker is going to come?'

Her deliverance appeared in the form of the leader of the association – 'Lady Ainsley,' murmured Lady Newby to Bridget – a rigid-shouldered lady who entered the room accompanied by a woman in drab clothing with a mannish sort of face. They walked to a dais beyond the top cluster of tables and Lady Ainsley compressed her lips primly together until silence fell.

'Ladies, thank you all for coming. I applaud your eagerness to support the efforts of this association in alleviating the deplorable plight of the poor in London. Allow me to introduce

Miss Blythe. She has petitioned to speak to us today as a representative from St Swithun's Workhouse and Soup Kitchen.'

Lady Ainsley stepped back to make way for the speaker. Miss Blythe stumbled as she climbed onto the dais and Lady Radcliffe tittered behind her napkin. Undeterred by her clumsiness, Miss Blythe cleared her throat.

'I am here to talk about a very important matter,' she said in a deep voice, 'that of poverty relief in this city. St Swithun's is only one of many institutions and it distresses me to describe the appalling things I see there each day. The people who come to our soup kitchen are in rags, barefoot, emaciated from hunger. In the workhouse itself, diseases of every kind run rampant and we cannot keep vermin out of the building.'

Bridget saw several of the ladies shudder in revulsion. They had not bargained on such a vivid account of the poor people's troubles; it was incongruous with this sunlit room filled with pretty hats and dainty china cups.

Miss Blythe carried on relentlessly. 'The accommodation situation is outrageous. They sleep four, five, six to a bed, the healthy sharing with the sick. We feed them as best we can but the quality of the food is unacceptable and the quantity is insufficient to satisfy so many hungry mouths. I come before you today to implore you to aid us. We need more funds to improve the services we provide. With your generous contributions, we could acquire more beds, better food, clothes, medicines, to help these poor souls. I beg you to pledge as much as you can spare.'

As she listened to the speaker, Bridget felt a vague sense of awfulness descend upon her, a dismay that clung to her skin like a thin layer of slime. It was guilt again, but of a different kind.

Miss Blythe persevered to her beseeching conclusion. 'The true horrors of St Swithun's must be witnessed to be believed.

I entreat you to come visit to see for yourselves. Your presence would be welcomed and your eyes would be opened. My sincere thanks for your time.'

The ladies did their best to hide their distaste behind sympathetic murmurs and there was a smattering of polite applause as Miss Blythe stepped down. They occupied the next few minutes signing pledges for what they believed to be the adequate amount for donation; their husbands would later write the appropriate cheques. The footmen were on hand to convey the pledges to Lady Ainsley, but Bridget felt compelled to deliver her own herself.

'Excuse me one moment,' she said to Lady Newby and the others, and she negotiated her way between the round tables to the top of the room. She approached Miss Blythe, who was hovering beside the dais, eclipsed by Lady Ainsley's more imposing presence.

'Miss Blythe, I am Mrs Lambourne,' she said. 'You spoke well, I commend you.'

Miss Blythe rubbed her wide jaw self-consciously. 'That is kind of you. I practised it a hundred times before going up.'

'The state of affairs at St Swithun's sounds very serious. Is the institution sufficiently staffed?'

'Far from it. We are too few to cope with the volumes of people that come through our doors. We are always in need of more hands. And provisions, of course.'

Bridget handed her the pledge. 'I do hope this will be of some use.'

Miss Blythe's eyes widened when she looked at it. 'Good gracious, this is most generous.'

'It is for a worthy cause.' She would deal with Garrett's indignation later. 'Tell me, when may I come visit?'

The woman's gaze snapped back up to hers. 'You truly wish to come? Begging your pardon, but I didn't think that anyone in this room would actually respond to that particular plea.'

'Having listened to your speech, I would not be satisfied with simply writing a figure on a piece of paper. I want to contribute in a more tangible way, if you believe I might be of some help.'

Miss Blythe smiled in astonishment, adding a touch of femininity to her masculine features. 'We would be ever so grateful for your assistance.'

They arranged for her to visit the very next day. When she returned to her table and proposed the scheme to her new companions, only Miss Caulfield expressed an interest and she was unavailable. Lady Newby and Lady Radcliffe both demurred and endeavoured to dissuade Bridget from the enterprise too, but she paid no heed to them. She was determined to keep this appointment.

The following afternoon, she instructed her coachman, Sawyer, to take her to St Swithun's Workhouse and Soup Kitchen, but she regretted the action when she emerged onto the street and was beleaguered by a gaggle of barefoot ragamuffins begging for coins; a carriage announced her status in society as loudly as a town crier with a bell. She distributed what she could and then hurried to the entrance of St Swithun's, a narrow door with rotting wood, peeling paint and rusted hinges.

As soon as she stepped through it, she felt bile rise in her throat. The air was full of the stench of unclean bodies. She swallowed and breathed shallowly through her mouth. She was in a long, low-ceilinged room which contained a scattering of mismatched benches and stools, vastly inadequate for the multitude of bedraggled people crowded inside, most of whom were forced to stand or sit on the grimy floor. A cacophony of coughs, groans and children's crying emanated from the teeming mass.

For the first time, the dangers of being exposed to such a situation occurred to her and she began to worry, not for herself but for her unborn baby. Her feet were taking a hesitant step back towards the door when Miss Blythe detached herself from the throng and came over to her. She strode with a confidence lacking in her demeanour yesterday; she looked far more comfortable in this environment where she was the unequivocal person of authority and not subordinate to a bunch of frivolous ladies to whom she had to grovel for financial support.

'Mrs Lambourne, thank you so much for coming.'

'I-I'm pleased to be here, Miss Blythe.'

'In this place I am just Frances,' Miss Blythe said with a wink.

'Then I shall be just Bridget,' Bridget replied, taking courage from the other woman's self-assurance.

Frances proceeded to show her around the soup kitchen. It was atrocious. The long room represented the entire extent of the institution's ability to provide outdoor relief – this 'kitchen' consisted of nothing more than boiling pots over a hearth tended by a couple of harried-looking women, and a few dirty bowls which had to be shared among the countless starving wretches who came to the door each day. The vegetables for the soup were already mouldering and there was nowhere near enough to feed all the clamouring mouths both inside and outside the ramshackle building. Bridget declined to enter the workhouse looming forbiddingly beside the kitchen, recalling Frances's allusion to rampant diseases, but understood that the conditions within were just as dreadful for those who were desperate enough to seek the dubious refuge which the indoor relief was supposed to offer.

'You are gravely underfunded,' she said, appalled by all she saw. 'I trust the revenue from yesterday's event will go some way towards rectifying the situation.'

'Not everyone was quite as generous as you. But it will still be an enormous help.'

'I shall speak to the association on your behalf and try to arrange regular donations from them. With more substantial resources, we could significantly improve the quality of the services provided at St Swithun's.'

Frances blinked. 'We?'

'Yes,' Bridget said with resolve. 'I would like to take a more active role here, if I can be of use. However, I must disclose that I am with child and fear I ought not return until after the birth. Until then, I shall campaign at more charity events and ensure the delivery of whatever supplies you require.'

Frances's sizeable jaw dropped. 'Good gracious, I don't know what to say.'

Bridget glanced over her shoulder at the miserable individuals slumped around the kitchen. 'Say you will agree.'

It shamed her to recollect her weeks of apathy in the drawing room when there was such work to be done. There would be no more idleness on her part.

# CHAPTER 6

As she perused a list of financial contributions obtained at the most recent meeting of the Ladies of Compassion Association, Bridget shifted her chair closer to the open drawing room window, seeking a puff of air to cool her flushed face. Everyone said it was the nicest May they had seen in years, and the gardens of Berkeley Square were swarming with gentlefolk enjoying sunny strolls, but she found the heat suffocating. At this advanced stage of her pregnancy, she just could not find a way to get comfortable.

After dabbing at her sweaty neck with a handkerchief, she picked up her pen, dipped it and wrote the total amount donated at the bottom of the page. She sat back, pleased; she intended this money to go towards new beds and blankets for the workhouse. She had already negotiated an agreement with the local greengrocers to supply the soup kitchen with produce at a reduced price, which Frances and the other women working there had received with deepest gratitude. Lady Ainsley seemed a trifle irked that the newest recruit to the association appeared to be supplanting her in terms of efficacy, but she could not deny that the association's goals were being achieved like never before.

The shout of a coachman drew Bridget's attention back to the window; a carriage had come to a stop on the street directly below her. Her mood darkened when she saw her mother emerge, the lady's appraising gaze sweeping up and down the grand facade of Wyndham House. The location spoke of status and money and met with her obvious approval.

Bridget grasped the little bell which had been placed near her for her convenience, the bell pull on the far wall presenting too much of a challenge in her expectant state. She rang it and Lizzie appeared.

'My mother has arrived and will be in need of refreshment. Please bring us some tea and biscuits.'

'Yes, mistress, at once,' Lizzie said with a curtsey and vanished.

Bridget looked out the window again. Wyndham House's imperturbable butler, Thrussell, and handsome footman, Peter, had come out onto the steps to greet the new arrival and see to her luggage. Lady Courcey superciliously accepted their welcome as though she were an exalted duchess instead of a mere baroness, then twisted around to bark an order at the two maidservants who accompanied her. It gladdened Bridget to perceive the freckled face of Ellen Ryan, her mother's lady's maid, but she did not recognise the other girl and could not imagine why the lady would have brought a second maid – Ellen was more than capable of tending to all her needs.

Peter lifted a trunk from the carriage and started to struggle up the steps with it. When Bridget heard Lady Courcey's sharp tongue turn in his direction, she frowned. She hoped her mother would remember that she was a guest now rather than the mistress of her own house.

The figures disappeared from view and their voices echoed in the hall below before footsteps sounded on the stairs. Thrussell showed Lady Courcey into the drawing room and then withdrew at a nod from Bridget. She rose unsteadily to her feet; her large belly made her feel off balance and she gripped the arm of her chair for support.

'Welcome, Mother,' she said in a clipped voice.

Lady Courcey came over and embraced her with care, the enormous bump protruding between them. Then she stood back and surveyed her.

'You have put on a good deal of weight,' she said, clearly not referring to Bridget's stomach area. 'The sooner that baby is out of you, the better. You cannot be a fat lady of society. People will talk about you.' She looked around the room. 'What a horrendous choice of colour for the curtains. Did they have nothing better?'

Bridget bit the tip of her tongue to prevent her retort, regretting for the hundredth time that her sense of duty as a daughter had triumphed over her detestation of her mother. She had felt obliged by society's expectations to invite Lady Courcey to London and be present when her first grandchild arrived into the world, even though she had no wish for the woman to be there, not after the irreparable harm she had caused the previous summer on the Oakleigh Estate.

Her chest tightened unbearably at the memory. Breathe, she reminded herself. You must continue to breathe.

Lizzie entered at that moment with a tray. She set the tea things on a low table and Bridget smiled at her in thanks. Lady Courcey squinted critically at Lizzie's departing back.

'Well, that maid will have to go,' she said as she and Bridget sat down. 'I cannot fathom why you have not got rid of her already.'

'Pardon me?' said Bridget, stunned.

Her mother's tone was matter-of-fact. 'You cannot keep such an ugly servant. Her skin is quite appalling. It is offensive to any guests who may see her.'

A blaze of fury rose up inside Bridget. 'I will not hear of it,' she said, keeping her voice controlled as she poured tea for them both. Her hand shook a little but she did not spill it. 'Lizzie is a girl of absolute reliability and irreproachable character. I quite depend upon her.' To prevent her mother from arguing the point further, she hastened on, 'Speaking of servants, I noticed that you brought two maids with you. I did not recognise the younger girl. Who is she?'

A sly look crept onto Lady Courcey's face as she picked up her cup. 'That is Cathy, one of the new maids at Oakleigh. It was necessary for me to fill a couple of vacated positions following certain events last summer.'

Bridget felt like her mother had just dealt a devastating blow to her abdomen. Lady Courcey was referring to her unfair dismissal of Cormac's two sisters, which had coincided with her eviction of his entire family from Oakleigh land after Bridget's love affair with him had come to light. The lady had gone to the exorbitant expense of bringing a superfluous maid, from the scullery no less, across the sea to England for the sole purpose of delivering this smug jibe.

Sickened, Bridget reached for her bell. 'You must be tired. Lizzie will show you to your bedchamber,' she said, disregarding the fact that neither of them had even touched the biscuits.

She sipped her tea and kept her eyes averted until Lizzie had escorted Lady Courcey from the drawing room.

Alone, her tears began to fall. Her stupor last winter had been excruciating but, now that she allowed herself to feel again, her remorse was equally crushing. She knew that if she lived to ninety years of age she could never make any mistake larger than the one that had destroyed the McGovern family.

She started when the door opened again and Garrett entered the drawing room. His timing was perfect if he had wanted to avoid greeting his mother-in-law. While courting Bridget, he had remained on the best of terms with Lady Courcey, drawing on the depths of his patience and charm. Now that his position within the family was utterly secure, he seemed more adjusted to the idea of risking the lady's displeasure. Bridget suspected that he had even forewarned his father, whose house this still was after all, of Lady Courcey's acerbic nature because Lord Wyndham had conveniently been called away to Swifton Hall, the title's country seat, just before her impending arrival.

Garrett took one look at his weeping wife and his mouth narrowed into a thin line. 'Ten minutes in the house,' he said, 'and the woman is already eliciting tears.'

He approached as though to put his arms around her but she wiped her cheeks and looked away. 'I am fine.'

They were at a sensitive point in their relationship. While she still could not forgive him for the cruel part he had played in Cormac's banishment and for his subsequent unsympathetic conduct, his own manner had wholly transformed when she had revealed to him that she was with child. Full of anticipation of the birth of his heir, he was now trying to be as tender towards her as he had been at the beginning of their courtship. But she was uneasy. If the coming baby was the result of a union that had taken place after she was married, then the due date was almost a month away. On the other hand, if it was the product of illicit relations before her marriage, then the birth would be quite a bit sooner. She did not dare to speculate how he might react should the event not transpire as he expected.

With a wounded shrug, he stepped back. 'I hope it was not an error in judgement to invite her. I don't wish for anything to disturb your comfort at such a delicate time.'

She refrained from pointing out that a state of comfort was entirely unattainable at this stage, or that she had always known Lady Courcey's presence would add stress to an already stressful event. Instead, she mumbled something about obligation and resigned herself to her fate.

They got a reprieve, however, when Lady Courcey sent word that she was suffering from a headache and would remain in her bedchamber until dinner. Welcoming this news with relief, Bridget set aside her figures for the Ladies of Compassion Association and took the opportunity to retire to bed herself. She ached all over her body and the baby was kicking so mercilessly that sleep would be out of her reach, but at least she could rest in preparation for the trials to come.

Lizzie – whose role had come to extend beyond that of housemaid as Bridget relied upon her more and more – had hardly helped her under the covers when an idea occurred to her.

'Lizzie,' she said, 'will you enquire after the lady's maid, Miss Ryan? Find out if she is currently attending to my mother and, if she is not, please ask her if she would come to my chamber.'

Lizzie scurried off and Bridget lay back on her pillows to wait. In the coming weeks, there might never be a suitable moment when she and Ellen could be alone, so she ought to seize this chance to speak with her in private while Lady Courcey was not nearby to overhear.

When Lizzie returned with Ellen, the lady's maid did not seem surprised to have been summoned like this – perhaps she had been expecting or even hoping for it. She took a seat next to the bed and Lizzie left them in solitude.

Bridget smiled. 'How are you, dearest Ellen? I have missed you.'

'And I have missed you,' Ellen replied with feeling. 'I am well and glad to see you in good health.'

Something relaxed inside Bridget, a coil of imprisonment and secrecy loosening ever so slightly. Ellen had always been an ally and knew more about Bridget's past than most. Last summer, she had helped Cormac sneak into the manor to be consoled by Bridget after his older sister, Mary, had ended her own life. Once

Ellen had become aware of the blossoming attachment between them, she had cautioned Bridget to be careful but she had also been discreet with the secret she kept – an uncommon trait in a lady's maid, a position notorious for gossiping to the mistress. Bridget wished she could have taken Ellen to London with her but she was Lady Courcey's servant and obliged to remain in her employ. Now, Bridget felt the burden of memory diminish, if only temporarily, at having her confidante beside her once more.

'How is everything at Oakleigh?' she asked, conjuring an uplifting image in her mind of her childhood home, the elegant building of warm red brick surrounded by stables, orchard, gardens, and green fields unfolding to the horizon.

'Very busy, since her ladyship chose to take up permanent residence there again. She entertained a number of guests over the winter. The land is flourishing too and Mr Enright told her ladyship that the limestone quarry is proving exceedingly lucrative for your inheritance.' Ellen paused. 'Do you think you will ever return?'

Homesickness pricked the back of Bridget's eyelids. 'It is impossible to say. I long to go back and yet sometimes believe it would be unbearable to set foot there after—after what happened.'

She could not even imagine the pain of standing beneath the oak tree in the orchard and recalling the man who had kissed her there, the lover she had lost and failed to find. So far, the enquiries she had sent to Ireland – to stables of manor houses in counties neighbouring Carlow, to townhouse mews in the cities of Dublin and Cork, to shelters, soup kitchens, workhouses – had yielded no positive responses. A needle in a haystack would have been easier to unearth. She swallowed the emotion that welled in her throat.

'Of course,' she said, 'it is out of the question altogether until the baby is old enough to travel.'

Ellen glanced at the large bump under the bedcovers. 'And how do you feel in anticipation of that particular arrival?'

'Scared,' she admitted. Garrett's father had secured the services of one of the most respected midwives in the city for the coming of his first grandchild, but childbirth was a perilous affair and neither a viscount's money nor a midwife's experience was any guarantee of a safe delivery. 'Although I am in such discomfort that I just want it to happen already.'

Ellen's expression was full of sympathy. 'When do you expect the birth to take place?'

Bridget hesitated. Should she speak the accepted truth or divulge what she suspected to be the very possible alternative?

'It might be as much as three or four weeks,' she said, then went on in a small voice, 'or as little as three or four days.'

Ellen's gaze connected with hers.

'Oh, my,' she murmured.

She made no recriminations and Bridget was grateful, though she still felt the inescapable shame which accompanied the thought of producing an illegitimate child. It had never been her intention – she and Cormac had promised to wed each other but had simply found it impossible to delay their reckless night of passion until after their vows, which Lady Courcey and Garrett had then thwarted. Still, she need not worry about society's perception of the situation. Should the baby come sooner than expected, it would nonetheless be born within the confines of a lawful marriage, if not that of its natural parents.

The main concern was whether Garrett would be able to tell if the child was his or not.

Ellen's own reflections had led her down a different track. 'So Maggie McGovern may yet have another grandchild. She would be happy to know it, if...' Her sentence trailed away into dismal silence, unfinished.

But Bridget could finish it.

If Maggie still lived on Oakleigh land.

If she and her family had not been evicted, forced to leave the only home they had ever known.

If they were still alive.

Bridget stared down at her hands resting on her pregnant mound and felt her heart twist as though an invisible fist had reached inside and wrenched at the fragile organ, tearing at the names imprinted on it. Maggie, who was Cormac's mother but had been as good as a mother to Bridget too. Cormac's three surviving sisters, Margaret, Bronagh and Orlaith, all still girls and unacquainted with the wider world. And little Patrick, the son Mary had left behind when she committed that terrible act – he had been mere months old when the family had been thrown out of their cottage. They had been condemned to a wretched existence of homelessness and poverty, and Bridget was to blame.

'Did you hear what became of them all?' she asked, her words barely audible.

'No,' Ellen said with a regretful shake of her head. 'None of them could write so there was no hope of expecting a letter, and any travellers who came through from nearby villages had no news of them. They just disappeared.'

Bridget gripped the bedcovers fiercely. 'Perhaps they made their way to the city, thinking that Dublin would offer them better employment prospects. Do you know if they had any destination in mind? Did you speak to them before they left?'

Ellen grimaced, the freckles on her nose and cheeks scrunching together. 'I was there when they left, and it is a scene I shall never be able to forget.' She sighed. 'The morning you were taken back to Dublin, while you were still locked in your

50

bedchamber, Liam Kirwan and I ran down to the cottage. Mr Enright was present too, looking like he'd rather be anywhere else, but as the estate's agent he had to supervise the eviction. Poor Maggie didn't seem to understand what was happening at all. Bronagh nearly had to push her out the door. It was dreadful to see her so dazed and broken. Margaret was trying to calm the two young ones, Orlaith and the baby, and I could tell it would be herself and Bronagh taking care of the family from then on, no doubt about it. I saw Liam press a few coins into Margaret's hand. It was all he had to spare from his stable hand's wages but she wept with gratitude. And after that they just wandered away with no notion where to go next.'

Her voice cracked. Bridget found she could not speak. She clutched Ellen's hand and they clung to each other, grieving for the unlucky McGoverns and the hardships they had been made to endure.

They drew apart when a knock sounded at the door. Lizzie peered around it, looking shocked to see their pale, tearful faces.

'M-mistress,' she faltered. 'Her ladyship's awake and calling quite insistently for Miss Ryan. She said—she said Cathy don't have brains enough to tend a beetle.'

Bridget sniffed and nodded. 'You had better go to her, Ellen. Thank you for coming to see me. That family is in my prayers.'

'And in mine. We can only hope and pray that good fortune finds them.'

Wiping a tear from her eye, Ellen rose, curtseyed and departed with Lizzie.

# CHAPTER 7

'I blame the poor quality of the city air,' Lady Courcey declared. 'The smoke is not conducive to my health.'

She, Bridget and Garrett were seated at the dinner table and Garrett had unwisely enquired after their guest's welfare, following her earlier retreat to her bedchamber.

'It is for the same reason that I have chosen to reside at Oakleigh on a more permanent basis,' the lady carried on. 'I am weary of Dublin's noxious environment. The country is far more wholesome to one's wellbeing.'

Bridget noted that her mother had kept her adoration of the countryside conveniently concealed throughout the seven years they had spent in Dublin, a good deal of which Bridget had spent pleading with her to take her home to Oakleigh.

Lady Courcey gave a delicate cough, then smiled angelically. 'I am for the most part recovered now though.'

'We are very glad to hear it,' Garrett said with the enthusiasm of one hoping to close down the current line of conversation.

In any case, she had turned her attention to the venison dish that was the centrepiece of that evening's dinner.

'Too tough,' she announced, pushing her plate away. 'Mrs Kavanagh knows how to cook it to perfection.'

'It is most regrettable that you feel that way,' said Garrett, cutting into his own portion of venison with more vigour than necessary. 'I am quite enjoying it myself.'

Bridget cast her gaze over the lavish range of dishes crowding the table, far too much for three people to consume, and compared it to the basic provisions she had scraped together for St Swithun's.

Pursing her lips, she said, 'We ought to appreciate what we have. There are many unfortunate souls who would be grateful for even a crumb from this table.'

Lady Courcey squinted at her. 'I suppose you are referring to that soup kitchen you mentioned in your letter. What possessed you to get involved in such ludicrous nonsense?' She swivelled towards Garrett. 'I'm surprised you are permitting her to indulge in it.'

'It is a commendable cause,' Garrett said mildly, neglecting to mention his and Bridget's heated argument about it. When she had first told him of her commitment to the Ladies of Compassion Association, he had objected to the notion of his wife demeaning herself among the common folk and had forbidden her involvement at such a practical level. He had only relented when she insisted that it was in fact fashionable for ladies to occupy themselves in charity work and promised she would not visit the soup kitchen or workhouse until after the baby was born. She supposed her passionate plea had made him realise that having such a purpose in her life played a significant part in preventing her from reverting to the dejected shell he had beheld in the drawing room.

'Hmm,' was Lady Courcey's doubtful response. She took a sip of her wine. 'This is not quite balanced,' she said with regret. 'I have a very sensitive palate. Buttimer knows my tastes well. His discernment ensures that Oakleigh's wine cellar is incomparable.'

Thrussell, standing behind Garrett's chair, stiffened at this and Bridget marvelled at Lady Courcey's talent to offend – she had managed to get under the skin of even the unflappable butler.

However, then her commentary shifted to a reflection on the most superb wine she had ever sampled (a mature bottle opened in celebration of Bridget's birth twenty years ago) and from there to the subject of children and the art of being a mother.

'You are going to love motherhood,' she said to Bridget. 'And if I may say so, I think you are going to make a fine mother.'

Bridget blinked. Was her mother making a statement that contained not one negative aspect to it? She looked at Garrett – the same incredulity was obvious on his face. Shrugging, he raised his glass.

'I could not agree more,' he said and drained the red liquid.

'Naturally, I shall assist you in every way I can,' Lady Courcey went on. 'I have had two decades of experience in the area so you could not ask for better guidance.'

Bridget gritted her teeth and stabbed at her own venison with her fork. It was delicious – whatever Lady Courcey had to say about the quality of the food, Bridget was more than satisfied with Monsieur Lévêque's abilities.

'There is no better person to whom a girl can turn for advice than her own mother,' said Lady Courcey sagely. 'Of course, you know that already. I have always been there to steer you along the right path. Without my help, you would have made quite a shocking blunder last summer, that is the undeniable truth. But I chose the right husband for you, didn't I?'

The lady leaned back in her chair and looked very pleased with her own success as a mother.

Right then, the baby gave an almighty kick inside Bridget and she imagined that it was as enraged as she was by Lady Courcey's arrogant words. This was beyond endurance.

She stood up so fast that she felt dizzy. She threw her fork on the table and it clattered off her plate and fell to the floor.

'I cannot tolerate this anymore!' she exploded.

Both Garrett and Lady Courcey stared at her in astonishment.

'What on earth—?' her mother began.

'You!' Bridget flung at her. 'I cannot tolerate *you* anymore!'

Lady Courcey looked indignant. 'That is no way to speak to your mother!'

Bridget glared at her. 'I have decided that I no longer have a mother. You haven't behaved like one in years so I shall not feel like I am missing anything.'

'You need to watch your tongue,' her mother warned, 'or it will get you into trouble.'

'What trouble?' Bridget crossed her arms over her protruding belly. 'There is nothing with which you can threaten me. You have already taken away all that I held dear. What would you do now, cut off my inheritance? Even if you could, I have no need of it. Spread ugly rumours about me? You never would, because that would besmirch your own name by association. You cannot touch me, my family or my status now.'

Lady Courcey, highly affronted, appealed to Garrett for support. 'Are you going to let her talk to me like this? Control your wife, for heaven's sake.'

Garrett raised his hands in a gesture that said he was taking no responsibility for this. 'I would never presume to interfere in the complicated relationship between a mother and daughter.'

Bridget continued to rant. 'You are a mean, bitter woman who finds fault with everything and loves no one. You have inflicted misery upon innocent people and *relished* it. You think you have been a good mother to me? You have brought about more heartache in my life than I ever deserved to suffer, flawed though I am. I am determined to be the exact opposite of you when my baby is born.'

'You ungrateful girl.' Lady Courcey's voice was low but the colour had risen in her cheeks. 'I have done everything in my power to provide for you, to secure your happiness. And this is the thanks I get?'

'You said the right word,' said Bridget with growing fury. 'Power. And you do not have it anymore. I want you to get out of my house this instant.'

'Don't be absurd,' said her mother, reaching for her glass of wine.

'I am being deadly serious!' Bridget shrieked and her mother's hand froze in mid-air. 'I never want to see you again! And you shall never set eyes on your grandchild. I do not want you to poison its life the way you have poisoned mine and the lives of so many others. Get out of my sight and do not ever try to come here again or I will throw you out into the gutter myself!'

Beginning to realise that Bridget truly meant what she was saying, Lady Courcey again implored Garrett to intervene. 'You must talk some sense into her. It is almost nine o'clock at night. Where could I go at this hour?'

He thought for a moment. 'A distant cousin of mine resides on Brook Street. She is an elderly widow and lives on her own. I could send a message to her. I am sure she would take you in, even at this short notice.'

Lady Courcey looked horrified that Garrett was choosing to take the part of his wife. She swung back to Bridget, aghast. 'You cannot mean to do this. Are you really going to drive me away? Your own mother?'

'Yes, I am,' Bridget said and beckoned to the butler, who had observed the entire scene without intrusion. 'Thrussell, please ask Miss Ryan to pack some of my mother's things, any essentials she will need for the next day or two. Then get Sawyer

56

to bring around the carriage. You,' she added, addressing her mother again, 'can send Ellen and Cathy back for the rest of your possessions whenever it is convenient for them.'

Thrussell bowed and departed from the dining room. Bridget felt a wave of heat pass through her and leaned over the table, resting on her palms and breathing heavily. Out of her peripheral vision, she saw her mother reaching towards her and snatched her hand away before the lady could touch it.

'Bridget, p-please,' said Lady Courcey, stammering a little.

Bridget gave her a derisive look. 'A strange word to hear coming from you. You are not used to begging, are you?'

'Please,' Lady Courcey repeated. 'Do not do this.'

'Go and wait outside in the hall,' said Bridget. 'Your very presence makes me sick to my stomach.'

'Pl—' Lady Courcey started again but Bridget interrupted by slapping her hand on the table.

'Didn't you understand me? Don't you respect anybody's feelings but your own? I said *get out*!'

Her voice had risen so high in pitch that Garrett jumped to his feet, ready to step between them if they came to blows. Bridget felt a pain low down and fancied that the baby itself was eager for a fight. But, with a rueful glance at her daughter, Lady Courcey stood and turned towards the door.

Suddenly, Bridget gasped. She had felt the pain again but it was ten times worse than before. She clutched at her belly and staggered; Garrett darted to her side and kept her upright. Lady Courcey whipped around and came forwards, arms outstretched to help.

'No!' Bridget snapped, clenching her jaw against the awful ache that was intensifying deep within her. 'Leave me alone!'

'But the child,' her mother said in anguish. 'It is coming too soon. You need me here.'

'I...do not want...you here for this,' Bridget managed to say and then sank to the floor. Garrett knelt beside her, supporting her against his chest. He looked up at Lady Courcey.

'You had better leave,' he said. 'Seek out Lizzie and tell her to send for the midwife as swiftly as possible.'

Lady Courcey had probably never been asked to deliver a message in her life but she nodded and hastened from the room. Bridget moaned and Garrett rubbed her back in reassurance.

'Do not fret, the midwife will be here before long,' he murmured. 'Our baby will be fine. You have no need to worry.'

And the baby was fine. After a short, difficult labour, the little girl came into the world in the early hours of the following morning. Bridget, through a haze of tears and emotions, knew with a single glance at her daughter's golden head and blue eyes that, though everybody else might accept the child had been born premature, neither she nor Garrett could be in any doubt of the truth.

His disappointment was achingly palpable. He had desired an heir, of course, but she suspected he had also hoped this birth would mend the rift between them, bringing them closer together in the way a child sometimes could. With the reality so blatant in her features, the baby could only serve to widen that distance.

At first, Bridget feared his wrath would be so great that he would turn them out of the house. On reflection, however, she realised he would not be that imprudent – in society's eyes, his loving wife had just provided him with his firstborn child. Even so, he made no effort to return to her chamber after the birth. Society, after all, could not see beyond closed doors. There would be no cause for suspicion within the household; the servants would probably attribute his disinterest to the baby's inferior sex.

Bridget cared not one jot. She kissed her daughter's fingers, each one perfect in miniature detail. The little girl would have no grandmother and an indifferent father figure but Bridget had more than enough love to compensate for them both. Whatever had happened to Cormac, wherever he was, at least one piece of him – a tiny, beautiful, wondrous piece – was right here in her arms.

'I will cherish her for you,' she whispered. 'Our sweet, beloved Emily.'

# Chapter 8

Cormac was plodding along the street, minding his own business, when a rapid patter of footsteps came up behind him and he felt his blanket being ripped from his shoulders.

He swore, whirled around and grabbed for the end of the tattered blanket as it whipped away in the thief's grasp. He got a secure hold and yanked it back towards himself. The thief didn't let go but lost his balance and fell on the cobbles with a thump that foretold of imminent bruises on his backside.

Cormac halted in momentary shock when he realised his opponent was a youth with skin as dark as soot and one milky eye, which stood out starkly against the black around it. His astonishment at such a foreign vision dissipated as a tussle for control over the blanket ensued between them. They were as malnourished as each other but Cormac was taller and had the advantage of a standing position. He pulled with all his strength and the blanket jerked out of the would-be thief's hands. The youth fell onto his elbows, then scrambled backwards and hopped up. Before he could run, Cormac seized him by his ragged shirtfront and cuffed him about the ear.

'Try that again and I'll make your other eye milky too,' he growled.

The youth wrenched out of his grip and darted away, hollering obscenities in his wake. Cormac shouted a few of his own in return and stamped off in the opposite direction, swinging the blanket back over his shoulders.

After a year on the streets, every inch of it was stained with filth, it reeked even worse than himself, and it had become so threadbare that its protection from the elements was minimal. But it was the only possession he had and he was damned if he was going to relinquish it without a fight, especially with autumn coming to an end and winter's cold fingers beckoning once more.

He strode on, keeping his eyes trained on his feet. He made no apology when he bumped into a chimney sweep, causing him to drop his brushes, and disregarded the angry bellow of a coachman when he crossed the street in front of a carriage. The idea of good manners was laughable, and perhaps a very tiny part of him hoped to be mown down by the wheels of a carriage. It wasn't like he had anything to live for.

He paid no heed to where he was going until he registered the sound of a polished accent that could not belong to any of the lower class folk he customarily encountered. He raised his head and realised that he had meandered into a more affluent area of the city. The streets were clear of waste, the doorsteps were scrubbed clean, and people of elegance populated the footpaths. The voice he had heard originated from a dapper-looking gentleman smugly telling his companion about a property he had just sold for a handsome price.

'On Mountjoy Square, you know. The fool was so eager to buy. He didn't seem to grasp that the city's south side is the prime location now.'

The gentleman caught sight of Cormac and levelled a disdainful glare at him. Cormac averted his gaze, turning in towards the wall of a millinery shop as the two men passed by.

In general, he avoided these prosperous parts of Dublin. No one took much notice of him in the areas of extreme poverty, but in this neighbourhood his presence was highly objectionable and he risked being apprehended by a constable. Still, he was here now and a recklessness made him decide to try his luck. Though the shame of it nearly crippled him, he hunkered down next to the door of the millinery shop and cupped his hands into a gesture of supplication. The fingerless gloves had unravelled down to his knuckles and his nails were almost as black as those of the gloves' previous owner. Just as he was wondering whether the old man would have labelled this wisdom or folly, an elderly lady exited the shop accompanied by her maid, who carried a hat box.

Cormac raised his hands towards the lady. 'Begging you for a little help, m'lady,' he said humbly.

She clicked her tongue in repugnance and jerked her head at her maid. The girl vanished back into the shop and reappeared seconds later with the owner of the establishment. She was clutching a broom which she waved towards Cormac in a threatening manner.

'You get out of here right now,' she barked. 'This is a respectable business. I don't want you repelling my customers.'

Imagining he could hear the old man's hoarse chuckle, he slouched away. But he didn't admit defeat just yet. He found another spot, this one by the locked gates of a park in the centre of a fine square, where it soon became apparent that the gates could only be opened by residents of the square who possessed a private key. Though a chilly wind made the branches of the park's trees whip about, the weather was dry and several of the local inhabitants seemed disposed to go for their daily constitutional. Every time footsteps neared, he peered up meekly and muttered an entreaty for a morsel of assistance. The gentlefolk either ignored him or gave him the briefest look of disgusted accusation for daring to mar their view before continuing on into the park.

Until the two young ladies came along.

He heard the heels of their ankle boots clipping smartly on the path, their voices chirping about a new shawl which one of them had purchased and the other was admiring. He cast his beseeching glance upwards, started to mumble his plea, and froze.

He recognised them. At first, he could not recollect where and all he could see was Bridget's face floating before him. Then he realised why he connected her with them – they were two of the guests who had visited Oakleigh for Garrett Lambourne's birthday celebrations. He fished about in his memory for their names. Miss Wallace and Miss…Gardiner, maybe?

The details began to filter back to him with more clarity. The group of ladies had chosen to go for a stroll down the avenue, even though it had been a squally day. Miss Wallace had asked him about the weather and he had warned them of a shower due to come down very soon, at which point Miss Gardiner had flirted with him, making some coy remark about him getting wet. It had been an inconsequential exchange but he couldn't help feeling flattered that he had attracted her interest and that this had perhaps provoked a whisper of jealousy on Bridget's part.

His insides ached to recall a time when he had held some small value as a human being, when he had been more than mud under someone's shoe. He drew his cupped hands back, tucking them under his arms. He had no desire to invite these ladies' attention.

They had noticed him nonetheless. Miss Gardiner's gaze slid over him with a wrinkle of her nose but Miss Wallace's eyes glanced away and then snapped back to him in disbelief. He did not linger a second longer. He clambered to his feet and stalked away, shoulders bent and blanket pulled tight around his ears. He didn't look back and she certainly did not call after him.

She couldn't have recognised him, not looking the way he did. His hair fell to his shoulders now, unkempt and so grubby that its fair colour was obscured to a dirty shade of ash. He was unshaven, a bedraggled beard covering his jaw, and his clothes were shabby and soiled. He bore no resemblance to the clean, groomed stable hand with whom Miss Gardiner had flirted.

But his appearance had struck a chord of familiarity with Miss Wallace. Still, she wouldn't be able to place where she had seen him. At least, he sincerely hoped she wouldn't. The idea that she might remember the man he had once been made him want to scream with humiliation.

He pounded the Dublin streets back to more familiar territory, having learned his lesson that only trouble came from straying into the city's wealthier districts. He decided to make for the docklands, even though this was a somewhat perilous venture, given that on his last visit a week ago he had stolen a bottle of French wine out of an unattended crate that had just been unloaded from one of the docked boats. He had traded it at the back door of an inn for a cold, greasy chicken leg and half a loaf of bread – the innkeeper would offer him no more than that, deducing that he had obtained the wine by dishonest means. He hadn't cared; the food had been glorious and for once he had gone to sleep on a doorstep without the usual ache of hunger gnawing at his belly.

But that was a week past and he had been famished many times over since then, with only rancid scraps from alleyways to satisfy him. The potential at the docklands was worth the danger – he would just have to trust that no one would identify him as the pilferer of the wine. Tying his blanket around his waist to liberate his hands, he skulked around the quays and warehouses, keeping a keen eye out for sentries or cargo ripe for filching.

Several hours of patience yielded nothing but an encounter with some startled rats scurrying behind a row of barrels. Dusk arrived and the dockworkers departed, all goods safely stored or dispatched. Dispirited, he wandered along by the waterside, hands and feet frozen and stomach empty. He would have given anything for the warmth of a glowing fire in the hearth and a bowl of stirabout on the table.

Suddenly, he heard the crackle of a real fire close by. Peering down an alley between two warehouses, he discerned a group of three or four men clustered around a brazier which blazed with light and warmth. The men were holding their hands over the fire and passing around a bottle of whiskey, each one knocking back a mouthful before handing it on to his neighbour. Cormac could tell that they were not homeless; they wore good winter clothing, looked well-fed and had clean-shaven faces.

He knew he ought to move on. His experiences over the past year had established that the majority of Dublin's populace were not inclined to be friendly to strangers and he did not expect these men to be the exception. But the fire looked so inviting and his extremities felt so icy that he found his feet moving forwards almost of their own volition. He crept down the alley, his eyes transfixed on the leaping flames. At first, the men did not notice him, occupied as they were in their drinking and loud conversation.

'—made up some story about having a sick child,' one of them was saying. He was thickset and bull-necked with enormous hands that could easily wrap all the way around the whiskey bottle. 'Needed the money for medicine. I told him his priority was paying back Cunningham what he owed and after that he could buy all the medicine he wanted.'

'Too right,' a thin-lipped man agreed, accepting the bottle and drinking, then passing it on around the circle. 'It's his own fault if one of them brats gets sick. Shouldn't have had so many in the first place. Don't know how they all fit in that poky house.'

Cormac edged nearer, not taking care to keep concealed. If the men looked in his direction, they would see him at once. But just a few more steps would bring him into the circle of heat from the fire. His whole body quivered with anticipation.

'I said I'd be back tomorrow to collect the rest,' the first man continued, receiving the bottle once more and taking a large swig. 'And I'm telling yous, more fool him if he doesn't have it by then.'

He was raising the bottle for a second draught when he caught sight of Cormac lurking nearby.

'Oi! Get out of here,' he said with a careless wave.

Cormac didn't move.

'Didn't you hear me?' the man snapped. 'I said clear off!'

The others turned to see what nuisance was bothering their comrade. With a nasty grin, the thin-lipped one picked up a heavy stick, probably intended for firewood, and threw it at Cormac. It glanced off his shoulder and clattered to the ground. The blow didn't hurt much but it incensed him nonetheless; he was tired of being treated like a dog, like a piece of rubbish, like a nobody. He was still a person and he wanted to be recognised as one.

Anger erupting inside him, he lurched forwards and swung at the man who had thrown the stick. Surprised, the man did not duck out of the way in time and Cormac's fist connected solidly with his mouth. The man fell backwards against the brazier and the elbow of his coat caught fire. He yelled and batted at his arm to quench the sizzling material. The other men were stunned at the unexpected attack and, in the time it took for them to register what had happened, Cormac seized his chance to assail another fellow, pummelling him in the chest and stomach. He had lost all reason, he didn't know why he was doing this; he just knew that he was filled with rage and that he had to take it out on somebody.

But now the men were beginning to react. One of them grabbed him around the waist and tried to pull him off his companion. The thickset man who had first noticed him was still holding the whiskey bottle and he swung it at Cormac's head. He felt the impact of it on the back of his skull and saw stars. He let go of the man he had been punching and staggered. In the next moment, he was dragged to the ground and pinned there. His vision swam and then he saw the man with the bottle standing over him.

'You're going to regret doing that,' he hissed.

However, before anyone could act, they heard a smooth voice coming from the entrance to the alley.

'Now, now, Munroe. Do not make any rash decisions.'

The man with the bottle, Munroe, looked up quickly at a person beyond Cormac's field of sight. 'Mr Cunningham, sir. I didn't see you, sir.'

'That is evident,' came the voice again. 'Do explain to me what you are doing.'

'It was self-defence,' said Munroe, swift to make his case. 'He just came at us fists flying. Nearly knocked out Lawlor's teeth.'

'I see. And I suppose the stick just hit him of its own accord?'

Munroe looked mutinous at the patronising tone of the unseen person. 'What's it matter? He's homeless. No one's going to care if he gets battered.'

'*I* shall care,' the voice corrected him and, at Munroe's incredulous expression, said, 'One does not pass up an opportunity when it walks so freely into our midst. We have a need to replace O'Connor after recent unfortunate events. A homeless man is a desperate man, and a desperate man can be a useful man. Let him get up.'

The man pinning Cormac to the ground released him and hauled him to his feet. He shook his matted hair out of his eyes and got his first look at the owner of the smooth voice. Cunningham displayed an impeccable sense of fashion, dressed in a tall hat, tailored coat and elegant gloves. He had a slender moustache and, for a man who seemed to command so much power, was rather short. As he strolled down the alley towards the group, it became plain that he was at least a head shorter than anyone else present. Nonetheless, the other men shuffled backwards respectfully at his approach.

He came to a stop in front of Cormac and gazed up at him.

'What is your name?' he asked in the same silky tone.

'McGovern,' said Cormac, taking his cue from how the other men were addressed.

'When did you last have a hot meal?'

'I can't remember.'

'Where do you sleep?'

'Anywhere.'

'What would you be willing to do to improve your fortune?'

Cormac eyed him. What kind of underhand dealings was this man involved in?

'I don't know,' he said honestly.

Cunningham seemed pleased with his answer. 'If you will agree to work for me, I shall pay you in food and board. You will have a roof over your head, clean clothes and three meals a day. Do you accept?'

'That depends,' Cormac said, with more bravery than he felt. He did not want to anger this powerful man but he also did not want to enter into the agreement blindly. 'What d'you do for a living?'

'I am a money lender,' Cunningham replied.

A number of things became clear to Cormac then. He now understood the conversation that Munroe had been having with his fellows before they spotted him. He fully comprehended how Cunningham was able to exude the authority that he did. He had a fair idea of what his own role would entail. And he knew that he was too weak, cold and hungry to refuse.

He nodded and Cunningham clapped his hands together once. 'Excellent. Munroe, take him back to the lodgings and get him cleaned up. He can start as soon as he has had a decent meal and a rest.'

Munroe, who was still fuming that his quarry had been snatched away from him, seized Cormac by the upper arm and marched him back up the alley. The rest of the men followed except for Cunningham. As Cormac exited the alley, he glimpsed the man staring down thoughtfully into the brazier, the light of the flames dancing across his face.

# CHAPTER 9

Cormac questioned the wisdom of his decision until a full plate of food was placed in front of him, and then he was too busy devouring it to ponder over right and wrong. He didn't even notice what he was eating, he just knew that it was hot and that it tasted better than anything he had ever eaten in his life. When he had satisfied his appetite, he was shown to a starkly-furnished room – no more than a narrow bed, a chair and a stained mirror on the wall – where he was able to bathe and shave, relieve himself in a chamber pot, and dress in a set of fresh clothes. After months and months of grime, it was overwhelming to feel so clean.

Among his discarded, ragged garments, he espied the threadbare blanket which he had guarded so fiercely for the past year. He fingered its frayed edges, the coarse material familiar and unpleasant to the touch. With a grunt, he tossed it into a corner of the room, intending to throw it on the fire as soon as the opportunity presented itself. Then, once he had brushed through his tangled hair, he collapsed on the bed, whose hard mattress felt like a carpet of clouds, and fell asleep without the dread that he might freeze to death before the morning.

But he was aware that this salvation came at a price and the next day he discovered just what he was willing to do to 'improve his fortune'.

He had hardly dressed when Munroe banged on the door of his room and stalked in.

'Take this,' he said, shoving a long, slim object into his hands.

He found himself holding a leather scabbard, from which he withdrew a dagger, plain apart from its sharp and gleaming blade. He stared down at it.

'Hide it inside your coat,' Munroe instructed. 'You might be needing it later.'

He fumbled as he slid the sheathed dagger into a pocket sewn into the lining of his coat, feeling very uncomfortable at the thought of carrying such a weapon. Why did Munroe believe he might need it? He tried to put it out of his mind as they left the lodgings but it was hard to forget when he could feel its constant pressure against his chest.

Munroe led him through a labyrinth of cobbled streets, many of which he recognised. He marvelled at the fact that, having previously stumbled along them in deep despair, he was now able to stride down them with some sense of purpose.

They turned onto a narrow street lined with cramped houses on both sides and came to a stop halfway down in front of a particularly grubby building. The brickwork was discoloured and the filthy windows had numerous broken or missing panes of glass. A scruffy child dawdled on the doorstep; when he saw Munroe and Cormac, he squeaked and vanished into the house.

'Just follow my lead,' Munroe said and approached the door, where another figure had appeared, presumably the boy's father. He wasn't a small man but fear hunched him over and he looked insignificant next to the strapping build of Munroe. He tried to block their way but Munroe pushed him aside and marched indoors. Cormac trailed after him with deep misgivings.

Munroe settled himself at a cluttered table in the kitchen and began rummaging through assorted bits of crockery, sewing, rags, and other domestic articles as though they were his own possessions. Cormac lingered awkwardly just inside the kitchen door. The man came in after them; he glared at Munroe but his hands were clutched together in profound anxiety. The child from the doorstep crept in too but the man pushed him out again.

'Go upstairs,' he hissed. 'And keep the others away too.'

The boy remained in the gap of the doorway, seeming like he was going to disobey his father, but the man reached out to smack him and he ran away down the hall. Cormac heard his feet thumping up the stairs, muffled voices in a room above, and then silence.

Munroe looked up at the man with an expression of severe disappointment. 'My eyesight must be getting worse, Doyle. For the life of me, I can't see any money set aside here for Mr Cunningham at all. Unless you have it hiding in a safe place somewhere else in the house? Do we need to search for it?'

Doyle shook his head.

'I remember saying I'd be back for it today,' said Munroe in a placid tone. 'D'you remember me saying that?'

The man nodded.

'Then where is it?'

Doyle's answer came out in barely more than a whisper. 'You might also remember the other part of that conversation where I told you I didn't have it.'

Munroe's eyes glittered with anger. 'Don't get mouthy with me,' he said, all pretence at civility disappearing in a second. 'You owe Mr Cunningham and we're not leaving 'til your debt's been paid.'

'I told you already, my daughter's ill. We need all our money to pay for her medicine. Without it, she might—'

'I don't give a damn about your daughter,' Munroe retorted, knocking over his chair as he shot to his feet. 'Makes no difference to me if she lives or dies. What I care about is ensuring Mr Cunningham's happy, and what'd make him happiest right now is to see the money you borrowed two months ago in his hand again. With the interest, of course.'

He moved closer to Doyle until they were only inches apart.

'Give me one more week,' said Doyle, his voice shaking.

Munroe's massive hands darted out and closed around Doyle's throat.

'Mr Cunningham gave you a second chance,' he snarled, 'and he never gives a third. If you can't give us money, we'll have to take something else that's worth the same value. What about your pretty wife? How much d'you think we'd get for her if we sold her to a brothel?'

Doyle's eyes bulged and he tried to speak but he could only make a choking sound with Munroe blocking his windpipe.

Throughout this exchange, Cormac had stood tensely by the door, feeling more and more unsure about his decision to accept Cunningham's offer. Munroe's behaviour was despicable. He supposed that threats were the only way a money lender could guarantee a return on his loans but was he, Cormac, capable of stooping to that level? Could he do this for a living?

He heard a muted whimper and looked down. A small, curly-haired boy, no more than two years old, had appeared in the doorway. His thumb was in his mouth and he gazed up at Cormac with wide, frightened eyes. He could not see Munroe and Doyle behind the door but the sounds his father was making were enough for him to know that he should be terrified of these strangers in his home.

Cormac had two choices. He could turn away from this scene, walk out the door and never return to Cunningham's lodgings, or he could assist Munroe in the task he had been assigned to do. In the first scenario, he would maintain his integrity but be back on the streets for his troubles. In the second, he would be able to hold on to the basic comforts of food and quarters which he had only just acquired, but he would run the risk of compromising his moral values in the process. Would he survive if he ended up homeless again, facing into another winter? Would he still be himself if he followed through this current situation to its resolution? What should he do?

An icy blast of wind through a broken window pane in the kitchen resolved his dilemma. He pulled his hidden dagger from its scabbard, dragged the small boy into view, and placed the blade at the boy's neck. Munroe and Doyle swivelled around and Doyle nearly fainted at the sight of his son being held at knife point. He shook his head frantically.

'All he needs is a little incentive, Munroe,' Cormac said in a low voice. 'Let him go so he can speak.'

Munroe relaxed his grip on Doyle's neck and the man took in deep, ragged breaths.

'Please,' he croaked. 'Please don't hurt him.'

'Tell us where the money is and I won't.'

Doyle put out a pleading hand. 'I'm begging you, don't do this.'

'Give us what you owe,' said Munroe, 'and he won't have to.'

Cormac contemplated the desperate man and then moved the dagger so that the tip of it was pressing into the boy's skin. The child began to wail. Anxious talking broke out above them before someone came running down the stairs. A young woman burst into the kitchen, wild-eyed at the sight before her.

'No!' she shrieked and stretched her arms out for the child, but Cormac jerked him out of her reach.

'Ye can have him back,' he shouted over the boy's cries, 'soon as we get what we came for.'

'Just give it to them!' the woman screamed at Doyle.

He scrabbled in the drawer of a dresser behind him, withdrew a teapot and fished out some money from inside it. He handed it over to Munroe and Cormac let go of the boy immediately. The woman snatched him up and buried her face in his curls.

Doyle stared at Cormac with bitterness. 'You didn't murder my son but you've probably killed my daughter. That was all the money we had left.'

'Mr Cunningham doesn't run a charity,' Munroe said and strode out of the kitchen.

Cormac followed, resisting the urge to look back at the devastation he had caused. Before today, he would never have believed himself capable of doing such a thing. But, faced once more with the prospect of destitution, he had committed a merciless, unscrupulous act that left him unrecognisable to himself. Disgust flooded through him and it was all he could do not to be sick on Doyle's doorstep.

'Nice work, McGovern,' Munroe said as they reached the top of the street. 'Cunningham'll be pleased with you. Looks like you're going to fit right in.'

Back at the lodgings, Cormac escaped to his room as soon as he could. Once the door was shut behind him, he dashed to the basin he had used yesterday for shaving and vomited into it. Crawling to his bed, he found he did not have the energy to pull himself up onto it so he just sat on the floor and leaned against the bed frame, legs weak and hands shaking.

He had just killed someone. If the daughter's condition truly was life-threatening, and should Doyle prove unable to procure the money from somewhere else to pay for her medicine, then Cormac's actions would be the major contributing factor to her death. He would be no less culpable had he gone upstairs and driven the dagger into her heart.

He pressed his fists into his temples. He was the lowest of human beings – he had inflicted pain upon others in order to deflect it from himself. If there was any humanity left in him, he would take that money and return it to the people who so badly needed it. Cunningham could manage without it. He should not have insisted that the loan be repaid at a time when the Doyle family could least afford it.

But Cormac quailed at the thought of defying Cunningham. At the very least, he would be thrown back onto the streets to starve and freeze again. If Cunningham was in a murderous mood – and Cormac was in no doubt that the money lender was capable of murder – then he might even lose his own life. What had happened to O'Connor, the man he had replaced? What 'unfortunate events' had Cunningham alluded to? An accident? Or an execution?

Part of him could not fathom how he had allowed himself to become embroiled in such sordid company. But another part remembered the alternative: the constant pain of an empty stomach...the agony of a cold so deep it went right through to his bones...the intense loneliness...the fear that he might die in a gutter and no one would bother to notice. He glanced at the tattered blanket, still puddled in the corner of the room. He could not return to that existence. He just could not.

Self-loathing surged within him. He knew he was being a coward, but his instinct for survival was even stronger than his compassion for others in distress. He did not attempt to justify it to himself. There was no point saying that almost any other person in this situation would have done the same. No point hoping that the Doyles had a friendly neighbour who might be able to help them. He had done a terrible deed and he could not deny it.

With a tremendous effort, he struggled to his knees and then to his feet. He looked into the mirror opposite him, his image visible despite the blemishes and cracks on the glass. His vivid blue eyes stared back, haunted by his appalling conduct. His shoulder-length fair hair, now that it had been washed, revealed once more that distinctive shade that only he and his sister Mary, out of all the McGovern children, had inherited from their father. What would Jack McGovern say if he stood before his son right now?

Cormac recalled the Grace of God Mission Society and their precondition for offering aid to the poor. He may as well have taken their soup when he had had the chance. He had lost himself anyway.

He stepped up to the mirror and drove his fist into the centre of it. Shards of glass scattered all over the floor.

# CHAPTER 10

The baby's wailing pervaded the nursery, high-pitched and hysterical.

'Oh, Emily,' Bridget crooned, swaying her daughter in her arms. 'Shush, don't fret, shush, shush.'

Her muscles ached; at six months, Emily was a plump, solid mass of flailing limbs. Bridget transferred the writhing body to her other hip and continued to murmur pacifying reassurances.

'You can entrust her to me, mistress,' the nurse said, hands outstretched, and there was more than a hint of 'I know better what to do with babies' in her tone.

Bridget remained polite. Mrs Crewe was only trying to fulfil the duties of her position, though it was one to which she had been appointed on Garrett's instruction and without Bridget's approval. 'Thank you, but no. I want to be able to calm her myself.'

Mrs Crewe's mouth compressed into a straight line. She could not seem to comprehend why a gently-bred lady would wish to concern herself with the messier side of raising children. Far better to surrender the child to a person of experience and only take her back once she had become quiet again.

But Bridget had promised herself from the start that she would not be one of those mothers. *She* would be the woman to raise her daughter, not a hired stranger, and she would cherish every aspect of that bond, from the gurgling laughter to the ear-splitting screams. Furthermore – Mrs Crewe's face had transformed into a picture of horror when she had been made aware of it – Bridget would require no wet nurse to feed her child. Some would consider it positively vulgar, but the sensation of her daughter's mouth suckling her breast was a marvellous wonder to her and not for one moment would she entertain the notion of giving it up for the sake of society's conventions.

However, she did rely otherwise on Mrs Crewe for her extensive knowledge and advice, for she had to concede that she knew very little about negotiating the intricacies of motherhood. She could remember when Maggie McGovern had given birth to Bronagh but she had been only seven at the time and had paid no attention to how Maggie had carried out critical tasks such as changing her soiled clothing or putting her to sleep.

On that point, even Mrs Crewe was struggling today. Emily shrieked and bawled with no sign of stopping, leaving Bridget with the desperate wish that her baby could speak and tell her what was the matter. She had been cleaned and fed and her temperature had seemed normal when Mrs Crewe had checked her forehead for fever. There appeared to be nothing wrong except that her small, red face was screwed up in unexplained distress.

When Bridget shifted Emily's weight again, Mrs Crewe's fingers convulsed.

'Would you mind very much leaving us alone?' Bridget asked her, striving for forbearance. 'I should like to accomplish this unaided, if you understand me.'

Clearly, Mrs Crewe did not understand at all, but she could not contradict her employer.

'As you say, mistress,' she said with forced composure and withdrew from the nursery looking aggrieved.

As soon as she was gone, Bridget let out a moan at the pain in her arms.

'Oh, Emily, Emily,' she said. 'Tell your mama what's amiss, my little gooseberry.'

She walked around the room while Emily continued to cry. With a glance at the closed nursery door, she bent her lips close to her daughter's ear. She started by speaking the prayers but switched to singing them, attaching an invented melody to give them a soothing quality and rocking Emily to the rhythm of the words. Over and over she recited the Our Father and the Hail Mary in the guttural lyricism of the Irish language. She was able to recall all of the Our Father but, to her chagrin, her memory could not summon up the full text of the Hail Mary. Every time she reached '*Tá an Tiarna leat*', she reluctantly had to skip the next two lines and go on to '*A Naomh Mhuire, a Mháthair Dé*'. Of course, there was no one in this country from whom she could seek illumination. For good measure, she crooned it all the way through in English as well.

Whether the prayers worked or Emily had simply tired herself out, she gradually grew quiet and nodded off, a slumbering boulder in Bridget's embrace. Thankful, Bridget laid the little girl into her cradle with infinite gentleness. Then she slipped her hand beneath the corner of the mattress and withdrew the wooden bird. It was an exceptional example of workmanship, a skilled carving of a bird about to break into song. She opened Emily's small fist and tucked the bird into it, letting the tiny fingers stretch across the bird's wing.

'Your papa wishes you a pleasant sleep,' she whispered.

She knew she could not get away with the sentiment for very long. Once Emily began to understand words, she would become confused if Bridget continued to make such oblique references to Cormac. But for now Bridget could console herself. And in the future, the bird would merely be a wooden toy of Emily's – she would not need to know where it had come from.

It was for Cormac that Bridget spoke the prayers, not wanting Emily to lose sight of the Irishness in her that came so much from her father. After the birth, Bridget had momentarily considered giving her an Irish name but then had thought better of it. Garrett knew Emily was not his, and knew it more each day as her eyes remained that astonishing blue and her golden curls grew in abundance. Bestowing an Irish name upon her as well would have rubbed salt in his wounds, which might have been no more than he deserved, but every single person of her acquaintance would have found it peculiar. Besides, Emily was a beautiful name.

Bridget stared down at the little girl. Where was her papa now? How Bridget yearned to know. Hope had risen in her a mere week before when a letter had arrived from Ireland, the address written in an unfamiliar hand. She had opened it with trembling fingers – would it contain information concerning Cormac's whereabouts? Was she moments from learning how to find him? Would she be able to get a message to him?

She had scanned the page swiftly, eager for good news. It had been penned by a Deacon Haybury who led the Grace of God Mission Society in Dublin. He could confirm that a young man called Cormac who fitted the description in Bridget's letter of enquiry had entered their building almost a year ago. Deacon Haybury himself had offered Cormac the chance to save his soul, but he had refused. The deacon could not say where the young man had gone next. He wished he could have been of more help, both to herself and to Cormac.

Bridget had pressed the letter to her breast and shed tears of relief and despair. To learn even this much – that Cormac had still been alive less than twelve months ago, that he had made it to Dublin – felt like a blessing, and yet the knowledge left her no better off than before. It had brought her to a dead end, just like all the other letters. Cormac was no nearer to her, no more tangible than the wooden bird carving.

The baby's fingers squeezed reflexively around the body of the bird. After leaving it there for a few minutes longer, Bridget eased it out of her grasp and slid it back under the mattress, hiding it from view. She kissed Emily's forehead and stole out of the nursery.

The nurse had lingered in the hallway and looked startled at her appearance, as if she had been caught listening at the keyhole.

'I just wanted to stay within earshot, mistress,' she said quickly. 'In case you called for my assistance.'

'Thank you, Mrs Crewe. She is sleeping now but I would be grateful if you would watch over her while I go speak with my husband on another matter.'

Mrs Crewe dipped her head in compliance and sidled back into the nursery.

Bridget walked down the long, cold corridor, shivering as a draught from a nearby window slithered across the nape of her neck. They were at Swifton Hall, the country seat of the Wyndham title and the home where Garrett had grown up. This was her first visit but she suspected there would not be many. As they had drawn near to the estate, she had sensed his whole body tautening like a length of rope stretched to its outermost limit. His mother had died here when he was a boy but she knew no more than that; he rarely spoke of Swifton Hall and never of his mother. The only reason they were here now was that Lord Wyndham had asked them to stay for the hunting and Christmas seasons and Garrett felt he could not refuse, given that Lord Wyndham had never voiced any objection to his son and daughter-in-law occupying the London townhouse on a full-time basis. The lord was out riding with his hounds at present but Garrett had remained behind today, informing Bridget that he wished to speak with her after luncheon. As though they were conducting a meeting of business, she had agreed to see him at three o'clock.

She found him sitting at a desk in the library, the fire in the hearth unable to penetrate the room beyond its meagre circle of warmth. She took up a position with her back to it and watched him peruse a document, the line of a frown creasing his brow.

'You desired to speak with me,' she eventually prompted when he made no effort to acknowledge her presence.

He waited a few seconds more before raising his gaze to hers, a childish attempt to assert his authority. 'I did,' he said and, unexpectedly, went on, 'I wanted to wish you a happy birthday.'

She had not forgotten the day but she had been certain he had.

'Oh,' she said. 'Thank you.'

'I have something for you.'

A birthday gift? Another surprise. She felt awkward about accepting it, considering the strained atmosphere that had burgeoned between them since Emily's birth, until he held out the document he had been reading. She approached the desk, puzzled, and took it from him. A quick glance at it explained all.

'Oh,' she said again, her voice harder.

He leaned back in his chair. 'It cannot have escaped your notice that twenty-one is a significant birthday for you.'

With all her thoughts absorbed in caring for Emily, it had, but she wasn't prepared to admit that. She shrugged.

'You now legally inherit the Oakleigh Estate and the Courcey title. Which means we have some papers to sign.' He gestured at the document.

She looked down at it. 'What exactly does this say?'

'It confers the guardianship of Oakleigh onto your mother in perpetuity. She will continue to be responsible for supervising the estate on your behalf, along with the assistance of the agent, Mr Enright, and you will have no need to concern yourself with it.'

She turned away from him and went back to the heat of the fire, still clutching the document but disregarding its contents. Her heart fluttered in her chest. Oakleigh was hers. By rights, she could assume the title of Lady Courcey this very day and take charge of the estate.

She felt like an imprisoned bird whose cage door had been unlocked. She was free to fly out through that opening and take wing with Emily to Ireland. Such an action could not be viewed as desertion; she would merely be fulfilling the legal obligation of her position.

Oakleigh was a place of agonising memories, there was no doubt about that. But it had also been where she had spent her childhood, a truly happy time when she had been surrounded by friendly faces and picturesque countryside. It was *home* and it would be a joy to raise Emily there.

Moreover, she was certain she would relish the challenge of managing the estate, of attending to her tenants' affairs and overseeing the productivity of the land. And she could not forget that that was the role her father had intended for her once it had become clear there would be no sons in the family.

The one setback which might clip her wing and knock her out of the sky was that her mother still lived at Oakleigh. Could she contemplate sharing a home with her, after the transgressions she had committed? No, she could not. She would have to send her away, perhaps to occupy the Dublin townhouse in Merrion Square again. Turning her out with nowhere to go would be a sweet serving of poetic justice but

Bridget supposed she was not that ruthless. In any case, she would have no need of the townhouse, not when she and Emily would be more than content to spend all their time in the heart of the country. It was an enchanting image and, astoundingly, it was within her reach.

She looked at Garrett where he still sat behind his desk, arms folded as he stared at her. As her husband, he had every power to compel her to do what he wanted because, in marrying him, she had rescinded her privilege to administer her property in her own right. She would need to determine the best way to negotiate her path to freedom.

'May I have some time to think about this?' she said.

'What is there to think about?'

'I must consider the terms carefully. After all, I have a duty to my tenants and to the legacy left to me by my father—'

'Take all the time you need,' he interrupted, his voice smooth. 'But allow me to assist you in your "decision". I am by no means disposed to permit my wife to live apart from me, not only on a different estate but in a different country. If, however, you choose to persist in that intention then be aware that Emily will remain in England with me.'

All of the air leaked out of her lungs. She inhaled to refill them but still struggled for breath. 'Are you...are you capable of callousness of that magnitude?'

'I am.'

'Why would you want her to stay, when you know...'

He narrowed his eyes. 'I want a son, a child of my own. And I cannot very well achieve that goal without my wife, can I? To keep you here, I must keep her here.'

He delivered this with a coldness more severe than the chilly air of the library. She stalked back to the desk and tossed the paper on its surface. He had forced her hand.

'I'll sign it. Of course I will,' she said, with no little frostiness of her own.

A look of grim satisfaction crossed his face. 'No time like the present.'

He passed her a pen. She came around to his side of the desk, dipped the pen in the inkpot, and signed at the bottom of the document. He took the pen from her and signed his own name, her authorisation not being complete without his signature.

'There is one more thing,' he said when she made a move to leave. His satisfied look had disappeared and the contour of his jaw had stiffened. 'Your mother's solicitor sent me all the records relating to Oakleigh and the entailment on the estate.'

'Fascinating reading material, I'm sure.'

'I have examined the stipulations of the entail in detail. You must already be aware, given your own position as heiress, that the inheritance of Oakleigh is governed by male-preference primogeniture.'

She raised her eyebrows.

'It was an extraordinary decision by your ancestors. Quite unorthodox. But it means that in the event of there being no male issue, the birthright will pass to any female progeny of the title holder. Hence...'

'Emily will inherit Oakleigh,' she said, awed.

'If we do not have any sons,' he finished, decidedly unimpressed.

She had an overwhelming urge to laugh. No doubt her great-grandfather had never envisaged a scenario like this when Oakleigh first came into existence. But, as it turned out, the daughter of a stable hand could someday preside over one of the finest properties in Ireland.

She was prevented from saying anything further by the sound of frantic running and the appearance of a servant in the doorway to the library. He looked ashen and dishevelled, quite out of line with the meticulous standards of Swifton Hall's staff.

'Sir, beg pardon!' he gasped. 'I must tell you—'

Garrett got to his feet. 'What is it?' he demanded.

'It's his l-lordship!' The servant gulped. 'We were on the hunt and I s-saw him clutch at his chest afore...afore he fell from his horse. I'm so sorry, m'lord.'

'M'lord'. The only way Garrett could be addressed thus was if his father was dead.

Garrett turned to Bridget. 'I need you,' he said, sounding surprised. Then his knees buckled.

# CHAPTER 11

Cormac twirled the dagger lazily, weaving it back and forth between his fingers. The wine merchant's eyes followed the blade, mesmerised by the sinuous motion.

'Ten pounds,' said Cormac.

The merchant licked his lips. 'I have five. I can give you the rest next week.'

'Ten,' said Cormac. 'Today.'

They sat on either side of a table in a dingy corner of the merchant's warehouse, stacks of empty crates all around them. Cormac's feet were propped up on the tabletop, casually crossed at the ankles, while the merchant's palms were splayed out on the rough surface.

'I'm due a shipment before the end of May,' he said in a pleading tone. 'It'll bring in money for me. Just one more week, that's all I'm asking for.'

Cormac's gaze was enough to make the merchant shrink back in his chair. He swung his feet to the ground, went around to the other side of the table, and sat on its edge.

'Are you left-handed or right-handed?'

The merchant blinked. 'Wh-what?'

Cormac repeated the question.

'Why?'

'I'm just trying to decide whether to be generous and take your bad hand instead of your good one.'

The merchant jerked his hands behind his back, leaving sweaty marks on the tabletop. 'No!'

'You're not leaving me with much of a choice. Mr Cunningham was very clear. The full amount with interest today or a penalty for the delay. He wasn't specific on the details but I've got an active imagination.'

He wrenched on the man's right arm, twisting it to expose the blue veins on his wrist, and pressed the sharp edge of the dagger to his flesh. The merchant cowered, his body nearly slipping off the chair as he sank further down into it, his arm outstretched in Cormac's iron grip.

'Please, no...' he whimpered.

'D'you have an alternative proposal? Ten pounds perhaps?'

The blade glided over the skin and beads of blood bubbled up and trickled down the sides of the man's wrist.

'I don't have the money! But I will when the shipment comes in, I swear!'

Cormac eyed the tip of the dagger, now shining red. 'Big shipment, is it?'

'Yes!' the merchant said, head bobbing eagerly. 'I'll be able to get the other five pounds for you as soon as it arrives.'

'I think we can do better than that, don't you?'

He wasn't long in making it back to the lodgings after that.

'Smart lad, this one is!' Munroe hollered to the other men who lounged around the dining area of the lodgings, enjoying their drinks and the attentions of the scantily-clad girls draped about them. Cormac sat on a bench wolfing down his meal and did not react when Munroe clapped him on the shoulder.

'Got the five pounds today and half of the shipment's profits next week. Far better outcome than the original ten. I'm telling yous, no one gets past this fellow!'

The men cheered and raised glasses to Cormac. He shrugged and said nothing.

'Cunningham was well pleased to hear it. Here you go.' Munroe placed a tumbler of first-rate whiskey on the table in front of Cormac with a flourish. 'Compliments of the chief himself.'

Cormac didn't reach out to take it. 'What'd he say when you told him?'

'That it was a lucky day when Lawlor threw that stick at you.' Munroe grinned. 'You've really made a name for yourself now. Might be someday soon you'll advance to the upper ranks.'

After a year and a half, Cormac was still a lower henchman, doing the grunt work. But Cunningham had a small ring of men around him, including Munroe, who handled mysterious dealings the underlings knew nothing about. Cormac suspected it involved giving loans to more respectable members of society, which required a level of intellect and discretion not found in your average lackey. A promotion to that level would indeed be a sign of faith in his abilities.

Munroe thrust the glass towards him. 'Take your time and enjoy. You've earned it.'

Cormac swallowed the drink in one, ignoring the burning sensation in his throat, and pushed himself up from the bench. 'Thanks. See you tomorrow.'

In his room, he lined up the plank against the back of the door and started practising. Every thunk of the blade into the wood was satisfying to his ears. He stood further back and aimed again. The dagger sailed through the air and lodged halfway up the plank. It wasn't quite where he had intended it to land, but he could feel the effects of the whiskey dulling his dexterity as the alcohol spread through his body.

A raucous roar drifted up from the dining area below. The men were settling in for the evening, boisterous after the news of his success with the wine merchant – no doubt a crate from the shipment's profits would end up in the lodgings for their consumption. Such bounty would go a long way towards easing their resentment of his unsociable behaviour. Not that he cared much for popularity anyway. He had their respect and that was enough.

He yanked the dagger out of the plank, remembering the similar force he had used on the merchant's arm. It was likely he had sprained the man's elbow, an injury more damaging than the shallow cut on his wrist. But the fool had resisted longer than Cormac had expected. He must not have been acquainted with the reputation that preceded Cunningham's man McGovern – most people he threatened were already aware that he was capable of terrorising a small child. They were the ones who succumbed to his demands most quickly. Then again, the merchant had probably found the devil he met today difficult to reconcile with the affable fellow full of pleasantries he had encountered when he came to Cunningham looking for help. Who would have believed that such a friendly chap would be willing to draw a blade on a man in dire trouble?

It was a poor way to repay him, Cormac supposed. Although he could not be certain, he was reasonably confident that the warehouse had been the same one from which he had stolen a bottle of wine a year and a half ago. The trade for that wine had staved off his hunger for a night – in token of that, a person of compassion might have viewed the confrontation with the merchant as an occasion to be lenient. But that was not how the world of money lending worked. If he had shown one sign of weakness, Cunningham's response would have been a ruthless punishment instead of a tumbler of whiskey.

Just as he threw the dagger again, a knock on the door disturbed his concentration. The shot went wild and the flat side of the dagger struck the wall before clattering to the floor.

He cursed and bent to retrieve it, then removed the plank and opened the door. One of the half-clothed girls from the dining area stood there, one hand on her hip, the other resting on the door jamb. She had long, black hair and full lips which were quirked into a suggestive smile. Her breasts bulged above the low neckline of her bodice, bursting to escape it.

'What d'you want?' he said roughly.

'I'm a gift,' she said. 'From the men below. They thought you deserved a reward for your hard work today.'

'Not interested.'

'Ah, now, don't go hurting a girl's feelings. Come on, you'll enjoy it.'

He started to close the door but she said quickly, 'Wait!'

He paused, levelling her with a gaze of absolute indifference.

'If I go down right away, they'll take the money back. Can I just come inside for a few minutes? I promise I'll leave after that. We can say you couldn't wait to finish.' She grinned.

He gave an irritated nod, let her in, and shut the door.

She sidled over to the bed and sat on the edge of it. He made a point of taking the chair by the window and laid the dagger on the windowsill.

'I'm Thomasina.'

He didn't offer his own name.

She looked at the scars on the plank. 'You've got good aim.'

'I'm working on it.'

She leaned back on her hands. Her open-fronted skirt was designed to show off pretty petticoats but, as she suffered from a deficiency of these, it revealed her stockings and a substantial amount of bare thigh instead. The end of a short shift was a negligible attempt to protect her modesty.

'Sounds like you're a man to be feared, according to the stories downstairs.'

He didn't bother to reply.

'How come you never hang about down below? Good-looking fellow such as yourself, all us girls have been eyeing you for months. I'd to fight the others off to get this job.'

'I like my solitude.'

She squinted at him. 'Is that really it? Or would you prefer if my name was Thomas?'

He frowned. 'No.'

'Just checking.'

She stood and wandered over to the window. One of her shift's diaphanous sleeves slipped down, baring the curve of her white shoulder.

'I like this time of year, when it's so late but there's still a bit of brightness in the sky. Look at that, past nine o'clock and I can still see down into the alleyway.' She turned to him. 'You ever been with a girl?'

'Why d'you ask?'

'I thought maybe you're afraid. But I'm good with the virgins. I can show you what to do.'

She was being persistent, he had to give her credit for that. 'No need to worry yourself.'

'So you have. Who was she? Not anyone in this building, that's for sure. Those hussies would be boasting about it if they had.'

He was silent.

'Go on, tell me. Have there been many? Or just one? Ah, I think just the one.'

She was reading his face too well and he didn't like it.

'Did you love her?'

'Can we change the subject?'

'That's a yes anyway. Did she love you or did you take advantage?'

That riled him up. 'I'd never—!'

'I hear you, calm down. Where's she now?'

He looked away. 'Not here.'

'That's good to know. I was thinking of checking under the bed. D'you still love her?'

'I'd like you to leave now.'

'Just a little longer. I don't want them to doubt whether it happened. Even if you were very quick, there'd usually be a bit of time afterwards to catch our breath.' She touched his arm. 'So you do still love her. How'd you come to be apart?'

'I'm not answering any more questions. You talk too much.'

'Well, you know the easiest way to get me to stop talking, don't you?'

She slid into his lap and he surprised himself by not protesting. Maybe it was the whiskey. Or maybe he was just goddamned lonely.

She ran her fingers through his hair. She smelled of smoke and sweat but there was something sweet there too, her natural female scent. She leaned in closer so that her round lips brushed his earlobe.

'They paid the full amount. You can do whatever you want. If you want to.' She wriggled in his lap and giggled as his body responded. 'And I think you do.'

To hell with it.

He pulled her to him and covered her mouth with his. She was quick to react, straddling him and rising up so that her hair fell like a curtain around his face. Their tongues stroked together and he savoured the feeling of connecting with another human being in a way other than threats and violence; it had no foundation in sincerity or sentiment but he told himself that didn't matter. He squeezed the fleshy mounds of her breasts while her own hands delved downwards, expertly negotiating buttons and fall to gain access. Her explorations were thorough, eliciting a ragged intake of breath from him as sensation overcame reason.

He stood and she wrapped her legs around his hips. He carried her over to the bed and laid her down on it.

'D'you have any preferences?' she asked.

She rolled onto her stomach, tossed back her skirt to expose shapely buttocks, and peeked over her shoulder with a coquettish wink. He caught hold of her hip and flipped her onto her back again.

'A traditionalist,' she said and for an instant seemed rather shy, as though she was not used to performing the act face to face. She opened her legs to entice him in and he accepted her invitation.

He just wanted to forget about everything in his life and focus on this one instant of reckless abandon. But the memories tugged at him, buzzing in his mind like insistent flies. Instead of a bed, a haystack. Instead of black hair, chestnut curls. Instead of lust, love. God, this was wrong. He was using the girl. And betraying Bridget in the process. But he was never going to see her again. And he was certain her bed was not empty.

It was anger which powered him through to the end. He groaned and fell to the side. She stretched like a cat.

'There now, don't you feel better?'

She could not be further from the truth. He closed his eyes. 'Get out.'

'Y'know, I thought you'd be rougher.' Her hands crept across his chest. 'It's half price if you want a second go.'

He opened his eyes and slapped her hands away. She stared at him, goggling.

'I said get out,' he growled.

'Fine, I can tell when I'm not wanted,' she said, even though that had patently not been the case for most of their encounter.

She started to slither off the bed but he seized her ankle to hold her back.

'Ow, that hurts!' she protested.

He pinched harder, making her squeak in pain.

'Nothing that's been said or done goes outside this room, d'you understand me? There'll be no sniggering with your companions later. And I don't want to see you or any of them darken my door again, d'you hear?'

He glanced over at the dagger which rested on the windowsill. For the first time, she looked fearful. She nodded and he released his grip. She straightened her clothes and darted from the room like she couldn't leave his presence fast enough.

He slid off the bed and went over to the window. He gazed at the blade for a moment. Then he picked it up, turned, and hurled it at the closed door. It landed exactly at the height of Thomasina's head.

# CHAPTER 12

Emily tottered towards Bridget, crying, 'Birdie! Birdie!' and waving her wooden bird gaily above her head. Bridget laughed and swept her up and around in the air.

'You can fly like the birdie too!' she exclaimed.

Emily shrieked with delight. 'Again!'

Bridget swung her around once more and then they collapsed together on the floor of the nursery in Wyndham House, her skirts billowing about them. She panted for breath; having just celebrated her second birthday, Emily was a ball of energy and every single day was an inquisitive, exhausting adventure of discovery.

Without warning, the door opened and Garrett appeared on the threshold. Bridget's heart lurched and she threw the hem of her gown over Emily's hand, concealing the object she grasped. Emily deemed this to be an entertaining lark and proceeded to crawl entirely beneath her mother's skirts.

Bridget glanced back at Garrett. Had he seen the bird? She thought not; he expressed no sign of recognition or anger. He advanced into the room while his valet, Brewer, hovered in the hallway beyond.

'I am going to the club,' he said, 'and I expect to be detained until late into the evening. It is best I stay there tonight instead of disturbing the house at all hours.'

'Very well,' she replied. She couldn't stand without revealing the bird so she remained on the floor, pretending that it was Emily's antics which prevented her from rising.

He stooped and dropped a kiss on her forehead. The tender gesture would have felt out of place only for what had occurred between them a month ago.

Upon the sad circumstance of his father's passing eighteen months previously, he had displayed a vulnerability which she had not seen in him before. To lose one parent at Swifton Hall had been bad enough; to lose the second there was intolerable and in his grief he had sworn they would never go back. To her surprise, the weight of the viscountcy had settled on his shoulders as an unwelcome burden.

'What man could ever desire to come into his inheritance when it necessitates the death of his own father?' he had burst out to her.

It had taken quite a while before he was able to accept his new place in the world, his ascent to the peerage and the obligations that came with such a status. During this adjustment period, he had relied upon Bridget to provide a sense of stability in their household. The servants had known to go to Lady Wyndham on matters that did not require their master's urgent attention. She had deflected many visits from acquaintances who wanted to sympathise or wish him well on attaining his birthright, conscious that he had no inclination to make civil discourse. She had liaised with Brewer to ensure that he was attended to whenever he called for it and left in peace whenever he did not.

She didn't think he had perceived her role of support and she hadn't looked for any acknowledgement of it. She was his wife and now a viscountess; it was no more than her duty demanded. Over time, he had emerged from his miasma of mourning, taking his seat in the House of Lords and socialising more regularly at his club again, and their lives had returned to a semblance of normality.

And then last month he had come to her. He had avoided her bed for so long that she hadn't expected his appearance and she had found herself wordless when he had entered her chamber and slipped under the covers beside her. But he had made no move to possess her. Leaning on his elbow, he had gazed at her with an expression free of any false emotion.

'I want to thank you,' he had said. 'You may believe I didn't notice, but I did.'

He had held her and kissed her and, when they had engaged in that intimate act, he had thought of more than his own pleasure, giving her a measure of satisfaction for the first time in their marriage.

Afterwards, she had been plagued by guilt, worried that the experience of such sensations by Garrett's caress was a treachery to the man who had first given them to her. All she could do was remind herself that she had not invited Garrett's attentions and felt no inclination to receive his advances that way again. Still, she could not deny that having a form of amity established between them was more restful. They were by no means a blissfully-married couple, but their relationship had lost some of its antagonism. She comprehended how badly he yearned for a child, a son, and she realised that she was not averse to the idea herself, knowing the joys that motherhood could bring. Perhaps their newfound tentative concord would lead to that happy event and to a lessening of the strife in their lives.

She looked up at him from her position on the nursery floor and offered him a cautious smile. He touched her shoulder and took his leave.

The next day, she paid a visit to St Swithun's, now a customary component of her weekly routine. The servants at Wyndham House had become well-versed in what was expected of them on these occasions. Her lady's maid, Audley, laid out her plainest gown and sturdiest boots and only assisted in lacing up her stays before leaving the bedchamber to let her finish dressing by herself. Neither Thrussell nor Peter stood at the front door to see her out. The carriage was not brought around; she would make her way there and back on foot. She could not avoid these trappings of her upper class position in the general scheme of things, but it seemed hypocritical to benefit from them on days when she would be in the company of people who would never have any hope of attaining such luxuries.

Upon her arrival to the soup kitchen – which now boasted four neatly-dressed women who tended the cooking fires and presided over a plentiful assortment of clean bowls and spoons – she was alarmed to find Frances in a state of some agitation.

'There was an official-looking fellow here this morning,' she told Bridget, even as she chopped up a cabbage to add to a boiling pot of water. 'Poking around and making enquiries.'

Bridget frowned. 'Enquiries about what?'

Frances tossed the cabbage pieces into the pot and wiped her hands on her apron. 'He asked about the poor folk, the numbers in the workhouse, the volume of people coming to the kitchen each day, how many able-bodied individuals are abusing the system, and so on. And he made some comments about the insupportable strain on the state due to the extensive funding it provides. As though it gives us that much.' She scowled. 'I think it's a bad sign. There are rumours of a commission being established to investigate it further. Not just here but all around the country.'

Bridget bit the tip of her tongue. 'Surely they couldn't be thinking of shutting us down? The relief we provide is immeasurable.'

Frances lifted one shoulder in an expression of doubt. 'Who knows what's on their minds? But it's causing concern in mine. Will you pass me another cabbage?'

As Bridget did so, she caught a whiff of the steam emanating from the boiling pot. In her distraction, Frances must have left a previous batch of cabbage cooking for too long; the unpleasant smell made Bridget's stomach turn. Choking back her nausea, she donned her own apron and set to work.

She returned to Wyndham House later that afternoon to learn from Lizzie that Garrett had come back an hour before her. Given how much time he had taken to spending at his club, he was rarely around to witness her dressed-down attire, but she knew it wouldn't please him to see it – especially the large soup stain she had acquired on the skirt – and she hastened to her bedchamber to change. However, a wail drifting down from the next floor sent her running up to the nursery instead.

She found Emily in floods of tears and inconsolable by the nurse.

'What has happened?' she demanded after a swift visual assessment confirmed that no physical harm had befallen her daughter.

Mrs Crewe patted Emily's head. 'Poor thing has lost her toy. I've told her it's likely to be under some piece of furniture but we haven't managed to find it yet.'

A block of ice formed in Bridget's stomach. 'Which toy?'

'That pretty little bird she's always playing with. Where are you going, my lady?'

Bridget was hurrying from the nursery before Mrs Crewe had finished speaking. She pounded down the stairs to Garrett's bedchamber. She almost stormed in without knocking but at the last moment gave a sharp rap on the door instead.

'Enter,' said his smooth voice.

She stalked in. A strong scent of cologne hung in the air and a fire crackled in the hearth; it was a cold day for May. He was standing before the window, his back ramrod straight. When he turned to her, his steely countenance said he knew she would come and he was ready for her fury.

She didn't have to ask if he had taken it. 'Give it back,' she said, low and ominous.

'No,' he replied.

She pointed an accusing finger at him. 'You have no right to keep it from her. Give it back.'

'I cannot.'

'You would choose to leave her in hysterics instead?'

'It is not a question of choice. I cannot return it to her now.'

'What do you—'

She froze. Then she swivelled to the fireplace.

'No!' she gasped.

She dashed to it and fell to her knees on the hearth rug. The blackened chunk of wood was missing its legs and its beautiful beak but the shape of one wing was still recognisable. She grabbed the tongs and endeavoured to clasp the remains in its grip. The wood disintegrated upon contact and the bird was no more.

A wave of anguish rose up in her throat but she pushed it back down. She would not let him see her cry. She dropped the tongs and stood to face him.

'The level of your cruelty is unimaginable.'

His fists clenched at his sides. 'You have no entitlement to speak of cruelty when it is your greatest weapon.'

'I beg your pardon?' she said, stunned.

'Don't act innocent. You are a mistress of cruelty.'

'I don't have the faintest idea what you mean!'

He gesticulated at the charred mess in the grate. 'That! And the Catholic prayers! And the Irish words!'

She baulked.

'Yes, I decided to spend some time with your daughter when I returned today. I may have no comprehension of the language myself, but I can still tell that her own grasp of Irish is near enough to that of English. It is *unacceptable*!'

He roared the last word at her. She took a step back but he strode forward and grabbed her by the shoulders.

'He is a phantom in this house. His presence is everywhere where you and that girl are and I will not tolerate it any longer. This is the last time you and I shall mention him. I tell you now that the prayers will stop, the Irish will stop, and any attempt on your part to pursue them further will result in punishment, not for you but for her. For all intents and purposes, and in all likelihood in reality, he is *dead* and you shall expel him from this house or, so help me God, I will make you regret it.'

He flung her away from him and marched back to the window. When he spun to confront her again, he had eradicated all emotion from his expression. With a detached air, he said, 'You may have already suspected this but, if you have not, let me enlighten you. I have a mistress. I was with her last night. She is not the first since the beginning of our marriage. I'll make no allusions to her or any others again, but know this: as long as you continue to hurt me, I will continue to hurt you.'

Her senses rioted in response to this unforgiving speech. Her vision blurred, her ears hummed, her throat closed to any intake of air. In the midst of her shock, she felt a grain of thankfulness that he had never become aware of the letters of enquiry she had sent to Ireland, fruitless though they may have been. Had he learned of those, she feared he might actually have raised his hand to her now.

When she finally trusted herself to speak, all she could think to say was, 'I understand.'

She stumbled to the door. On the threshold, she turned and looked back at him.

'I did not know when to deliver this news to you. But I shall return your honesty in kind. Though I cannot say it with absolute certainty, I believe I am with child.'

And she walked out without waiting to see his reaction.

# CHAPTER 13

Cormac strode along the docks, conscious of the dual weights of the dagger against his chest and a bag of coins against his thigh. He had just made his final visit to the wine merchant, who had relinquished the last of the negotiated profits with a poorly-disguised glower. It had taken nearly four weeks for him to amass the full amount from the sale of his cargo but Cunningham had instructed Cormac to be lenient at this juncture, given the substantial revenue to be gleaned from the bargain. Cormac had adopted a courteous and relaxed demeanour as he collected the remainder of the money but the merchant, holding his right arm in a gawky manner, had bid him farewell with a murderous tone to his own civil words.

Dusk was setting in, a blanket of pink-orange sky suspended over the River Liffey. The lingering rays of sun gilded the rigging of a ship moored nearby. Crewmen scurried over its deck and passengers queued on the dock, waiting to board. A lone seagull wheeled overhead and landed on the ship's tallest mast, shrieking softly.

As he went by the open double doors of a warehouse, he heard scuffling within and a girl's tremulous remonstration floated out. 'I s-said no kissing.'

The deep voice of a man responded, 'Come on, love, one little kiss won't hurt.'

'Kissing c-costs extra.'

He forced himself to keep moving. A whore's affairs were no concern of his. However, he had barely passed the end of the warehouse when there was a muffled crash, followed by a scream that was cut short.

He hesitated. It was none of his business; the sensible course of action would be to stay out of it. But the girl's voice had stirred something inside him, something he had not allowed himself to feel for a long time. A brotherly instinct. She sounded very young, as young as Margaret or maybe even Bronagh. Not much more than a child. What had happened to her that she had been reduced to the most disreputable of occupations at such a tender age?

He whirled around and marched back to the entrance of the warehouse. The customer might have paid for the girl's services but he had no right to mistreat her. Cormac stood in the doorway and let his eyes adjust to the gloom. A pile of overturned crates lay strewn on the dusty floor of the warehouse. Next to them, a man in dirty clothes and scuffed boots was kneeling over a ragged, redheaded girl and pressing his mouth hard on hers. She was whimpering and struggling to heave him off herself.

Cormac approached the pair, grabbed the man by the back of his coat, and hauled him off the girl. She scrambled out of the way, gasping.

The man gaped at Cormac in disbelief. 'What the hell d'you think you're doing?'

'She said no kissing.'

The man looked ready to throttle him. 'Get your interfering nose out of my business,' he growled and made to turn back to the girl.

Cormac laid a restraining hand on the man's shoulder and withdrew his dagger. He winced at how swift he was to produce the weapon; the act had become far too natural for him.

'I think you should leave,' he said calmly.

The man's eyes widened as they focused on the razor-sharp blade. 'Who're you?'

'I work for Cunningham. D'you know who that is?'

The man's face filled with foreboding. However, he tried to put on an air of bravado as he said, 'I paid good money for the wench. She's got to do her job.'

Cormac beckoned to the girl, who was cowering next to the fallen crates. 'Give him back his money.'

She fumbled in her shabby bodice and dropped some coins on the floor. Cormac stared at the money in pity; she had been selling herself for next to nothing. The man plucked up every single coin and passed his hand through the dust to make sure he had not missed any. With a last resentful look at Cormac, he lumbered out of the warehouse and into the dusk.

Cormac offered his hand to the girl but she shrank back further against the crates. He realised he was still gripping the dagger and quickly put it away, then held out his hand again.

'I won't hurt you,' he said.

After another faltering moment, she reached out and he helped her to her feet. She touched a cut on her arm, casting a grimace at the upended crates. The wound did not appear to be deep though and it had already stopped bleeding.

She peered up at him from beneath pale eyelashes. 'Why'd you do that?'

'He was a thug. If he doesn't play by the rules, he shouldn't be allowed to play. How old are you?'

'Eighteen.' She had to be lying; she looked a lot younger than that.

'How long have you been doing this?'

She hung her head in shame. 'That was my first time.'

'Might I suggest you make it the last too?'

She continued to look down at the floor. 'I can't. I need the money.'

He didn't say anything else. He just stood there and surveyed the pitiable young thing in front of him. She was the exact opposite of Thomasina. That black-haired seductress had known her talents in the bedchamber and had flaunted them to the best of her ability. This girl huddled in on herself like she was embarrassed by her own body. Her red hair hung in dull, straggly clumps, the bones of her arms stood out starkly, and there was a yellowish tinge to her skin and eyes. She had to be either living on the streets or in the most basic of shelters.

He understood the desperation of her situation and did not try to offer any platitudes. How could he tell her to find a more honourable way to survive when he himself had been unable to take that advice in his own hopeless circumstances?

He imagined what it would feel like if it were one of his sisters who had been reduced to this vulnerable state, forced to sacrifice the purity of her body in order to feed herself. Once again, he experienced a strong, brotherly impulse to protect, followed by an intense wave of homesickness which threatened to overpower him. Ever since he had left Oakleigh, and especially since he had joined Cunningham's crew, he had actively blocked out all thoughts of his family and his past. But this girl, this pathetic, would-be prostitute, had broken through his defences and set loose a thousand memories which all clamoured for recognition inside his head. Mary's temperamental expression, fluctuating from irritable to tender in a heartbeat. Margaret's faraway smile as she daydreamed about true love. Bronagh scowling after receiving yet another reprimand from the cook. Orlaith's diligence and affection in caring for her chickens. And his mother. Darning in her rocking chair, praying over her rosary beads. Scolding him, hugging him, weeping in his arms.

All of a sudden, he felt so emotionally shattered that his legs went weak and he had to sit down on one of the crates. The tremendous effort he had put into barring himself from thinking about any part of his old life was too much to sustain any longer. It had consumed him, made him forget who he was, led him to commit unspeakable acts. Now there was nothing left but a broken shell that even his mother would not recognise. He felt drained, ashamed, conscience-stricken.

It was easy to pinpoint the rotten source of his circumstances. Cunningham was the poison running through his veins. He had twisted his view of the world, made him believe that he had nothing left to lose, that it was acceptable to hurt others, that inflicting harm and unhappiness was a small price to pay for a hot meal and a bed. But the cost of these luxuries had been enormous; he had damaged the lives of countless people, and he had lost his integrity in the process.

The solution to this horrifying revelation came to him in an instant. He had to get away from here. Not just from the warehouse, not just from the city, but from the country. If he ever hoped to find his way back to the person he used to be, he needed to distance himself as much as possible from this place of violence and corruption and from the fiend who cultivated that sordid environment.

Standing again, he groped in his pocket and withdrew the bag of coins he had collected from the wine merchant. Wordlessly, he held it out to the redheaded girl, tugging on its string to reveal its contents. During his internal battle of emotions, she had started to cry, but now her tears stopped as she stared, amazed, at the money.

'What—?' she said in a tone of utter bewilderment.

'Take it,' he urged and thrust the bag into her hands. 'You need it a lot more than that goddamned bastard does.'

She was too flabbergasted to either ask him who he meant or to be offended by his language. After the briefest flash of uncertainty, she crammed the bag deep inside her bodice. She hovered on the balls of her feet, about to run, so he grabbed her wrist to hold her back.

'Use it carefully,' he warned. 'Mind you don't find yourself here again.'

She nodded. He released her and she fled. When he was certain she was gone, he approached the warehouse's entrance. From the doorway, he had a clear view of the ship he had seen earlier. A pair of gangways now stretched from the dock to the deck and the waiting passengers were crossing over them in two groups, the well-heeled separated from those of more modest means. It looked like they were about to embark on a night voyage.

He considered the ship and made his decision. There was no point in delaying and he had no personal belongings to go back for. Regardless of where the vessel was headed, it was perfect for what he needed.

He thought of the money he had just given away and wondered whether he ought to have retained some of it for himself. But he couldn't very well pay for his new life with money stained by his past actions. So he would have to figure out how to get on board without a ticket.

He emerged from the warehouse and strolled back along the docks. Dusk had darkened into night and one of the crewmen on the ship was holding up a lantern to light the way for the boarding passengers. There were more lanterns hanging at sporadic intervals along the ship's deck; by their dim illumination he could make out the full length of the vessel. The gangways seemed to be the only method of boarding it. But that would not do for a stowaway.

Going as close to the edge of the dock as he dared without raising suspicion, he scrutinised the structure of the ship. A portion of the rigging for the sails was attached to the hull, stretching down almost to the waterline; the ropes would make decent footholds for an adept climber. If it was the same on the other side, where there would not be so many watchful eyes, then that would be his access point.

He ambled further up the docks until he was out of sight of the ship. Glancing around for any onlookers and finding none, he swung his legs over the wall of the dock, lowered himself from the edge by his fingertips, and dropped the last few feet into the water. The cold was instantaneous but bearable. He tried very hard to ignore the questionable quality of the reeking River Liffey.

It had been a long time since he had gone swimming, but he and Bridget had spent many carefree days frolicking in the Sruhawn on the Oakleigh Estate in their youth. He struck out in the direction of the ship, slicing through the water as quietly as he could. The weight of his clothes made progress slower but not impossible. When the vessel came into view, he took a deep breath, ducked below the surface, and swam the rest of the way underwater. He did not break the surface again until he had come alongside the flank of the ship facing onto the river.

Sucking in lungfuls of air, he floated in the water as he scanned the hull in search of the rigging. He spotted it, swam over, and grabbed onto the mesh of rope. Water dripped from his heavy clothing as he hauled himself up and he expelled an involuntary grunt with the effort of it. Panicked, he clung to the rigging and waited for an inquisitive head to peer over the side and raise the alarm. No one appeared, but he counted for a hundred seconds before he deemed it safe to climb again.

When he reached the gunwale, he hoisted himself inch by inch above it until he had a view in both directions of the deck, which was lit by another scattering of lanterns. Luck was with him; it was deserted. The crew's attention must still be occupied with the gangways at the far side of the ship, while the passengers were probably ensconcing themselves indoors for the night crossing.

He scrambled over the gunwale and hunted around for an adequate hiding spot. Further down the deck, he noticed a long chest shrouded in a sheet of tarpaulin. He feared the chest might have a locked lid but, upon closer examination, he found that the tarpaulin was its only cover and it was secured by knotted rope. His fingers were numb from the water and it took him several minutes to work through a number of the complicated knots. He stayed on the alert for the sound of footsteps and kept glancing over his shoulder, expecting to be discovered at any moment, but the deck remained empty.

He eventually loosened enough of the tarpaulin to investigate the inside of the chest. It was filled with coils and coils of rope, neatly looped and stacked together, but there was just enough space for a man's body to squeeze in on top of them. He slithered into the gap and flattened himself against the uppermost layer of ropes, bending his knees to fit. Then he did his best to rearrange the tarpaulin so it did not look like it had been disturbed. He knew he had left wet footprints on the deck, as well as puddles of water from his sodden clothes, but that could not be helped; he hoped they would dry out before anyone happened to pass this way.

He let out a long, slow breath as he registered exactly what he had just done. He supposed Cunningham was at this moment wondering why McGovern had not yet returned to the lodgings after visiting the wine merchant. He would be enraged once he realised that neither his lackey nor his money would be coming back. The promise of his retribution alone was enough reason for Cormac to never show his face in Dublin again.

The final spell of waiting was interminable, and he spent it chewing his lip in dread that he would be found and ejected from the ship before it ever departed. But then he felt the vessel stir as though rousing from slumber, and at last it was moving, away from the shore of his home country, away from the mess he had made of his life.

# CHAPTER 14

The euphoria of his successful escape lasted about as long as it took for the ship to pick up pace, indicating that it had departed from the docks and was out on open water. Then his qualms began to set in.

It was all very well to renounce the contemptible existence he had led in Dublin for over a year and a half – he didn't regret that decision for an instant. However, his impetuous actions now found him holed up in a tight space with no food or water for an indeterminate period heading towards an unknown destination.

'This is no time to lose your nerve,' he muttered, prodding ineffectually at a coil of rope that was poking into his hip.

True, he had no notion which city, or even which country, would be the ship's next port of call. Nevertheless, anywhere had to be better than the godforsaken place it had just left. He pictured the coloured globe Bridget's governess had used in her geography lessons, and which she in turn had shown to him whenever she felt the urge to educate him in more than the rudiments of reading and writing. The ship was not large enough to be undertaking a transatlantic crossing to the Americas. Somewhere up or down the coast of Ireland was a possibility, but the more likely course was across the Irish Sea to Scotland, Wales or England. There was an outside chance it might be making for the northern shores of France but he prayed that wouldn't be the case. Bridget had never taught him a word of French.

Once he arrived there, wherever 'there' would be, his initial challenge would be to alight from the ship undetected but, if it came to it, he could always disembark by the same route he had taken to come aboard. After he got back onto dry land, his main priority would be to find work of some kind, but this time he would ensure that it was honest labour involving no daggers whatsoever. He was an able-bodied young man who knew how to work with wood and horses – these talents had proved inadequate in Dublin but there might be better opportunities for him on foreign soil.

In the short-term, he was more concerned with the inevitable onset of thirst and hunger. At a minimum, several hours stretched ahead of him without any form of sustenance and he hoped once again that the ship was not destined for somewhere as distant as France. Hunger he could manage – heaven knew he had enough experience in that area – but thirst could only be endured for so long. Did he dare venture out of his hiding place if it became too severe? He could attempt to pass for a steerage passenger and obtain a cup of water from the ship's supplies. It was an option, but he would bide his time for now. Perhaps the ship would dock before he needed to court that danger.

The minutes dragged by. A single set of footsteps pounded past the chest in a hurry to get somewhere else, and then all was quiet again.

He shifted restlessly. The ropes dug into his back and his cold, wet clothes stuck to his skin with nauseating clamminess. As they dried, the stench of the river water became more prominent and he tried to take shallower breaths. To distract himself, he imagined how the legitimate passengers were occupying themselves on their voyage. The less well-off had probably located the least uncomfortable parts of steerage to lay their heads, while the more affluent were no doubt well settled into their cabin quarters and availing of hot beverages. He swallowed, disregarding the dryness of his throat.

After a while, it grew even more difficult to breathe. The small space was stifling and he had drawn the tarpaulin so tight against the lip of the chest that there was no chance of any fresh air getting in. Could he risk opening it a little? Deciding that the threat of detection was minimal, he tugged at the tarpaulin from the inside until he had created a narrow gap between it and the edge of the chest. He put his face to the slit and breathed in. A cold breeze stung his nose but it was blessedly fresh. He pulled the tarpaulin to make the opening wider and adjusted the way he was lying to let the air waft across his cheeks.

The sensation was sweet at first but soon he became aware that his new position was causing an ache in the lower half of his left leg. It was turned at an awkward angle and he could feel a cramp building in the muscle. He tried to massage it but he was too restricted under the flat tarpaulin to reach down to it. He cursed fluently under his breath in Irish. It would be agony to suffer through the rest of the journey like this.

The cramp spiked painfully and forced him to act. He would have to get out of the chest and walk around to ease it. Wincing at another excruciating spasm, he listened hard for any sound of people nearby. He could hear nothing except the waves. He would scarcely be on the deck for two minutes before ducking back under the tarpaulin again. It was an acceptable risk to take.

He squeezed out from beneath the heavy tarpaulin and stood gingerly on the deck. The throb in his leg heightened and he hobbled in a circle to alleviate it. Looking out across the water, he could only distinguish an inky expanse spreading in every direction. Above, stars dotted the equally black sky. He shivered in his half-damp clothes and rubbed at his aching calf. At length, the pain dissipated until it was no more than a faint twinge. Relieved, he was just stooping to climb back into his hiding place when...

'Good evening.'

He froze.

Stupid, stupid, stupid. How foolish of him to emerge from his concealment. Now what would happen? Would he be incarcerated in whichever city the ship docked next? Or would he be brought back to Dublin where, imprisoned or not, he would have to confront Cunningham's wrath? Either way, he had wasted his shot at a fresh start, for nothing more significant than a leg cramp. He gritted his teeth and turned around.

Instead of a crew member, he found himself facing one of the passengers. The young man belonged to the wealthier social class on board, judging by his well-fitting coat, high shirt collar and white cravat, although he wore no hat. He was about Cormac's own height and he had neat brown hair and pale blue eyes which looked at Cormac with a quizzical expression.

'Good evening,' he said again.

Because he could not think of anything else to say, Cormac replied, 'Good evening.'

The young man took a step closer. 'You're a stowaway, aren't you?'

Cormac sent a wry glance down at the chest with the tarpaulin folded back. 'What gave it away?'

The man smiled. 'Do not look so worried. I'm not going to report you.'

Cormac felt some measure of relief but did not allow himself to relax. 'Why not?'

'I don't want to draw attention to myself either,' the man said cryptically. He stuck out his hand. 'I'm Oliver.'

Cormac thought it odd that a gentleman would introduce himself by his first name instead of his surname or title but he shook the fellow's hand nonetheless. 'Cormac.'

'It is a pleasure to meet you,' said Oliver, with the amiability of one who believed he had just made a firm friend.

Making an encouraging gesture to follow suit, he strolled over to the edge of the deck and leaned on the gunwale. After a moment's indecision, Cormac joined him. He knew he ought to be concerned that someone else might come along, one who would be less merciful towards stowaways, but something about this young man had sparked his curiosity. Maybe it was the fact that he had chosen not to acknowledge the vast social divide between them, which was an attitude Cormac had only ever witnessed in Bridget and her father. As he rested his forearms on the smooth wood, he felt embarrassed by the smell of the Liffey on his skin and clothing, but Oliver seemed not to notice. He was gazing ahead as if he could see all the way to the horizon, even though the weak light from the ship's lanterns illuminated only a small area of water before melting into the darkness beyond.

The sea breeze stirred his neat hair as he turned to Cormac. 'So I assume you did not elect to hide in a ship's chest for your own amusement. Are you a fugitive from the law? Should I fear for my safety?' He spoke with the serenity of one enquiring about the weather.

Cormac's lips twisted sardonically. 'A few hours ago, perhaps. Not anymore.'

'Turning over a new leaf, are you?'

'You could say that.'

'Who were you a few hours ago?'

'Someone I didn't want to be any longer. Someone I never wanted to be in the first place,' he added, his voice laced with bitterness.

118

'And you blame another individual for this?'

He shot Oliver a surprised look.

'Or am I mistaken?' the young man said mildly.

'No, you're not.' This stranger had, with disturbing perception, hit it quite right.

'Who was the party at fault? Your parents? Your employer? Your lover?'

He was so nonplussed that he answered with the truth. 'My lover.' He supposed 'my employer' would also have been accurate, but Bridget had been the one to reject him, thrusting him into a desperate set of circumstances. 'Though I guess she wasn't really mine.'

'Ah. Another man's wife?'

'Fiancée.' He sighed. Thinking about her made his chest feel like there was an iron strap tightening around it.

'What happened?'

'We had an affair. Her mother, my employer, banished me from the estate when she found out.' Had he actually summarised the whole complicated disaster in so few words?

Oliver exhibited no condemnation at his confession. 'So that was what induced the unfavourable alteration in yourself?'

Having no inclination to delve into a more detailed account of his misdeeds, Cormac said, 'That's the long and the short of it.' He looked sideways. 'Why are you so interested?'

'When I saw you, I perceived a kindred spirit. I thought it might be nice to empathise.'

'Nice?' He raised his eyebrows. His tale had not been one of uplifting inspiration.

'Helpful,' Oliver amended. 'Tell me, what are your prospects at this current juncture? Are you travelling to someone who can assist you?'

'No.' Cormac watched the waves below them splash against the hull of the ship; a sprinkle of sea spray moistened his cheeks.

'I've just forsaken the last place in the hope that the next one won't be so unforgiving.' He frowned in recollection of Oliver's comment. 'A kindred spirit? So d'you also have a delightful story to tell?'

'I do, indeed. It is about as amusing as your own. Would you care to hear it?'

'Go ahead.' He was now quite intrigued by this enigmatic young man.

'It has the same root as yours. A lover.' Oliver tugged at his cravat and collar to loosen them, exposing his pale throat. 'I was besotted. And my Vic was besotted. Although, as it turned out, not with me. I was cast aside for another man after I discovered them together. Oh, yes, and then my beloved parents died.'

Cormac gaped at the calm delivery of this shocking disclosure.

Oliver smiled without humour. 'It has been the best six months of my life.'

With an uneasy feeling in his gut, Cormac wondered if the fellow was a bit unstable for a wild glint had crept into his eyes. 'I'm very sorry to hear that. D'you have any other family?'

'My uncle and aunt live in England. I am journeying to them now.'

'England?' said Cormac, diverted. 'That's where this ship's heading?'

'Yes.' Oliver did not look pleased at the prospect. 'My uncle and aunt will be waiting for me when we dock. I have never met them but I know they have no children of their own so doubtless they will smother me and expect me to take over their substantial estate when they die.'

'Are they very rich then?'

'Richer than I'd care to admit. My uncle is an earl. But I do not want to inherit, how tedious it would be.'

It was a singular statement to issue from the mouth of a gentleman.

'What would you prefer to do instead?' Cormac asked, mystified.

'I have always wanted to be a poet. However, my parents believed that the literary life was beneath me and encouraged me to study law instead. My Vic was the only truly happy point of my existence. And then...' He trailed off, his Adam's apple bobbing as he swallowed.

Cormac shifted in discomfort. 'Maybe things'll improve once you settle in England. You might meet a new girl and...' His voice too faded away.

Oliver shrugged with a sardonic expression. 'I do not believe so. But I suppose I shall have to make peace with my fate.'

His hands flexed, as though anxious to be occupied. Fishing in his pocket, he withdrew a knife with an ornate handle, flicked it open, and began scratching idly on the gunwale.

'It could be worse, y'know,' said Cormac. 'Least you've somewhere to go once we've crossed the sea. My first challenge is going to be figuring out where my next meal'll come from. I'm not trying to feel sorry for myself,' he hastened to add. 'I'm just attempting to give you some perspective.'

Oliver didn't look up but he seemed to contemplate Cormac's advice seriously. After a long pause, during which there was no sound but the waves and the scrape of metal on wood, he said, 'If you were in my place, what would you do?'

Cormac hesitated. With reluctance, because he knew it was not what Oliver wished to hear, he replied, 'I think you're duty-bound to go to your uncle and aunt, for a time anyway. But after a while, if you explain to them you're not content, they might let you write your poetry instead.'

Betraying his first hint of melancholy, Oliver murmured, 'You and I both know that will never happen.'

He blew at the shavings that had accumulated on the gunwale. The breeze caught them and they whirled away into the night, revealing the single word he had scored into the wood.

'Victor'.

Startled, Cormac glanced from it to Oliver, but the fellow offered no clarification regarding this unforeseen revelation. Pocketing the knife, he drew in a gulp of air and expelled it by jerky degrees. When he spoke again, it was so quietly that Cormac could barely hear him.

'It will be nothing but obligation and obedience, a lifetime of pretence for a withered soul.'

He stared at Cormac with sudden intentness. 'Here are a few details you ought to know. My full name is Oliver Davenport. The date of my birth was the eighth of February, 1809. Twenty-five years ago, my father, Mr Gerard Davenport, came to Ireland where he met my mother, Miss Caroline Prendergast. They married and had three children. Two died in infancy, only I survived to adulthood. In March of this year, my parents drowned in a boating accident on a lough near our home in Meath. Our estate was sold and I am now travelling to Bedfordshire to live with my uncle and aunt, Lord and Lady Bewley. Oh, and my quarters here on the ship are in B5. Here is the key to my cabin.'

He withdrew a key from his pocket but, baffled, Cormac did not take it.

'Why do I need to know all of this?'

'Because I am weary of my life,' said Oliver. 'You may have it if you want. And my thanks to you. It was comforting to have a friend at the end.'

He dropped the key on the boards of the deck and turned swiftly to the gunwale, grasping the top of it to heave himself over the edge. Letting out an exclamation of shock, Cormac darted towards him and seized his shoulders just before he plunged overboard. He hauled him back and they fell onto the deck, Oliver struggling in his grip with a growl of frustration.

'Get off me!'

They tussled back and forth on the wooden boards, Oliver fighting to extricate himself while Cormac refused to relinquish his hold. At last, Oliver gave up and went limp.

'You win,' he said. 'Will you let me go now?'

'Only if you stay well away from the edge,' Cormac warned.

Oliver gave a grudging nod and Cormac released him. The fellow scrambled back and stood, brushing down his fine clothes with fastidious displeasure.

'What were you *thinking*?' Cormac demanded, panting as he got to his own feet.

Defiant, Oliver said, 'I'm done with thinking. And feeling. And existing.'

He thrust his hand into his pocket, pulled out his knife, and dragged the blade across his throat in a deep slash. Blood spurted from the gash, staining the white skin and pristine cravat bright red. Horror-struck, Cormac caught him as he sagged towards the deck. Oliver's pale blue eyes widened in surprise and fear, losing focus as his head lolled to the side. Cormac sank to his knees and yanked the sodden cravat over the wound in a frantic effort to staunch the stream of blood.

'Jesus Christ, don't die! Come on, damn you!'

But the air in Oliver's lungs gurgled pathetically out of his ravaged windpipe and Cormac found himself supporting the weight of a dead body in his arms.

He averted his face and heaved the contents of his stomach onto the boards of the deck. His mind screamed, one endless howl of shock and incomprehension. Had that really just happened? An act so abominable, so inconceivable, that his head swam as he attempted to deny its occurrence. He took a deep breath to steady himself and inhaled the reek of blood and vomit, making all denial impossible. For the next few seconds, he concentrated on not getting sick again. When he was in control of his bodily functions once more, he tried to assess the alarming situation into which he had been plunged.

Oliver Davenport, this stranger whom he had known for little more than ten minutes, had just killed himself. What had compelled him to do such a monstrous thing? Granted, he had suffered the recent death of his parents and the loss of his beloved Victor, and he had faced the prospect of being the unwilling heir to his uncle's estate. But did that merit giving up on life altogether? He had relayed no warning that such desperate thoughts had been preying on his mind. For most of their encounter, his demeanour had been nonchalant. Even towards the end, he had seemed downhearted, but not suicidal by any means. It was unthinkable that the young man who had shaken his hand with such affability was...gone.

Cradling Oliver's lifeless form, he was forcefully reminded of another senseless tragedy. His sister Mary had ended her own existence with a noose around her neck. Both she and Oliver had chosen the most extreme course of action without confiding in anyone else. How could they believe that suicide was the only option, when that sin condemned the soul to perpetual damnation? Oliver may have thought he had lost everyone worth living for, but Mary had still had her family, she had still had her son Patrick. He felt anger rise up in him at their inherent failings, their inability to reach out for help, their refusal to fight on. In the next instant, he berated himself for thinking ill of his sister. She, like Oliver, had been intolerably unhappy and, in both cases, he had been too blind to see what was coming.

He became aware of something hard beneath his knee and looked down to see Oliver's pocket knife on the deck. It had slipped from his hand as life escaped him and now lay there in lethal inertia. Cormac picked it up gingerly, the slick smear of crimson oozing down the handle and onto his fingers. It hadn't been Oliver's planned means for his demise – was it a more ghastly end than drowning? Cormac experienced a queer surge of guilt; his well-meant intervention had doomed Oliver to make that choice.

At that moment, he heard a crewman bark an order towards the front of the ship. He suddenly recollected where he was and a wave of panic swept over him. Should somebody stumble across him right now, they might see a suicide but they could also very well see a murder. Once they coupled their suspicion regarding the incident with the fact that he was not even authorised to be on the vessel in the first place, he could anticipate a punishment no less than death. He needed to act fast.

What should he do with Oliver's body? If he abandoned it, then it would be discovered, alarms would be raised, and stringent security checks would make it almost impossible to leave the ship undetected. He supposed he could hide it, perhaps in the very chest he had used to take cover himself – there was a strong likelihood that the ship would have already docked and the passengers alighted by the time it was found. But concealing the corpse would definitely make it appear as though a murder had taken place and he did not know whether he would be able to get away in sufficient time. If he were caught and connected with the crime, again he could expect to follow Oliver sooner rather than later.

A third course of action would be to get rid of the body entirely. He could dump it over the side of the ship and wipe away the evidence on the deck, and no one would ever know the atrocity had occurred. But when the crew checked the ship's passenger records after docking, they would realise that they were short one passenger and there would be a missing person inquiry. And of course, he remembered with a jolt, Oliver's uncle and aunt would be waiting for him at the docks. Once he did not show up as expected, they would become distraught and instigate an inquiry of their own.

It was only then that he recalled Oliver's words: 'I am weary of my life. You may have it if you want.' He had been so shocked and nauseated by the bewildering turn of events that the young man's extraordinary comments had flown out of his head in the immediate aftermath. Now he tried to analyse what they could mean. The intention was clear enough but the logic behind them was impossible to fathom. Had Oliver really believed that he, Cormac, could step into someone else's shoes just like that? It was a ludicrous notion.

He chewed the inside of his mouth, wincing at the acidic tang of vomit. Could it work? Of course not. How could one man assimilate himself into the life of another without the people around him seeing through the deception at once? Then he remembered that Lord and Lady Bewley had never met their nephew and therefore would not be familiar with either his looks or his personality traits. At the present time, Oliver Davenport was nothing but a name to them; given that Cormac was only four months older than him, he could feasibly slip into the role without their knowledge. There was the issue that Oliver came from an upper class family and Cormac did not, but he had a decent handle on his reading and writing and was familiar enough with the manners of the aristocracy – having served them for so many years – that he thought he could pass for a lord's nephew without an excessive degree of difficulty. So impersonating Oliver Davenport would not be an unachievable task.

But what about not being Cormac McGovern anymore? The man he had been, the life he had led for over two decades, would be eradicated as though it had never existed. Then again, what was so estimable about his life that was worth preserving? He had failed his family by ending up in a position where he could no longer support them and neglecting to uphold the values he had been taught since infancy. Indeed, for the last year and a half he had lived as though he were a different person. Perhaps Cormac McGovern was already gone. Which would make the decision before him quite easy after all.

Feeling like a criminal, he groped around on the deck and found the key to Oliver's cabin. Holding it between his thumb and forefinger as though it were a serpent about to strike, he weighed his options for the future. If he continued on as himself, he could remain hopeful for better luck across the sea but still ran the risk of falling back into a seedy life similar to the one he had led in Dublin, or else returning to the misery of homelessness. If he accepted Oliver's proposal, he had a chance of infinitely improving his quality of life. He would rise to an elevated position in society that would never have been possible for him to reach as Cormac McGovern, lowly stable hand turned beggar turned money lender's lackey. He would also have access to money which he could send home in secret to his family and start to make amends at last for the pain he had brought upon them. He had to admit he was becoming more open to Oliver's idea.

But there was still the question of what to do with the remains. Whatever path Cormac chose, he would be obliged to do something despicable. Abandoning, hiding or disposing of the body were all hideous acts for the one who had to do the dirty work and undignified ends for the one who had died. With an ironic pang of realisation, the thought struck him: had he let Oliver depart this world in the manner he had wished to, his own situation would now be a lot simpler.

Wavering in indecision, he was almost too preoccupied to heed the voices issuing from around the corner of the deck towards the ship's stern. But they broke into his consciousness as they grew louder and shriller.

'Oh, Millicent! This sea crossing is ghastly, isn't it?'

'Yes, I do not know when I have felt so ill. What a horrid experience.'

'You were right to suggest we come out on deck. The fresh air should do us some good.'

'But it is a touch too breezy here. We ought to try the next side, Gertrude, it might be more sheltered.'

Dismayed, he heard the heels of the two ladies clicking nearer. He was out of time – he had to make his choice now. He stared down at Oliver's slack face, the hideous wound on his neck, his fine clothes ruined by blood. This disillusioned young man's attempt to live his life had been unsuccessful but he had sanctioned the passing of its ownership to another. Cormac viewed this as justification enough to take a shot at it himself.

He thrust the cabin key into his own pocket, struggled to stand with Oliver's body in a macabre embrace, and heaved it over the gunwale. It fell into the sea with a sickening splash. He hoped it would sink before anyone within earshot investigated the source of the noise. Oliver's pocket knife followed him into the water. Next, Cormac whipped off his coat, mopped at the pool of blood and vomit on the deck and, just as the seasick ladies rounded the corner to his side of the deck, threw it overboard as well. A faint discolouration remained on the wooden boards of the deck but he would have to trust that no one would recognise it for what it really was. He realised his dagger was still in the inside pocket of his coat and felt no compunction over its loss. A watery grave was the best end for it.

'May it rust there,' he muttered bitterly.

The two ladies turned their heads in surprise as they registered his presence on the deck. After bowing politely in their direction, he spun on his heel and strode away from them. He needed to get inside fast. Anyone he met would regard it as suspicious to be out-of-doors on a ship without wearing an outer layer of some kind. Furthermore, if they looked more closely, they could not fail to discern the blood stains on his hands.

Ducking through the first door he found leading below decks, he descended a stairwell and hurried down a passageway lined with numbered doors. A steward passed him going the opposite way; Cormac slowed his pace but did not make eye contact. After stalking along two more passageways in mounting agitation, he finally located a small sign proclaiming the quarters for B5. He unlocked the door, entered, and shut it behind him with an exhalation of relief.

He found himself in a small but comfortable cabin containing a bed and a table with a pitcher, basin and towel. There were no windows but a lit lamp hung in an alcove beside the door. A trunk stood beneath it.

He dropped onto the bed, his heart racing. Had he truly just done that? He was both appalled and exhilarated by his actions. It had been a dreadful incident but now he was journeying to a lord and lady who were going to take him in as their own nephew. This guaranteed two vital aspects of his future: he would not have to go back to starving on the streets and he would not be required to threaten poor people for money anymore. Both of these certainties were worth the horror of tossing a dead body overboard.

He knelt by the trunk, unfastened its clasps and rummaged through its contents. There were sets of clothes, pairs of boots, a coat and a hat, as well as a small case holding items for shaving and grooming. Underneath this at the bottom of the trunk lay a slim notebook with a navy cloth cover. He flicked it open and swallowed. Oliver's poetry. The handwritten words rose from the pages, clouding the air with their despair. *The torment of drawing breath, already breathing death.*

Cormac's exhilaration evaporated. With a heaviness in his chest, he closed the notebook. In respect of Oliver's memory, he would keep it in his possession, to preserve the remnants of the anguished spirit who had crafted those hopeless verses.

He needed to start preparing himself for his arrival in England. Crossing to the table, he poured water from the pitcher into the basin. He scooped up a mouthful to rinse the sour taste from his mouth, and another to slake the dryness in his throat, and then set to scrubbing the blood stains from his palms and the odour of the River Liffey from his hair and skin.

Once he had dried himself with the towel, he extracted the grooming case from the trunk. With the aid of a small mirror, he shaved the layer of stubble that covered his jaw. Next, he found a scissors and, recalling Oliver's tidy haircut, chopped at his own long hair until it had amassed in golden piles at his feet. He trimmed it as best he could, though the style was a bit rough and he had no way of telling how it looked from the back.

Last of all, he needed to dress like a gentleman. He stripped out of his garments and crammed them into the trunk, along with the mound of cut hair; he would find a way to dispose of them all at the earliest opportunity. He donned shirt, waistcoat, coat and trousers, admiring the fine quality of the material. By a stroke of fortune, there had been less than an inch in the difference between his and Oliver's heights and the sleeves and trouser legs, while a little short, were not noticeably so. He dubiously picked up a cravat and wondered how to tie it. Following a number of failed attempts, he managed to fashion it into something resembling a neat knot. He completed his ensemble with a pair of leather boots, which were only a touch on the tight side.

After that, all he could do was wait for the vessel to dock and for his new life as an impostor to begin.

# CHAPTER 15

Bridget entered the nursery to find Garrett bending over the cradle, shaking a silver rattle and making uncharacteristic baby noises.

'You are the best boy, yes, you are,' he chattered, and an answering gurgle came from within the cradle. 'Goo goo ga, that's right, good boy.'

The sounds were incongruous with the man she knew and yet that man did not stand before her.

He had transformed upon the birth of their son. The thing he wanted most on this earth had come to him at last and he had become disposed to be kinder towards everyone, even Emily, rendering him unrecognisable from the devil who had destroyed the wooden bird and roared at Bridget and announced his infidelity with such indifference.

In that last respect, she was reasonably certain those activities had ceased. During the past three months since James had been born, Garrett had spent so much time at home and away from his club that he could have had little opportunity to invite the interest of any mistress. That did not mean he had returned to Bridget's bed, however. She had provided him with a son and he therefore had no further use for her. All of his attention was now focused on giving James a wealth of love which she had never believed to be within his capacity and which she could only assume he had stored away until the advent of this vital individual into his life.

Her own heart overflowed with adoration for James too. Not for one instant would she say that she loved her son more than her daughter – Emily still meant the world to her. But James had two advantages which Emily did not: he was male, and he had the benefit of two loving parents, not one. The atmosphere in Wyndham House was positively festive.

James, who would be the seventh gentleman to hold the title of the Wyndham viscountcy, had been named for his grandfather, the fifth in that line. Blissfully unaware of the great honour that would one day rest upon his shoulders, he babbled from the depths of his blankets. Bridget approached the cradle and gazed lovingly down at him. He had a shock of black hair on the crown of his head but thus far not much growth towards the front. He wriggled and produced a gummy smile at the sight of her, but it disappeared as a fretful cough shook his little body. Garrett leaned over and touched his forehead.

'Still hot,' he said.

The boy had been out of sorts over the previous two or three days with a rather high fever. Garrett, taking on the role of overprotective father, had scarcely left the nursery in all that time. Concerned that the fever had not yet passed, Bridget placed her palm on James's forehead too.

'I think we ought to send for the physician again,' she said.

'I agree. I shall do so directly.'

He started to turn away but hesitated. He cleared his throat and looked at her. 'Before I go,' he said, 'there is something I wish to say.' He cleared his throat once more, as though he found it difficult to get the words out. 'I believe I owe you an apology.'

Startled, she said nothing. Was he bedding a mistress after all? A sense of disappointment settled over her, not for her own sake, but because such an admission would mean that the happy mood in their household had been yet another lie.

But then, to her shock, Garrett said, 'I have treated you badly during our marriage. Neither of us is blameless in the whole affair, but I have come to accept that I made things worse.' He smoothed his thumb over the surface of the rattle; it was wet at the top where James had been sucking on it. 'We should not have wed. You were right, and I see that now. I saw it quite soon after the event but of course by that stage it was too late.'

She gaped. What on earth had prompted this confession? This man had been her husband for three and a half years and yet she still could not become accustomed to his mercurial ways. Recalling the last period of reconciliation they had enjoyed before the onset of his fury over the wooden bird, she resolved not to be deceived by a false sense of peace this time.

The rattle jangled softly as Garrett turned it over in his hands. 'I was blinded at the time by my anger and humiliation. To be jilted by a woman...' He shrugged. 'I wanted to exact revenge, to hurt you the way you hurt me. On top of that, you were my possession. I had no intention of standing by and allowing you to be snatched away from me. I had to win.'

She experienced a spark of anger herself. This did not sound like much of an apology, and all he was doing was dragging up agonising memories which *he* had stipulated must never be alluded to again.

'You don't need—' she began, hoping to forestall any further attempts on his part to 'apologise'.

He held up his hand to cut her off. 'My revenge came with unwelcome repercussions. I had no more wanted to get trapped in a loveless marriage than you had, but that is precisely what happened. I was mistaken in thinking you had been the victim of a mere infatuation, a wild impulse to rut in the hay that would be swiftly overcome once you regained your senses. I knew you had loved me once and I thought you could love me again, despite the events of that summer.'

She tried, and failed, to mask her incredulity. He smiled wryly.

'I was a misguided fool, yes, but you still owe me some thanks. Have you thought about what would have happened had I not married you? You would have been a fallen woman with a bastard child.' He didn't let her argue the point, but pushed on, 'You wouldn't have found him. I would have made sure of that. At least our marriage gave legitimacy to Emily's birth. Her life could have been a great deal more unpleasant, had she not been born in wedlock.'

Bridget's hands curled tightly in the folds of her skirts. 'I'm afraid your understanding of what constitutes an apology is drastically different to my own.'

'True, I'm not doing very well at it,' he admitted. 'Let me backtrack. This is meant to be my acknowledgement of how I was at fault. What I'm trying to say is I ought to have seen that your feelings could not be so easily overcome.' He sighed. 'I recognise now the depth of your regard for him. I once experienced that feeling too, not with you, but with another woman.'

He delivered this so casually that he appeared unaware of its impact, not seeming to realise that she had received it like a punch to her gut. She had known he had dallied with other women, but had he truly loved any one of them as much as she loved Cormac? She didn't think it could be possible – but then she glanced down at James, his small fist inserted in his mouth, and remembered that Garrett did indeed have that ability, even if he had never demonstrated it towards her.

'I did a lot of damage that summer,' he said now. 'And while I don't know if I would have acted any differently where he was concerned, I am sorry for what has transpired between us since.'

He set the rattle down in the cradle, touching the back of his knuckles against their son's cheek.

'But now we can say that some good has come from our union at last. You have my deepest gratitude for that.' He let out another sigh, this one a long breath of joy and devotion. 'I shall send for the physician now.' He made to move away but looked back down at James with a frown.

'What is it?' she asked.

He reached into the cradle and drew back the blankets, exposing more of the boy's skin. His face went ashen.

Bridget peered in and gasped. A red rash had begun to spread from behind James's ear and along his neck. She stared up at Garrett, horrified.

'Measles,' he muttered. 'Dear God, it's measles.'

Her mind raced through all the facts she knew about the disease. *Contagious* came top of the list.

'Have you ever—' she started.

'Yes, you?'

'When I was two. But Emily—!'

Emily, a month shy of three years old, had never contracted the measles. To remain one minute longer in this house would endanger her as well as James.

Without further communication, she and Garrett hastened from the nursery, he to summon the physician and she to seek out Emily.

Within the hour, Emily was bouncing around the seat of the carriage and straining to peep out the window, excited at the unexpected expedition through the teeming London streets. Bridget restrained herself from constantly checking the girl's forehead and skin for signs of fever or rash. She had kept Emily far away from the nursery until they had left the house so the risk of exposure was minuscule – but anxiety still compressed her lungs like a pair of stays pulled too tight.

136

She had ordered the coachman to take them to the Newby residence. Lucy, who had become such close friends with Bridget that they were firmly on first name terms, accepted Emily into her home without hesitation, verifying that everyone in the household had survived the disease and would not be in any danger.

'What a dreadful misfortune!' she exclaimed, her large nose scrunching in consternation. 'I do hope James will recover quickly.'

'Thank you, dearest, I am so grateful,' said Bridget. 'I shall come back as soon as possible to see Emily but I cannot say exactly when—' The words clogged in her throat.

Lucy clasped her hand in both of her own. 'Take all the time you need. She will be perfectly fine here with Angela and Valerie.'

Emily confirmed this by beaming from ear to ear when Lucy's two young daughters appeared from behind her skirts. Even so, it was agonising for Bridget to leave her little girl behind and she nearly ran for the carriage, feeling torn between her two children. But right now James needed her more.

The next few days passed in a blur. Hazy faces went to and fro around her: Garrett, the physician, and an unfamiliar maid to replace Lizzie, who had to be sent away because she had never suffered the measles before either. Their voices drifted about Bridget, distant and vague, like they were calling to her from the bottom of a deep well. The only thing she was in tune with was her son – his plaintive cries, his wracking coughs, his sore, red eyes, his hot, rash-covered skin. She willed his tiny body to fight the disease. Her own body felt numb. When she spoke, her lips seemed moulded of wax, hardly able to move.

'Save him,' she croaked to the physician. 'Please save him.'

Could God be so cruel, to bestow such happiness upon her family and snatch it away again so quickly? Three months was nothing, the blink of an eye. She did not know yet what sort of person her son was. Would he have a sweet tooth for jellies and cakes? Would he ride a horse well? Would he be the kind of child to run crying to his mother when he got hurt or bear it with a man's silent endurance? How she yearned for the day he would come home from Eton conjugating Latin verbs, reciting Homer's Iliad, and boasting about his school's win over Harrow in their annual cricket match. And when he grew up, she hoped he would be a gentleman in every respect, incomparable in courteousness to ladies and servants alike.

She knew it was all over when she saw Garrett slumped on the floor of the nursery, back against the wall, head in his hands, sobbing so hard that his whole frame shuddered with grief.

She floated over to the cradle in a fog of bewilderment, oblivious to the murmured sympathies of the physician. She looked down. He had been making so much of a commotion with his crying and coughing that the inert, silent form seemed unnatural. She stroked the black tuft of hair. Her eyes misted, becoming sightless, and in that moment her world was reduced to two senses: the touch of that soft, soft hair and the sound of her devastated husband's weeping. One was achingly familiar. The other she had never witnessed before in her life, not even at his father's death.

'White gloves,' she said dazedly.

'Beg pardon, m'lady?' the strange maid mumbled by her side.

'White gloves,' she repeated. 'And a white coffin. That is what is required for a child's funeral.'

Her voice cracked and the tears spilled over.

The following day, she went to Newby House to retrieve her one surviving child. Emily clung to Bridget's knee as the carriage hit a rut in the street on the way back, jostling them about. The little girl fingered the black crape of her mother's dress and looked up with blue eyes full of confusion.

'Baby James not at home?' she asked hesitantly.

'No, gooseberry, I'm afraid he's not.'

'Where he now?'

'He's gone to live with the angels in heaven. Do you remember me telling you that?'

'When he coming back?'

'He won't be coming back. He is going to stay in heaven where God will take such good care of him.'

Bridget gulped and clutched Emily to her breast so the girl would not see the wetness in her eyes. Emily continued to ask questions and she answered them in muffled tones, trying as best she could to express what had happened in a manner the child could understand. An absurd notion, given that she herself could not understand why her precious boy had been taken from her.

Thrussell met them at the door of Wyndham House, his sorrow under control save for an escaped sniffle. As they crossed the threshold into the entrance hall, Garrett came down the stairs. Emily's face lit up and she ran forwards.

'Papa!'

Before James's death, Garrett might have been benevolent enough to give the little girl a swift hug or a pat on the head. Now his livid expression made her falter and shrink back from him.

The reason for his resentment was palpable: the stable hand's child lived, but his own had not. Any scrap of affection that might have existed between them was irrevocably lost.

Bridget put a soothing hand on Emily's small shoulder. 'Let's not trouble Papa right now,' she murmured.

Garrett brushed past them both, anger and anguish radiating from him in equal measure.

'I am going to the club,' he said and vanished out the door.

# CHAPTER 16

Cormac hunched over a hefty volume in the library, hungrily scanning its pages. Though the subject matter was not part of the education Lord and Lady Bewley had prescribed for him, it was essential reading nonetheless; every member of the aristocracy possessed this knowledge, so he needed to understand it too lest he be caught off guard at some inopportune moment.

The book contained a comprehensive description of the peerage of the United Kingdom, listing the various grades of nobility and the principal families therein. A viscount, it revealed, ranked higher than a baron but lower than an earl. He tried to absorb the information in general terms but could not help applying specifics. Bridget had risen above her station when she married Garrett but Cormac, in his current role, was due to inherit an earldom which would place him above that supercilious gentleman. It was so extraordinary that he laughed softly to himself.

'Amusing material, my boy?' came a voice from behind him.

He shut the book with a snap and spun around. Lord Bewley stood at the library door. He had a head of fine, white hair and he leaned on a beechwood cane with a brass, T-shaped handle. Despite these signs of infirmity, he was hale and hearty for his advanced years and the cane was more of an affectation than a crutch. His eyes crinkled as he smiled.

'I am pleased to see you being so diligent with your studies, Oliver, but the humans in the house would enjoy your company on occasion. What are you reading?'

Cormac gave an embarrassed shrug. His tailored clothes glided comfortably with the movement.

''Tis—I mean, it's nothing important, Uncle,' he said, pronouncing the words with care. 'I apologise for my unsociable behaviour.'

'Never apologise for striving towards an educated mind. It is an admirable quality and I am happy to encourage it. Having said that, I must interrupt your scholarly exploits to request your presence in my study for a brief meeting.'

Concealing his curiosity, Cormac slid the book back onto its shelf before following his 'uncle' out of the library and down the cavernous hallway to the study. Bewley Hall was the ancient seat of the Davenport family and its enormous rooms, luxurious furnishings and extensive grounds spoke volumes of the earldom's noble status and ample fortune. Moreover, Cormac had learned that the assets connected to the Bewley title spread much further than this, encompassing several properties around the country and a fine establishment in London too. He had believed Oakleigh to be an impressive estate but it paled in comparison to what the Earl of Bewley could boast of in his possession.

They entered the study to find Lord Bewley's land agent, Mr Sandler, already waiting with a benign expression on his squashed face, his sizeable forehead and equally substantial chin constraining his other features into the narrow space between them. He handed a thick ledger to his master as Lord Bewley sat behind a broad desk covered with neat stacks of letters, a few books, and an elegant inkstand. The earl indicated that Cormac should occupy the seat opposite him, while Mr Sandler took up a position a discreet distance behind Cormac's chair.

Lord Bewley cast a fleeting glance through the pages of the ledger and then put it aside. 'I shall not prevaricate on the matter, Oliver. I wish to speak to you about the entailment of my estate.'

Cormac hoped he would be able to follow the intricacies of what the earl meant to discuss. Inheritance law was just one small part of the vast education he had acquired over the past twelve months, which also included mathematics, politics and philosophy – not to mention the appropriate etiquette in dressing, dining and conversing, and, entirely unanticipated, the proper steps to all the popular dances of the ballroom. While he managed to muddle through most of it well enough, Latin and Greek had proved to be beyond his capabilities and he had found it necessary to invent a lie about Oliver's parents' aversion to conventional tutoring as an explanation for his inadequate edification. Though Lord and Lady Bewley had not expressed any reproach, they had put forward their recommendation that the discrepancies be remedied and had retained a personal tutor for that purpose. It had been far from a simple undertaking but he had made considerable improvements across the year in his objective of becoming a refined gentleman. Lord Bewley must have thought so too; this was the first time he had summoned his 'nephew' to his study and Cormac sensed it was for an interview of some significance.

'The critical detail I must reveal to you,' said Lord Bewley, 'is that there is, in fact, no entailment.'

Cormac gathered that this was an unusual circumstance and adopted a suitable air of surprise.

'You may well be taken aback. The original entail expired in my grandfather's generation and he neglected to renew it. He was fortunate that my father answered his prayers for an heir and I, in turn, obliged my father. The countess and I, on the other hand…'

He trailed off. Cormac knew that Lord Bewley would never blame his wife for their lack of offspring – having spent a full year in their home, he was in no doubt that theirs was a happy marriage of love and understanding. But the truth remained that, no matter how much they desired it, they had never been blessed with children.

'Without an heir of my own blood,' Lord Bewley continued, 'my deceased brother's son is the next in line, and the noble title must pass that way regardless. However, in the absence of an entailment I am not obliged to bequeath my material estate to you, Oliver. I am free to bestow it upon anyone of my choosing. I could give it to an urchin in the village if I so wished, though naturally I do not wish that. I intend to leave the estate in capable hands upon my death. Mr Sandler, for example, would be an ideal candidate, having occupied the role of land agent here for almost two decades. His extensive knowledge of the Bewley lands and the tenants who live and work upon them is surpassed by none but myself.'

Lord Bewley gestured respectfully towards the agent. Mr Sandler made a noise of humble dissent but Cormac kept his eyes trained upon the earl. He suspected that the real Oliver Davenport had never known of these particulars and wondered what point Lord Bewley was leading to. Instinct told him he need not be concerned that his deception had been discovered; he was positive that Lord and Lady Bewley wholly believed he was their flesh-and-blood nephew.

Confirming this, Lord Bewley said, 'You have resided with your aunt and me for a year now. I confess we found you a little rough around the edges upon your arrival. You had received a somewhat coarser upbringing than we had anticipated, but doubtless we have the less civilised environs of Ireland to thank for that.'

Cormac tried not to bristle. He understood that Lord Bewley harboured no personal ill will towards Ireland or its people but, like all the other English Cormac had encountered, the earl accepted without question the assertion that the Irish were an inferior, unsophisticated race, and therefore no more could be expected of his nephew than to have appeared in the state he had.

'We communicated our hope that you would rise to the standards befitting a gentleman bearing the name of Davenport, for this family is old and revered, both here in Bedfordshire and further afield. And I am delighted to observe that you have acquitted yourself creditably, embracing your improvement in all respects, from erudition to comportment, with aplomb. In short, we are very proud of how much you have progressed.'

Cormac felt gratified by the praise. 'I never cease to be grateful to you and Lady Bewley for affording me these opportunities to better myself. I am glad to hear that you are satisfied with the results.'

'More than satisfied,' said Lord Bewley, steepling his hands on the desk. 'You are a fine young man, unafraid to admit what you do not know and eager to cultivate your advancement. It is plain that, if you continue upon this trajectory, you will indeed be worthy of your inheritance.'

'Thank you, Uncle,' said Cormac. He contemplated how to phrase his next statement in the most eloquent terms. The words were coming to him more easily, the more he spoke the tongue of the upper classes. 'I shall endeavour to meet your expectations to the best of my abilities.'

Lord Bewley gave him a look of unmistakable fondness. 'I know you will.'

# CHAPTER 17

She stood beneath the branches of the oak, a smile of welcome lighting up her face. He felt his own mouth broaden into a grin as he strode towards her; he could not wait to sink his hands into her luscious, chestnut hair. Just before he came within arm's reach, her smile faltered. The ground shifted under their feet and, glancing about in alarm, he realised they were on the pitching deck of a ship. He grabbed onto the gunwale to keep his balance. Sea spray splashed his cheeks. He looked back at her and saw that her jaw had dropped in horror.

'What did you do?' she gasped.

He had no time to answer her. The hand was already snaking around her throat, gripping a blade with a razor-sharp edge. It drew across her tender flesh and red blood blossomed on pale skin.

'No!' he bellowed. 'Stop!'

But she was already slumping to the deck, her dark brown eyes glassy and empty. Her collapse revealed Oliver, a maniacal sneer stretching his lips. He pointed the bloody blade at Bridget's body.

'That was your fault,' he said. 'And so is this.'

He raised the knife to his own throat.

Cormac roared again for him to stop but the words were choked off. He touched his neck and felt the gash there, the blood welling up and spurting out, the breath leaking from his body...

He woke with a start, shaking from head to foot. He reached up to his throat and found it intact. His hand rose further and discovered that his cheeks were indeed wet, though not with sea spray. He was dashing the tears away when a voice spoke, making him jump with fright again.

'Oliver, dear?'

Lady Bewley hovered in the shadowy doorway of his bedchamber, her plump figure silhouetted by the glow of the candlestick she held. As she came further into the room, the flame illuminated the deep concern in the fleshy creases of her face.

'A-aunt,' he stuttered. 'What are you—'

'You were shouting,' she said, her voice full of sympathy. 'Was it another nightmare?'

He had roused her before with his night-time struggles but she had always waited until the following day to make solicitous enquiries. He must have been shouting violently indeed to draw her to his chamber at this late, dark hour.

'I—yes—I'm so sorry for disturbing you.'

'There is no need to be sorry.' She set the candlestick on the bedside table and sat on the edge of his bed, taking his sweaty hand in her own. 'I only wish I could ease your suffering. You do miss your parents most dreadfully.'

She and Lord Bewley believed that the deaths of Gerard and Caroline Davenport haunted his dreams, and he allowed them to think so. He could not, after all, tell them that it was their true nephew who visited him nightly, along with the lover he yearned for with the despair of eternal separation. But her words served as a wretched reminder that his own parents were lost to him too; his father had passed away a long time ago and his mother might as well be dead, living on Oakleigh land where he was forbidden to ever set foot again. She was as unreachable as the suicidal Oliver, whom he tried to save every night in the nightmarish landscape of his tormented mind.

Quite beyond his own volition, a sob escaped his throat.

'Oh, you poor dear,' Lady Bewley said and pulled him to her.

He found himself unable to resist. He let her wrap her large, comforting arms around him, press his head to her shoulder and stroke his back, and he cried in her embrace like a boy with a grazed knee. He was undeserving of such solace but he accepted it greedily, wanting for just a short time not to feel the loss of all the dearest people in his life.

They said nothing else. Somehow she knew the moment when he was ready to be released and she freed him from her grasp with no more than a gentle kiss on his temple. She picked up the candlestick and left the chamber, gliding away like a guardian angel.

The next morning, he entered the breakfast room with some trepidation, wondering how much she had told Lord Bewley of what had happened during the night. But neither the earl nor the countess acted like anything was amiss and he went to the sideboard, relieved. While he was grateful to Lady Bewley for her consoling presence, he was also acutely embarrassed that he, a grown man, had fallen apart to such a degree. The less said about the undignified affair, the better.

He filled his breakfast plate with the usual twinge of guilt. He still found it hard to tolerate the vast amounts of food at his disposal, and the criminal waste of what was left uneaten, when he was conscious of the awful poverty that existed across the sea in his home country. In the beginning, he had guzzled more than his fair share at every meal, fearful that he would wake from his hallucination to find himself back on the streets of Dublin, emaciated and starving. Unfortunately, his stomach had not been accustomed to such a rich diet and, after a disagreeable period when he did not stray far from the chamber pot, he had learned to control his intake. Now, his body was well-nourished and stronger even than it had been when he had worked as a stable hand.

'Lord Sinclair will be calling today,' Lord Bewley announced as Cormac took his seat at the table. 'He and I mean to resolve the dispute over the boundary line in the forest.'

Lord Sinclair's estate bordered Lord Bewley's along its northern side and some confusion had arisen over where the boundary lay through a section of woodland that Lord Sinclair was having cleared for tillage. All was amicable between the two lords but the neighbour was punctilious to a fault and had insisted that the matter be dealt with promptly.

'Mr Sandler will also be present at the meeting,' said Lord Bewley. 'In the meantime, I should like you to visit two of the farms beyond the village. They are having an issue regarding fallen fences and wandering livestock which I want you to settle. Mr Comerford will accompany you as he is already familiar with the situation.'

It seemed that Lord Bewley, having declared his intention to bestow his estate only upon one worthy of the honour, now expected Cormac to earn that honour by contributing to its management. Both daunted and eager, Cormac accepted his duty with due deference. He was glad to hear that Mr Comerford would be his companion – apart from the fact that Mr Sandler's second-in-command would steer him away from any major blunders, the man actually had some Irish ancestry, a connection which Cormac secretly treasured. Never mind that the fellow was as gruff as an ill-tempered bull.

'Have some coffee, Oliver,' Lady Bewley said, pouring a cup from the copper pot and pushing it over to him. 'It's fresh.'

'Thanks, Ma,' he said without thinking and nearly knocked over the cup. 'I mean, Aunt,' he corrected at once and busied himself with swallowing the scalding liquid almost in one gulp.

When he dared to look up, Lord Bewley was gazing blandly out the window and Lady Bewley was rising to replenish her plate at the sideboard. As she turned from the table, he caught a glimpse of the private smile that lifted the corners of her mouth.

After breakfast, Cormac and Mr Comerford set out together, following a lane that led away from the grounds of Bewley Hall and towards the local village of Gildham. A light haze had burned off and left a glorious summer day in its wake, the sun beaming down on an undulating carpet of verdant fields. Though Cormac regarded England as a foreign country, he could not deny that its landscape resembled the Irish countryside so much that it was almost like riding across Oakleigh land. His heart tugged at the wistful memory of home.

There was silence between them apart from the jangle and creak of harness and saddle and the steady beat of hooves on dusty ground. Mr Comerford, a bachelor past his prime who sported a remarkable set of mutton chops, was not a man inclined to indulge in casual conversation. Cormac didn't think the fellow was inherently churlish, only that he hadn't quite grasped the nuances of human interaction.

Deciding to take the proverbial bull by the horns, Cormac charged into discourse. 'These surroundings remind me of the area where I grew up. Tell me, what part of Ireland was your grandmother from?'

Mr Comerford made a gravelly noise in his throat as though he had not yet used it that day. 'Kerry.'

They trotted on another hundred yards.

'Do you still have family there now?'

'Some distant cousins.'

This time Cormac waited a mere fifty yards before asking, 'Did you ever visit it?'

'Once, in my early twenties.' Mr Comerford surprised him by adding gruffly, 'A striking place. Have you ever been there?'

'No.' In reality, he had never left Carlow until his banishment and had only spent that brief spell on the Willowmere Estate in Kilkenny before heading to the unforgiving city of Dublin. In the past of the young man he was impersonating, he could make the safe assumption that Oliver had lived the majority of his life in Meath or Dublin and would never have had occasion to visit the most south-westerly county of Ireland. 'I have heard tell of its wild beauty though and it sounds comparable to the rest of the country, a breathtaking panorama of every shade of green that can be found in the moss and the leaves and the clover. It is no wonder Ireland is called the Emerald Isle.'

He experienced another deep pang of homesickness and pushed it away, while Mr Comerford, unmoved by his poetic digression, lapsed back into taciturnity.

They passed through Gildham, a peaceful hamlet with a church and parsonage, numerous cottages with pretty gardens, and the dwellings of several craftsmen, including the skilled lacemakers for which Bedfordshire was known. Some of the inhabitants recognised Cormac as the nephew of the earl and hailed him in their strong accents.

It had taken him a long time to adjust to being among the English. Thirty-four years had elapsed since the failed rebellion of 1798 but the fire of revolution continued to simmer in every Irishman's heart. He hated the way England had such a stranglehold on Ireland, crushing its people and traditions at every opportunity. Still, he had to acknowledge that most of the English people he encountered were not the ones to blame for the hardships put upon his countrymen. Lord Bewley might claim some responsibility, being a peer in the House of

Lords, but these locals had probably never travelled far beyond the environs of Gildham. In fact, just like the land on which they lived, they were not so dissimilar from the folk he had left behind.

This impression was borne out when they arrived at the first farm and the farmer's wife, Mrs Marsh, insisted they sample some of her freshly-made cheese before going about their morning's business. As she was setting a stacked plate on the table, two small boys, barefoot and giggling, dashed through the kitchen, snatched a couple of squares of cheese, and scampered out the door. Mrs Marsh picked up her skirts and ran after them, scolding at the top of her lungs. Cormac hid a smile; the bustle and racket was so reminiscent of Mrs Kavanagh's kitchens at Oakleigh.

After filling their bellies with the flavoursome cheese, he and Mr Comerford met with the two parties involved in the wandering livestock dispute. Farmer Marsh was accusing his neighbour, Farmer Fletcher, of neglecting to maintain his fences, with the consequence that Fletcher's cattle had strayed into Marsh's fields and trampled a substantial portion of his crops, but Fletcher protested that he had only fortified his fences the previous winter. The four of them went out to inspect the fallen fence in question and, having scrutinised the area, Cormac thought he could identify the problem.

'This patch is very boggy, despite the good weather,' he said, digging his booted heel into the ground with a squelch of confirmation. 'That means it must be even worse in wet conditions. The heavy rainstorms this past spring can't have helped matters. The fence posts are loosening as a result, which then enables the animals to push them down.'

'What choo propose we do about it, sir?' Fletcher said dubiously.

Cormac reflected on the lessons he had received from his tutor on the subjects of estate management and agricultural concerns, as well as his own experience building fences in the past.

'Plant vegetation,' he said. 'Trees, hedges, something with strong roots to hold the soil together. That ought to secure the fence in a more solid position. In the meantime, we can erect a makeshift fence thirty feet that direction,' he pointed towards some higher ground, 'as a temporary measure.'

He shrugged out of his riding coat. Mr Comerford and the two farmers gaped at him.

'What choo doing, sir?' said Marsh.

'An extra pair of hands will get the job done quicker.' He grinned at their astounded faces. 'Let's get to work.'

Much later, he and Mr Comerford returned to Bewley Hall, mucky, sweaty and tired. His companion betrayed no opinion on the day's events but he himself was quietly exultant. It had felt good to stretch his muscles in such physical exertion and he believed he had found a reasonable solution to the farmers' grievances. As they entered the house, the butler, Sheppard, informed him that Lord Bewley once again required his presence for a meeting. He hurried to wash and change his clothes – assisted by his valet, one of the most extraordinary aspects of his new life – and then made his way to the study. As he went down the corridor, he passed a striking display of lilacs assembled in a patterned bowl. He held his breath and did not let it out until he had gone past the display and could be sure the scent of the flowers could no longer reach him.

A thin woman with a set of keys dangling from her waist hovered outside the study door. She was so skinny that the bones of her elbows and shoulders stuck out, even beneath the layers of her black uniform.

She was the housekeeper of Bewley Hall and also Mr Sandler's wife, though the pair's typical interaction with each other would not make that connection apparent. Professional at all times, they were aloof in their public exchanges, and just once had he glimpsed them behaving in any kind of demonstrative manner. Not long after his arrival to Bedfordshire, he had spent a full afternoon out in the stables – the only place where he felt he could take a breath from his false existence – and afterwards had thought it best to come into the house by a side door so as not to drag mud and straw all over the floor of the entrance hall. He had caught sight of the housekeeper lingering in an inconspicuous alcove along the passageway, Mr Sandler by her side. He seemed to be reassuring her about something and, in a sweet gesture, he had taken her bony hand, kissed her knuckles, and pressed her palm to his cheek. She had looked pacified and gratified by his attention. Then her gaze had slid past him and alighted upon Cormac and she had jumped back at once. Cormac had given them a genial nod to indicate that he had no objection to such familiarity between husband and wife, and he had walked on, envying their intimacy. He was not as lonely as he had been in Dublin, but bearing a secret he couldn't share with even a single soul was its own form of isolation.

That wasn't to say that the intimacy of marriage was beyond him altogether. In fact, it was positively on the cards if he chose to remain at Bewley Hall. Lord and Lady Bewley had made no attempt to disguise their anticipation of the great many grandnephews and grandnieces they looked forward to doting upon and had already suggested he appraise the jewels on offer during the next London season. About a month ago, he and Lord Bewley had been drinking brandy at the dining table after dinner when the earl had brought up the subject with his usual frankness.

'Amorous congress,' he had said, causing Cormac to nearly spit out his brandy.

Coughing and swallowing, he had sputtered, 'P-pardon?'

'I have no wish to appear indelicate, but we are men and there are no ladies here to offend. Did my brother ever speak of such matters with you?'

Cormac had just shaken his head, incapable of words.

'You are at an age where it would be safe to assume you have had some dalliances with the opposite sex. Am I correct?'

He had felt himself go red to the tips of his ears. He wasn't sure how comfortable he would have been engaging in such a conversation with his own father, let alone this elderly gentleman who was no blood relative of his. He had mumbled something unintelligible but the earl had evidently understood.

'I am not here to censure but to counsel. All I ask is that your conduct befits a gentleman and that your discretion befits the lady. Be prudent and, once you marry, be loyal.'

It had been a chivalrous speech and it had made Cormac examine his past entanglements with a perturbed conscience. An heiress and a prostitute – both had been consensual but he could judge neither to be a success when one had discarded him and he had discarded the other. Ashamed, he had promised himself that his next conquest would be undertaken with much greater consideration.

But preferably in the far distant future.

'I appreciate your sound advice, Uncle,' he had said. 'In light of it, I beg to be allowed whatever length of time may be necessary to make myself deserving of that lady to whom I will be unfailingly loyal. May we defer any contemplation of a visit to London until I have accomplished that?'

Lord Bewley had raised his brandy glass in a gesture of approval. 'That is indeed an acceptable request.'

No more had been said on the matter since, but being summoned to the earl's study twice in two days made Cormac worry that Lord Bewley might have begun to view the situation in a more accelerated way.

Mrs Sandler shuffled aside as Cormac approached the door to the study. 'Good day, sir,' she muttered.

As he nodded in greeting to her, the study door opened and both Mr Sandler and Mr Comerford emerged.

'A word with you, Mr Sandler, if you please,' the housekeeper said, and she and her husband walked stiffly away down the hall.

Mr Comerford made a grunting sound that might have been construed as a salutation to Cormac or a gripe about bellyache, and he too disappeared.

Cormac knocked on the door, waited for Lord Bewley's call of invitation, and entered.

'Have a seat, Oliver,' said the earl from behind his desk. He idly stroked the brass handle of his cane, which rested against his knee. 'You must be weary. I hear you have been involved in an inordinate amount of physical exercise.'

Cormac sat, his first misgivings beginning to stir. Was he about to receive a condemnation of his actions?

'Do not look so anxious,' Lord Bewley said with a good-humoured smile. 'I am very pleased. Mr Comerford has given me a glowing account of your efforts today.'

Glowing? Cormac sent a glance of bafflement towards the closed door. Mr Comerford obviously liked to play his cards close to his chest.

'Very well done, my boy.' Lord Bewley tapped his cane on the desk. 'And you will be happy to hear that all has been settled with Lord Sinclair as well. He is the most pedantic fellow I ever met but that is well and good, I suppose, where land boundaries are concerned. Carruthers will handle the documentation with thorough attention to detail. We do not want to cause headaches for future generations.'

Cormac shifted with uneasiness but Lord Bewley didn't notice, absorbed as he was in locating a specific letter from the neat pile in front of him.

'Here, take this.' As Cormac stretched out his hand, he continued, 'It is from your mother's sister.'

Cormac froze in the action of taking the paper. Oliver's aunt? He had not even been aware of the connection. He drew back slowly and unfolded the page but could not make himself read the words. This was it. His duplicity was about to be discovered; he was moments away from being arrested and sent to prison.

'I have never met your mother's side of the family, as you know,' said Lord Bewley. 'I understand she was descended from a line of rather impoverished Irish nobility but, when it came to sanctioning my brother's marriage to her, that was not a material issue for me. He was in love with her and she with him. I could not have opposed the match on grounds of eligibility when they were so suited to each other.'

Even in the midst of his fear, this remark brought a realisation that caused Cormac's gut to twist in sadness: Oliver Davenport had perished needlessly. He had deemed death to be preferable to a life suffocated by obligation, but Lord and Lady Bewley were eminently decent people – they would not have forced their nephew into a situation that would have made him unhappy. And Lord Bewley himself had said he was under no commitment to bequeath his estate to his heir presumptive. They might have been disappointed but they would have allowed Oliver to pursue his dream of a poet's life. With a wave of remorse, Cormac experienced afresh the loss of that anguished young man.

Lord Bewley recalled him to the present with his next disastrous statement. 'Mrs Gibson has intimated that she should like to visit Bewley Hall.'

That was the worst news possible. She would lay eyes upon Cormac and scream the house down that he was not Oliver.

'I surmise, however, that seeing her dear nephew is not her objective, as she alleges, but seeing what her dear nephew is due to inherit. And, I further deduce, claiming that he has a Christian duty to provide aid to his poorer relatives.'

Lord Bewley's lip curled at the notion of such vulgarity and Cormac seized the opportunity to circumvent the impending calamity.

'She ought not come then,' he said and added in wild invention, 'I regret to disclose that this is not the first time she has attempted to inveigle funds from our family. My parents were kind-hearted enough to satisfy her requirements on several occasions but she always coveted more. There was no love lost between her and my mother.' Guilt pricked at him but Gerard and Caroline Davenport could not contradict him. 'I have no great desire to see my aunt when her purpose is so distasteful. Perhaps, if you are amenable to the proposal, I could send a small sum of money to placate her.'

The irony of the circumstances was that this unexpected complication might lead to a solution to a private concern of his. He had been wondering for some time how to surreptitiously send money back to his family in Ireland, now that he was in a position of affluence. Mrs Gibson had opened up the avenue to his accessing the necessary funds.

Lord Bewley set aside his cane and reached for the inkstand. 'Yes, I think that would be the best course of action. I'm certain Mrs Gibson would then find that a journey across the sea would not be so agreeable to her after all.'

Cormac sat back in his chair, affecting a relaxed pose. Although the immediate danger had passed, the tension did not leave his body. He had been growing comfortable in his role but now he realised he must always be watchful; his was a highly precarious position and he could be exposed at any time.

# CHAPTER 18

'That was most entertaining!' declared Lucy.

'Yes,' Cassandra enthused, 'the sets and costumes were magnificent!'

'I felt the music was not as strong as some of his other compositions, but otherwise I enjoyed it,' said Alice in her soft voice. 'What did you think, Bridget?'

Bridget bobbed her head at her companions. 'I agree with you all, though I believe the portrayal of the plight of the lower classes was vastly underemphasised.'

The four ladies were returning from the theatre in a single carriage, which Lucy's husband, Lord Newby, had put at their disposal for the evening.

'Dearest,' said Lucy, rubbing Bridget's arm with affection, 'you always do advocate so generously on behalf of the common man.'

Cassandra sniffed. 'I cannot imagine why. The creatures have no one to blame for their poverty but themselves.'

Bridget's mouth tightened but she restrained herself from berating her friend; though Cassandra was a wealthy countess, she could not boast of a broad education. 'Perhaps if you accompany me to St Swithun's sometime, you will observe that that is not the case.'

Cassandra looked horrified at the idea of setting foot in the workhouse, but Alice said, 'I do believe I should like to come with you. I have deferred a visit for far too long.'

Lucy's interjection reflected Bridget's own thoughts. 'Sweet Alice, you have too gentle a soul for such a venture. One look at the miserable wretches and you would dissolve into tears.'

Alice seemed near to weeping at the very thought. 'Oh dear, it may be that you are right. How do you bear it, Bridget?'

'And why do you even bother?' said Cassandra.

The halting of the carriage prevented Bridget from answering. The Newbys' footman opened the door and announced, 'Wyndham House.'

She gathered her mantle around her shoulders. 'Goodnight, ladies, and thank you all for an enjoyable evening.'

'Do not forget my party in two days' time!' Cassandra trilled in farewell.

'Indeed, I shall not,' Bridget called back as she stepped down from the carriage.

A blast of chilly January air hit her and she drew her mantle tighter around herself. Breath billowing out in front of her, she climbed the front steps of the townhouse where her own footman greeted her at the door.

'Thank you, Peter,' she said after he had closed the door and shut out the cold. As he took her mantle and bonnet, she said, 'My goodness, it's bitter out there. Tell me, how has your mother been since the stove was installed?'

'Very well, m'lady. I can't thank you enough. That stove's been a godsend. She says the house ain't never been so cosy and her lungs have cleared right up.'

'I am so pleased to hear that. Do let me know if there is anything else we can provide for her comfort.' Bridget moved further into the entrance hall and perceived the stillness within the house. 'Is my husband not here?'

'No, m'lady, he hasn't returned home yet.'

Perhaps Garrett had chosen to remain at his club for the night. In a neutral tone, she said, 'You may go to bed now. Leave the door locked but unbolted. My husband will let himself in if he comes back.'

After Peter had bowed and retreated, she picked up a candlestick from the hall table and ascended the staircase all the way to the third floor. There, she paused outside a door, listened for a moment, and stole into the chamber.

The air was warm from the small, slumbering body sprawled on top of the large bed. Bridget crossed the room and the candlelight flickered over her daughter's face. More than six and a half years had passed since her arrival into the world, but Bridget still found herself captivated by every endearing aspect of her, from her tiny button nose to her slightly chubby cheeks, flushed now with sleep.

But it was her hair that made everyone gasp in admiration. Thick curls, even thicker than her mother's, fell in natural waves down her back. And their extraordinary shade, such a golden hue that they shimmered in even the faintest light. Of course, there were the inevitable comments: how unusual, both parents so dark and the child so fair, that had to be a very uncommon occurrence? Bridget's reply remained consistent – that it was more common than one might expect – but she was certain people talked. No matter. Her conduct in society was exemplary; other than the colour of her daughter's hair, there was no foundation for that one vague rumour.

A single curl had fallen across the little girl's mouth and it fluttered out and back with each gentle breath. Heart full, Bridget bent over to kiss her forehead. Emily made a snuffling noise but didn't wake up. She had kicked off the covers at some stage in her sleep so Bridget pulled them back up over her shoulders to prevent her from catching a chill. Then she left the room without a sound.

She descended the stairs to her own bedchamber on the second floor. Audley, her lady's maid, assisted her with her nightly regime, placing her jewellery in the box on the dressing table and taking out a fresh nightdress from the chest of drawers. Once Bridget had slipped it on, she dismissed Audley and climbed into bed, humming one of the more memorable tunes from tonight's theatre performance.

That was when she realised with a jolt that it must be past midnight and tomorrow had now become today. The humming died in her throat and she looked back at the chest of drawers. The lowest drawer contained some of her saddest memories, and only once a year did she permit herself to look inside.

She slid back out of bed, stumbled across the room, knelt by the drawer, and pulled it open. A small pillowcase rested at the top; she withdrew it with a sigh. Embroidered on the front was his name: James. She kissed the stitched letters and rubbed the soft fabric against her cheek.

Next there were several baby gowns, tiny and neatly folded. She took them out one by one and stroked them before setting them on the floor. At the bottom of the drawer lay a velvet pouch. She untied it and a lock of soft, dark hair fell out onto her lap. The tears came and she didn't stop them, allowing herself to grieve for her little boy. He would have been four today.

She was not sure how long she sat there crying but at length the tears subsided and she felt better for the release of emotion, despite the pain that had accompanied it. She touched the lock of hair to her lips, tucked it back into its pouch, and returned everything to the drawer.

As she climbed into bed for the second time, she heard the distinct sound of the front door opening and shutting two floors below. A few clumsy bangs and a muffled oath told her that he had been drinking heavily tonight. Footsteps mounted one set of stairs, and the next. She held her breath and listened to their erratic movement across the landing, trying to determine their direction. They faltered and then there was a knock on her door.

She exhaled in resignation. 'Come in.'

Garrett sidled into the room and closed the door behind him, tilting back against the door panels as though his sense of balance was uncertain. She waited for him to speak first.

'It is very cold outside,' he said with the barest hint of a slur. 'I think it might snow.'

She arranged her expression into one of polite interest.

Running a hand through his black hair, he approached her bed and sat on the edge of it. A strong smell of spirits wafted from him.

'I have not forgotten what day it is,' he murmured.

She stared at him, dumbfounded.

He frowned. 'Do not look so surprised. Do you think I am heartless?'

She could not find the words to form a reply.

'He was my son,' he muttered. 'And I loved him.'

That was true but he had no right to be injured by her astonishment when he had for so long suppressed any hint of such emotion. After James's death, he had turned into a statue of ice, shunning her and Emily while simultaneously making it his ambition to frequent every drinking and gaming establishment in London. The loss of their boy had broken him and obliterated any hope of a peaceable marriage between them; all they had left was a fabrication for the eyes of society. During these past long years, they had each carried a burden of sorrow in solitude, the weight of it doubled because he had refused to share it. She didn't think she could ever forgive him for that, but now was not the time for reproach.

'May God look after our boy,' she said, her speech as indistinct as if she had been the one imbibing alcohol.

'Amen,' he said.

He shifted his weight and she thought he was going to leave, but instead he slid closer and leaned over to press his lips to hers. At first, she kissed him back, hoping it was merely a goodnight kiss. However, when the kiss became prolonged and his tongue pushed through, she stopped responding and he pulled back from her.

'What is wrong?' he asked, annoyed.

'I do not think this is appropriate,' she said, 'considering what day it is.'

'On the contrary. Today is James's birthday. I know it is a sad day but it should also be a hopeful one. Why don't we look to the future where there could be another little boy dressed in the clothes you keep tucked away in that bottom drawer?'

'We cannot replace James!' She was aghast at the suggestion.

'Of course not, I did not say that. But he is no longer with us and I think in honour of his memory we should try again. I want a child.'

'You already have a child,' she said and instantly bit her tongue, wishing she could bite back the words too. What a foolish thing to say. It was an unspoken rule within the house that they should never allude to Emily as his daughter if it could be at all avoided.

His eyes flashed. 'I desire a son,' he said, his quiet voice making the assertion no less threatening. 'One I can acknowledge. I want you to give me an heir.'

He put his hand on the bedcovers over her thigh and his head lowered towards hers again. She closed her eyes and submitted to him.

# CHAPTER 19

Garrett did not choose to remain in her bed so the next morning Bridget woke alone. After Audley had helped her to dress in sombre clothing, she went upstairs to her daughter's bedchamber. Now that Emily was older, Mrs Crewe's services were no longer required and the nurse had been replaced by a governess, Miss Davison. Bridget had been apprehensive about engaging the young lady, aware of the notorious role a governess could play in the carnal proclivities of the master of the household. But it had turned out to be a fortunate appointment for Miss Davison's features had proved too plain to tempt Garrett's interest and she had come to adore her charge. Though it was not within the remit of her educational duties, she revelled in combing through Emily's curls every morning, in which position Bridget found them as she entered the chamber. At her appearance, Emily slithered out of Miss Davison's grasp and ran into her arms.

'Mama, I dreamed last night that you and I grew wings and were able to fly over all the rooftops of London!'

'How wonderful that would be.' Bridget plucked at Emily's small chin. 'We would never have to worry about tripping over the cobblestones. Our poor horses would be left unemployed though. What would they do without a carriage to pull?'

'They could grow wings too and join us up in the clouds,' Emily replied as though this were the most sensible thing in the world. She surrendered again to Miss Davison's clutches and sat patiently on a stool while the governess arranged her hair.

'Not the red bow,' said Bridget. 'Please choose something plainer for today.'

'Why can't I wear my red bow?' Emily asked, disappointed.

'It would not be very fitting, gooseberry. Today is your brother's birthday.'

Emily took in the solemnity of her mother's dark-coloured dress and understood.

'Not the red bow today, Miss Davison,' she said gravely. 'I shall wear my navy one instead.'

The two women exchanged a sad smile over her fair head.

Bridget and Emily went down to breakfast, the little girl still chirping about her dream. When they entered the breakfast room, they found Garrett seated at the table reading a newspaper. Emily ceased her chatter and gazed down at the floor.

'Good morning, Papa,' she mumbled to her toes.

'Good morning, Emily,' he said tersely. He had no pet names for her.

They took their places at the table. As Bridget buttered some toast for Emily, the little girl spoke up, her expression thoughtful.

'Am I still a sister even though baby James isn't here anymore?'

Bridget glanced at Garrett, whose face had hardened.

'You will always be his big sister and he will always be your little brother,' she said. 'That will never change.'

'I wish the measles hadn't made him go to heaven,' said Emily. 'I would have enjoyed showing him how to paint when he was old enough.'

Garrett shoved his chair back and left the room without another word. Bridget was anguished to see how Emily's face fell.

'It's supposed to snow today,' she said. 'Wouldn't that be exciting? If enough falls, you could build a snowman in the gardens.'

Emily brightened at once and dashed to the window to check for falling flakes.

They heard Garrett depart the house soon after, gone to spend the day lounging about his club or whiling away the hours at Parliament or perhaps attending a meeting with his solicitor or his agent – enduring James's birthday anywhere but at home.

After breakfast, Bridget relinquished Emily into Miss Davison's care for her morning lessons and sat at her writing desk to respond to two letters.

She dealt with the easy one first. It was to her friend, Madeleine Wallace, now Mrs Matthew Parnell following her marriage to an acquaintance of Garrett's. She was still living in Ireland and happily married with two children. She related all the gossip about the girls Bridget had known back in Dublin, while Bridget in turn updated her on the latest London fashions. Their correspondence amounted to nothing more than vacuous nonsense but Bridget had to be content with that. Much as she yearned to unburden her long list of heartaches to a sympathetic friend, there was no one who would be able to understand, least of all the frivolous Madeleine.

The other, more troubling, letter was from her mother. She had not seen Lady Courcey since the night of Emily's birth and had not heard from her in nearly all that time. But a month ago, just before Christmas, Lady Courcey had finally written. She had wished the family a happy and peaceful season and expressed the hope that they were all in fine health. She had spoken of the Oakleigh Estate and how well it was prospering. Then, in a startling demonstration of humility, she had begged her daughter to forgive her and allow her to visit them in London. The closing line had intimated that she was not in the best of health and that she was finding the winter cold and lonely.

The tone of the letter was so melancholic that Bridget wondered whether her mother had sunk into a depression. How ill was she? Perhaps that was why she wanted to make amends.

But how could she make amends? Some acts were unforgiveable. Apart from her transgressions against her own daughter, Lady Courcey had been responsible for the appalling fate of the McGovern family, forcing them into destitution and rendering their chances of survival almost nonexistent. And the most unconscionable part was that the lady had known full well the ramifications of her actions and it had not inhibited her in the slightest.

Bridget's hand was heavy as she reached for her pen.

Mother,

Thank you for your correspondence. I am glad that the estate is thriving under your guardianship.

We are all in good health. Emily is six and a half now and full of chatter. She is very intelligent and loves to paint.

I am sorry to hear that you have been poorly; I trust that Mr Abbott is taking good care of you.

I regret to say that I cannot grant you the forgiveness you desire. You have hurt too many people and the wounds have not yet healed. But I maintain the hope that one day they will be healed and we shall be able to bridge the gap that necessarily came between us.

However, that day is not today. Please do not write again. You will hear from me when I am ready to communicate once more.

Your daughter,
Bridget

She sealed the letter and set it aside to be sent with the other household messages.

Later that morning, she pulled on her sturdy boots, her plainest bonnet and a weathered cloak, and left the house on foot. A few snowflakes had started to drift down but that did not deter her; this was one commitment she could never neglect.

She arrived at St Swithun's out of breath and flushed from the vigorous walk. There was no clamouring crowd outside the soup kitchen and the building itself was dark and deserted. Despondent as always at the sight, she trudged past it to the entrance of the forbidding workhouse.

It was the new Poor Law which had brought about the grievous state of affairs. Two years previously, Parliament had passed an act banning all outdoor relief – from then on, the poor could only seek succour within the confines of the workhouses, and the conditions inside those were made as unpleasant as possible to discourage all but the most desperate from entering them. Bridget and Frances Blythe had done everything they could to incite the Ladies of Compassion Association into righteous protest against such barbaric measures, but the ladies' complaints had been lacklustre at best – they were only concerned with the appearance of altruism rather than the actual improvement of the lives of the misfortunate souls they purported to aid. Bridget had even petitioned Garrett to speak against the proposed act in the House of Lords but she knew it was futile; he wouldn't entertain the notion for an instant when it would mean aligning himself with the minuscule minority. The whole endeavour felt like trying to break through an iron door with a feather. The soup kitchens around London were shut down, charitable financial assistance to the workhouses was repressed as much as possible, and St Swithun's became as good as a prison for the creatures forced to take refuge there.

Nevertheless, Bridget persevered. She still had two able hands to distribute food and a smile to offer comfort. She would volunteer in whatever manner she could and damn the people who were unwilling to support their fellow man and who were unable to see that their own good fortune was merely by chance of birth.

Frances had been appointed as an assistant matron in the workhouse once the soup kitchen had closed and she never failed to inspire Bridget with her tenacity and kind-heartedness. She was the only member of staff in the place who tried to insert an element of humanity into the proceedings, which made St Swithun's just a little less unbearable than the other workhouses around the city.

Today, she assigned Bridget to the men's dining hall, while she would serve the women and children under the age of six in a separate hall. The dinner bell rang and, under the watchful eye of a warden with a truncheon at his belt, the inmates shuffled in, queuing up in a straggly line to collect their meal of boiled beef, bread and a pint of beer.

Bridget invited the first person, an elderly man with hardly any teeth, to approach her bench. He received his plate and mug with shaky hands and whispered, 'Thank you, m'lady,' in a quavering voice before sitting at a table near the back of the hall to mash the gristly meat and hard bread with his gums.

She handed out the rations to each man and boy. Some took them from her in silence, others with murmured thanks. She smiled at everyone, whether they raised their eyes to her or not, and tried to put a little extra on the plates for the younger boys.

At length, the line began to peter out and the hall filled with a low din of muttering and clunking of dishes. The last man in the queue had a lopsided gait and shambled up to her with a scowl.

'About time,' he grumbled.

She presented him with a smile and his plate and mug.

'What're you smiling at?' he demanded, making no move to take them from her.

She was taken aback. 'I—nothing. Your dinner, sir.' She held them out again.

He closed his hands into fists. '*Sir*? Don't you mock me. You think I don't know where you come from? The kind of people you come from? If they were here, there ain't no chance you'd be calling me *sir*!' He spat on the floor.

'I meant no insult,' she said and placed the dishes on the bench for him to pick up himself.

'Your very presence is an insult,' he said, his words dripping with vitriol. 'Don't you know you're good for nuffin but lying on your back in a rich man's bed and pushing out his brats?'

She gaped at him. What had she done to deserve this kind of abuse?

'That's enough, Joe,' came another voice and she was relieved to see Frances appear by the man's side; she must have already finished dispensing food to the women and children. She grasped his arm but he shook her off and seized Bridget's left wrist. She jerked in surprise and pain.

'You think you're such a saint,' he growled, 'coming down here for a few hours to take pity on us poor folk afore going back to your fine house, thinking you've done your duty. You ain't nuffin but a fraud.'

Frances's attempts to drag him away were ineffectual. He twisted Bridget's wrist so that her palm was facing down, exposing the engagement ring on her finger: a large ruby encircled by pearls.

'Look at that! Why fool yourself? You ain't making a bleeding bit of difference!'

By this stage, the warden had come to intervene. He forced Joe to let go of her with a blow of his truncheon between the shoulder blades. He hauled the belligerent man out of the dining hall but she could still hear him shouting expletives all the way down the corridor. For such an infraction, he would spend up to twenty-four hours in the refractory cell, which the inmates called the 'dark hole'. He must truly have been incensed to risk a punishment so grim.

Her hands were shaking and she felt winded as though the truncheon had landed on her own back. Frances steered her into a back room, away from the staring eyes of the men and boys.

'Don't you fret about him,' she said in bracing tones, rubbing Bridget's upper arms briskly. 'He's just bitter because life dealt him a bad hand and he thinks you're holding a royal flush. He saw you as an easy target for venting his frustration.'

Bridget could not speak. Her wrist hurt abominably.

'Let me get you something to drink,' Frances said and bustled away.

Bridget blinked back the tears that threatened to fall. Joe had misjudged her, but of course she could tell neither him nor Frances the truth. She was not here for self-gratification. The real reason she threw herself into her charity work was because she nurtured the hope that if she was being kind to these poor individuals then maybe, if there was any justice in the world, in some unknown place there were other compassionate people who were aiding Cormac and his unfortunate family. She would do this work for decades if it meant that some sort of balance might be restored.

That was, if any of them was still alive.

# Chapter 20

By the next morning, the pain in her wrist had somewhat receded. It still looked swollen but thankfully not enough for Garrett to notice. If he heard that there had been real danger at the workhouse, she feared he would forbid her to go there again. Therefore, in order to give the impression that all was well, she kept her promise to attend Cassandra's gathering that evening. She would be going without Garrett, of course; he seldom made the effort to socialise with her acquaintances.

She travelled to Radcliffe House with Lucy and her husband. Lord Newby was fifteen years Lucy's senior and usually uncomfortable at this type of assembly, where dancing was a favourite activity, but he bore his discomfiture with stoicism. They ascended the steps to the open front door and a pair of fetching footmen conducted them into the grand entrance hall where their hostess came forwards to meet them. Cassandra was wearing an extravagant, green gown with a waist so narrow it was a wonder she could breathe, while an emerald-encrusted tiara nestled in her hair. She never did anything by halves; when she threw a party, her guests always remembered what she wore.

'You are all most welcome!' she greeted them before casting a look of amused disappointment towards Bridget. 'Lord Wyndham could not make it again? What a pity, your husband has far too many clashing engagements! Alice is already here, do come and join her.'

She led them into the drawing room where they found Alice hovering forlornly in a corner.

Cassandra cried, 'I declare, Alice, we cannot have you alone like this a day longer. We must find you a husband. And I do believe I have just the gentleman, a new fellow from Henry's club who will be in attendance tonight. I shall have to introduce you both. Excuse me, while I go ask Henry about him.' And she fluttered off in pursuit of her husband.

Alice turned pink. She had neither beauty nor fortune and, at the age of twenty-eight, had almost resigned herself to spinsterhood, but the colour in her cheeks indicated a small degree of optimism.

A footman passed by with a tray of champagne flutes and Lord Newby secured glasses for each of the ladies. Bridget took hers with her left hand, winced at the sudden stab of pain in her wrist, and switched the glass to her right hand.

Lucy perceived her grimace and said with concern, 'Good gracious, do you have an ache?'

Bridget glanced at Lord Newby. He attended the same club as Garrett and the two men were in frequent company together; she had no wish for her tale to reach Garrett's ears. Lord Newby seemed to understand, however, that his presence was not desirable and tactfully moved away to converse with a puffy-cheeked gentleman.

Once the three ladies were alone, she gave her companions a brief account of what had happened at St Swithun's. As to be expected, they were both horrified.

Alice exclaimed, 'An attack on your own person, how shocking!'

Lucy added, 'There is no question that you ought to cease your involvement at once.'

Bridget stood her ground. 'One man's desperate act is not enough to frighten me from my duty.'

'You should confine your obligation to making charitable donations,' said Lucy with a shake of her head.

Bridget was saved from defending herself further by Cassandra's reappearance.

'Excellent news, ladies. The gentleman's name is Mr Oliver Davenport and he is the sole heir to a vast estate in Bedfordshire. Now, wouldn't that be a fine match for Alice? He and his aunt and uncle are in London for the season. Here he comes now with Henry.'

Bridget, Lucy and Alice craned their necks towards the doorway, where Lord Radcliffe was just entering the drawing room in the company of...

Bridget's heart stopped and she gasped so loudly that all the people in the room turned to look at her.

'Are you feeling unwell again?' Lucy asked, clutching her elbow.

The room spun around Bridget; she could not breathe. *Cormac?* For a moment she believed she might faint, but Lucy's pinching grip kept her alert and upright.

'I'm fine,' she managed to rasp. 'Just a twinge in my wrist again.'

She sat in a chair that Lord Newby offered her but refused some smelling salts from Alice. The other guests looked away once they could see she was not in any immediate peril and their collective attention returned to the newcomer at the party. Without their gazes upon her, she could try to recover some semblance of composure.

She could not have been more shocked and winded than if somebody had pushed her down a flight of stairs. Cormac, *her* Cormac, a stable hand, was being ushered into the room and introduced to some of the highest people in London society.

And he looked like one of them too, resplendent in the stylish evening wear of a wealthy gentleman. But it was not just the clothes that made him look the part; he held himself like a nobleman, tall and proud. His comportment was impeccable and he greeted each guest with incomparable courtesy.

This sophistication was so unlike the Cormac she knew that she had to blink and stare at him again. It was unquestionably him but some things were very different. His skin, which used to be so tanned from the sun, had grown paler and his fair hair had been cut shorter so that it did not fall into his eyes anymore when he bent his head. And he was bending his head an awful lot – every woman in the room seemed to want to make his acquaintance and he bowed respectfully to each one, appearing flattered and humbled by their attention.

She was flabbergasted. Where on earth had this suave Cormac come from? Far more crucially, where had Cormac himself come from? The last she had known of him was that he had refused the help of the Grace of God Mission Society – how did he proceed from that deplorable situation to attending a gathering at one of the most fashionable residences in London? It was astounding. She would have been less surprised if Emily had turned into a rabbit.

She blanched when she saw Cassandra approach Cormac and coax him in their direction. She was not ready for this. She must be in a dream and he was no more than an apparition from her past. This could not actually be happening.

'—and it is my delight to introduce you to Lord and Lady Newby.' Cassandra sounded as distant to Bridget as though she were speaking from the other side of a closed door.

'I am most pleased to make your acquaintance,' said Cormac, bowing to Lucy and her husband.

It was unmistakably his voice but it, too, seemed altered. His accent was more cultured and there wasn't a trace of his former rural twang. Even the language he used was more formal than his old way of speaking.

'And this is Lady Wyndham,' said Cassandra.

Bridget rose from her seat and did the only thing she could do – she offered her hand and murmured, 'My sincere greetings, Mr Davenport.'

'A pleasure, Lady Wyndham,' he said and bent over her gloved hand with the charm of a gracious stranger. This was Cormac but he was far removed from the Cormac she had once known so well.

He let go of her hand very quickly.

'And may I present Miss Caulfield?' Cassandra went on with an ostentatious flourish in Alice's direction.

Alice went as red as beetroot and tripped over her words as she squeezed out her greeting. It was evident that she was quite taken with Cormac, and why not, for he was more dashing than any other gentleman in the room. Bridget had always thought him good-looking, but now, polished up as he was, he had become exceptionally handsome.

After these introductions, Lord Radcliffe commandeered Cormac for the company of a cluster of gentlemen by the fireplace, providing Cassandra, Lucy and Alice with the chance to put their heads together.

'Did I not tell you?' said Cassandra. 'I can think of no better match for a woman seeking a husband.'

'He is very attractive,' Lucy remarked, somewhat breathless. 'What an eligible gentleman. Indeed, Alice, you could not go wrong with this Mr Davenport.'

Alice's eyes widened. 'Oh, but he will never consider me. You saw how the other ladies behaved, they will all want him. And I have no fortune.'

Cassandra waved the argument away. 'Have I not already said he is to inherit a substantial estate? He has more than enough money for you both.'

It was Lucy who noticed that Bridget was not contributing to the conversation. She touched her arm solicitously. 'Is your wrist hurting very much? Do you need to go home?'

'No, not at all,' Bridget replied swiftly. Departing this party was the last thing she wanted to do. She had to observe more of this new Cormac and, if possible, speak with him alone. The initial shock was beginning to wear off and now she was consumed with a blazing desire to find out how he had come to be here. 'I do not need to leave. I did feel unwell for a moment but it has already passed.'

Just then, the bell sounded for dinner and the guests drifted into the dining room, which was filled with several round tables, each laid out with twelve place settings. Bridget went in on the arm of Lord Newby and Lucy was escorted by her husband's puffy-cheeked companion. Bridget and Lucy sat, while the men remained standing until the rest of the guests had arrived to the table. To Bridget's left were two ladies and two gentlemen whom she recognised as Cassandra's distant cousins, and the last four places were claimed by Cassandra, Lord Radcliffe, Alice and...

'Mr Davenport, do come sit here by Miss Caulfield! You must tell her about the beautiful countryside in Bedfordshire for she is very fond of nature.'

Cormac held out a chair for Alice with a smile – the matchmakers were on the road to success already – and, as all the men sat down, he took his own seat which happened to be opposite Bridget, leaving her in a good position to watch him and listen to his conversation during the meal.

He himself turned out to be the main topic of discussion. The female guests in particular were eager to learn more about him and paid rapt attention as he answered questions on everything from his political standpoint to his favourite sport. This kind of treatment was customary for any new addition to their circle but it seemed to be even more intense with Cormac, no doubt because he was unattached and so pleasing to the eye.

'Mr Davenport,' simpered one of the ladies on Bridget's left. 'Some of us find it difficult to believe that there is no Mrs Davenport. Is there any reason why you have not yet married?'

'Miss Norwell, how very forward of you!' Cassandra remonstrated and then turned to Cormac with a gleam in her eye. 'Although I suppose it would be rude not to answer, now that the question has been asked.'

He chuckled. Bridget was amazed at the effortless way he was able to flirt with these brainless women. 'I'm afraid the answer is quite dull. I have simply never sought a Mrs Davenport. My aunt and uncle preferred me to concentrate on learning to manage the estate in Bedfordshire before becoming distracted by such matters. Having said that, I do believe that marriage was one of their motives in our coming to London this year. They are of the opinion that I should consider settling down in the near future and that I may find a potential wife here in the city.'

A flurry of whispers passed between Miss Norwell and the other female cousin and then they both looked up and beamed.

'I am astonished that you have never been to London before,' said Lucy. 'Why is it you are only making your first visit now?'

'There are two reasons for that,' he said, taking a sip from his wine glass. 'First of all, I was born in Ireland and most of my upbringing took place there, so for a long time I never had the opportunity to visit this splendid city. Then, when I did move to England, I persuaded my aunt and uncle to delay my acquaintance with London as long as possible.'

'Why would you do that?' Cassandra asked incredulously.

'I suppose I felt that, having grown up in another country, I was somewhat rough-edged and needed to refine my style and manners before venturing among you fine people.'

He looked embarrassed as he said this and even more so when a chorus of protestations arose vouching that he had the most gentlemanly conduct in the world. Bridget doubted if much of his story was genuine but she suspected this last bit almost certainly was. While always well-mannered, the Cormac she had known wouldn't have had the first idea of when a gentleman should remove his gloves or which cutlery he ought to use when dining. If he had shown up in London with his former rustic manners, he would have been laughed out of the city.

'Why did you grow up in Ireland?' said Alice. 'Were your parents from there?'

'My mother was Irish. When she married my father, he decided to stay in Ireland rather than bring her back to England. She would have been heartbroken if he had forced her to leave her home.'

Bridget experienced a wrench of sorrow as she compared this tale to her own life, while the ladies made hushed comments to each other about how romantic and selfless the elder Mr Davenport had been to make such a personal sacrifice for his wife.

'Are they still there now?' That was Alice again; she must indeed be smitten to overcome her shyness long enough to pose three questions in a row.

'I regret to say that they have both passed away,' he said and sympathetic murmurs rose up on all sides. 'They drowned in a boating accident. Lord and Lady Bewley were the only family I had left so that is when I came to live in England.'

Barely trusting her voice to work, Bridget summoned up the courage to ask, 'And how many years ago was that?' She hoped she might extract a snippet of real information that could help her decipher his true story.

He looked at her across the table with a tilt of his head and she could swear he knew precisely what she was thinking. 'About four and a half years ago.'

Lucy said, 'Do you plan to return to Ireland in the future?'

'I would very much like to go back again sometime,' he replied, and the conversation moved on to the topic of travelling abroad, and choice holidaying destinations, and had Mr Davenport ever visited the continent.

After the dinner had ended, the party transferred to the ballroom so the dancing could commence. Mr Davenport was by far the most popular candidate for a partner and every lady tried to catch his eye, hoping he would write his name into her dance card. Bridget marvelled at the way Cormac moved out on the floor. Even though she had never seen him dance back at Oakleigh, she was positive he could not have been knowledgeable in such steps back then. He must have received lessons in the meantime. Which raised one of many burning questions: what sort of life had he led in the intervening years that he'd had occasion to obtain dancing lessons? Who in God's name were Lord and Lady Bewley? Had he invented them or were they real people? Was he coercing them into pretending to be related to him? Or had he hoodwinked them into believing he was their nephew? Idea after idea, each one more ridiculous than the last, churned through her head until it was sore.

A quiet voice interrupted her thoughts. 'Good evening, Lady Wyndham. Would you do me the honour of taking the next dance with me, if you are not already engaged?'

Her stomach flipped over. 'Oh, I—no—I mean, yes—that is to say, I am not engaged.'

Cormac looked like he was trying to hide an amused smile as he offered her his arm and said, 'Shall we?'

He escorted her out onto the floor and they took their place on one side of a quadrille square. She glanced up into his familiar blue eyes and felt her breath catch in her throat. It was a surreal moment, standing next to someone whom, until tonight, she had feared to be dead. She was bursting to ask him dozens of questions but she would have to choose her words with care in case the pairs of dancers on the other three sides overheard.

'Are you real?' she whispered as the musicians struck up the tune and their hands clasped together. Despite the two layers of gloves, the contact made her heart skip a beat.

'Indisputably so.'

They took a turn within the perimeter of the square, his movements as graceful as if he had been born to be a gentleman.

'Who is Oliver Davenport?'

'I am.'

'But who is he really?' she pressed.

He hesitated. 'Too long an explanation for one dance.'

She swallowed, unsure what to make of that. The dance separated them for several bars, obliging them to partner with the couple opposite them. When they returned to each other, the adjacent pairs took up the pattern, giving her the opportunity to ask, 'How did you come to be here?'

'Here at the party, here in London, or here in England?'

She was taken aback by his casual tone. How could he not see the gravity of the situation? 'Did you come here seeking me?'

He looked disgusted. 'Don't be so self-obsessed. Believe it or not, you aren't the reason for my being in London.' It was their turn again to participate; they circled smoothly around the square. 'I didn't spend the last seven and a half years pining for you. I made a new life for myself and our paths just happened to cross at this moment. You will not even see me again after tonight.'

Crushed by this rejoinder, she endured the rest of the dance in silent turmoil, which he did not seem disposed to disrupt. When they were nearing the end of the quadrille's final figure, she said at last, 'Don't you want to meet another time? When there are not so many people around?'

'What good would that do?'

His bluntness was scalding. Doing her best to conceal her distress, she said, 'So you do not have any wish to become reacquainted?'

'How is Garrett?' he said pointedly in response, just as the music finished and the dancers reformed the square. He gave her a stiff bow, not allowing her time to answer, and all she could do was curtsey and watch him walk away.

What a dreadful encounter. It left her feeling lightheaded again; she had a sudden and desperate need for air. A set of French doors led from the ballroom to a secluded terrace outside; retreating out to it, she found it empty of guests. Grateful for the solitude, she closed the doors behind her, blocking out the clamour of the dancing and chatter.

A light snow had fallen and the terrace and its balustrade were coated in white. It was bitterly cold but she did not feel it – she was smouldering with emotion. Now that she was on her own, she could let her feelings spill out. She began to weep.

The relief was overwhelming. Cormac was alive. For more than seven years she had lived every day in the fear that he was not, and to learn the truth was a release from that imprisonment. How he had become an apparent gentleman of society was unfathomable to her but it mattered less than the realisation that he was alive and very well.

She started in alarm when she heard the French doors open again and whirled to see Cormac emerging onto the terrace. She tried to wipe her tears away but it was too late to hide them. Was that regret on his face? He shut the doors as she had done, though that was not quite proper now that they were a man and a lady alone.

He approached her, withdrew a handkerchief from his pocket, and held it out. 'Am I the cause of these tears?'

There was no need for her to reply. She took the handkerchief and dried her eyes.

'I had better apologise for my discourtesy during the dance,' he said. She noticed that he did not drop the formal language of the upper classes even though there was nobody to hear but her; she supposed it must come to him naturally now after so many years playing the part.

She shook her head. 'You had every right to speak as you did.'

A pregnant silence fell between them. Unable to bear the weight of it, she asked, 'You say you did not seek me out, but did you know I was going to be here tonight?'

'No, though when I came to London I suspected I might happen upon you.'

'I all but fainted when you entered the drawing room.'

'You did look quite appalled. The sight of me must have indeed been a shock to you.'

She said tentatively, 'Did you not feel something similar?'

He paused. 'It took a moment to adjust,' he said, but she was convinced he was underplaying the emotion he must have experienced. No one could share a past like theirs and not have a strong reaction – whether positive or negative – when they saw the other again.

A few stray snowflakes floated onto their hair and clothes but she paid them no mind. 'You received your invitation to the party through Lord Radcliffe?'

'Yes, we became acquainted at our club.'

'You are fortunate it is not the same club as Garrett's. Had he encountered you, he would have exposed your masquerade immediately.'

'I made advance enquiries to avoid such a scenario.' For the first time, he seemed apprehensive. 'Can I trust you not to divulge my secret?'

With all her sincerity, she said, 'I swear I will not do anything to hurt you. But will you tell me how you have managed to rise in society by no legitimate means that I can think of?'

The set of his jaw was enough; she was not entitled to know that information. He cast around for a change of subject. 'Are you well yourself?'

'As well as I can be.'

'Do you have a family?'

Her heart twisted and she turned her face away so that he would not see her pain. 'I have a daughter. Her name is Emily.'

'How old is she?'

'A little over six and a half.'

'Quite the hasty marriage.' His voice was hard.

That grieved her, his assumption that she and Garrett had conceived Emily directly after they had married. But, dear God, how could she find the words to tell him the truth?

They were startled by the sound of the French doors opening once more. This time it was Lucy who appeared, silhouetted by the candlelight from the ballroom. She checked at the sight of Bridget and Cormac on the terrace alone – they were standing rather closer than propriety dictated. Bridget balled up the handkerchief into her fist and Cormac took a respectful step away.

Acting unperturbed, he said, 'Lady Newby, is it not? I have been introduced to many new faces tonight but I believe I have it right.'

'You do, indeed, Mr Davenport,' said Lucy. 'Are you enjoying the evening's entertainment?'

'Most assuredly, yes. Lady Radcliffe knows how to throw a fine party. However, I anticipate my joints will be stiff tomorrow. Perhaps next time I shall not attempt to participate in every single dance.'

Though it took an enormous effort on her part, Bridget added her laughter to Cormac's with the cordiality of two people who had only made their acquaintance a few hours ago. Lucy laughed too before throwing a quizzical glance at Bridget.

'I came to look for you. I cannot imagine what you are doing out here in the freezing cold!'

Bridget could think of no quicker excuse than, 'My wrist was bothering me again. I thought to put some snow on it.'

'You injured your wrist, Lady Wyndham?' Cormac asked.

She reddened. 'It is nothing. I hurt it in an incident yesterday.'

Lucy linked arms with Bridget. 'Lady Wyndham is our heroine of the workhouse.'

Genuine surprise filled his features. 'The workhouse?'

'Oh, yes,' said Lucy. 'She is the most philanthropic person of our acquaintance, devoting herself wholeheartedly to the cause of the poor. Not even a deranged man's assault can discourage her.'

'How very admirable,' said Cormac. 'And please accept my best wishes for a speedy recovery. Ladies, I shall return indoors. I would advise you not to stay out much longer in this weather.'

He bowed to them both and headed back to the ballroom.

Lucy gazed after his retreating back. 'Good gracious, he really is a fine-looking man. He has such beautiful eyes. We must do everything we can to match him with Alice before that Miss Norwell can get her claws into him. He and Alice would make a lovely couple, do you not think?'

'Mmm,' said Bridget noncommittally.

# CHAPTER 21

'So, Oliver,' said Lady Bewley, executing a precise rap on the top of her soft-boiled egg, 'you sampled the delights of London's season last night. I trust that went well?'

Cormac, whose own thoughts had also been dwelling on the party at Radcliffe House, looked up. 'Yes, it was an enjoyable evening.'

'No doubt you encountered a great many pleasing young ladies,' she said with a twinkle in her eye.

From the top of the table, Lord Bewley winked at Cormac. 'Beware,' he said. 'She is scheming again.'

Cormac withheld the weary sigh that threatened to escape him. 'I believe you are right, Uncle.'

'Well?' Lady Bewley prompted. 'Were they agreeable to you?'

'They were, I suppose, but what is the hurry? Do you need me to find a wife within a month of our arriving in London?'

They both stared at him in surprise.

'Forgive me,' he backtracked. 'I did not mean to be impertinent.'

Lady Bewley reached across the table and patted his hand. 'There is nothing to forgive. We have been putting a good deal of pressure on you about this, more than we should. From now on, we shall step back and let you take your time. It is important that you find the right woman, a proper lady who will make a worthy lifelong companion for you.'

Bridget's face swam into his mind but he banished her at once. 'I promise I shall keep looking. If I search hard enough, I am sure she will appear.'

'Make certain you choose a lady who is willing to have a large family,' said Lord Bewley with a chuckle. 'Your aunt and I are looking forward to spoiling our many grandnephews and grandnieces.'

'I shall take that into account,' Cormac said, laughing along with him, though his gut clenched at the daunting task they had set upon his shoulders.

'I hope the company at the party was stimulating, at any rate,' said Lady Bewley. 'Impartially speaking, did you make any interesting new acquaintances?'

Irresistibly, Bridget surfaced again. 'I met Lady Wyndham, who helps at a workhouse,' he said before he could help himself. That particular detail had stuck with him ever since he had heard it.

Lady Bewley, who was herself involved in charitable works in Bedfordshire, perked up with interest. 'Does she indeed? How intriguing. Did she mention where the workhouse is situated?'

'I did not ask for further information.'

'I would be most eager to hear about the workhouses here in the city, for they must accommodate hundreds of poor souls. Perhaps you could arrange for Lady Wyndham to come visit me? I should very much like to talk with her about her endeavours.'

He nodded, but found he had no appetite anymore and pushed his plate away.

As soon as breakfast was over, he escaped to the gardens of Raynesworth House. Situated on Park Lane, the Earl of Bewley's London residence reflected the affluence of its distinguished address, and its grounds were no exception, comprising an expanse of lawn, well-tended flowerbeds among winding paths, and a walled orchard. Cormac paced along one of the paths, sloshing through the melting remains of the previous day's snowfall, and took deep breaths to calm himself.

These discussions about taking a wife were becoming alarmingly frequent. It had been all very well to agree to the suggestion back in Bedfordshire when the potential wives were in distant London – but now they were right in front of him and he was expected to choose one. Could he make such a long-term commitment to his false persona? There would be no way out if he got married; he would be Oliver Davenport forever and Cormac McGovern would be no more.

And what of his unfortunate bride, whoever she might be? She would have to remain ignorant of his deception, meaning that their marriage would begin upon a bed of dishonesty. Now that he could afford to have scruples again, the very notion of it revolted him.

He approached the walled orchard and pushed at the door, which resisted due to a sheltered snowdrift on the other side. Shoving his way through, he found himself in a small enclosure with fewer than a dozen apple trees and a stone bench in one corner. It was a decent size for a garden in a well-populated city, but paltry in comparison to the sprawling orchard at Oakleigh.

And that, of course, directed his thoughts once more to Bridget.

He would have liked to convince himself that her existence was immaterial to him now, but in reality he had been vigilant for a glimpse of her ever since his arrival to London. He had sought her chestnut curls whenever he passed a lady on the street or at the park or in a ballroom, hoping and fearing it would be her.

And then he had entered the drawing room at Radcliffe House. It had taken every ounce of his willpower to retain his composure, but at least he had had years of practice in maintaining a facade. He had managed to preserve his self-control, while an ignoble part of him had experienced a small amount of vindictive satisfaction in her stunned bewilderment.

She was greatly altered, he had perceived that at once. Though an outsider would deem her an image of perfect loveliness, he discerned the waxen quality of her too-pale cheeks, the drooping lines of sadness around her mouth, the haunted look in those dark brown eyes. This profound change in her had consumed him all night, making sleep impossible. What unhappy things had befallen her since they had last met?

And why should he care so much?

He supposed he was drawn to her because for a decade and a half she had been the brightest point of his life; seeing her again stirred up feelings which had long lain dormant. But what were those feelings now? There was such a great deal unresolved between them that he found them impossible to identify.

He knew he should hate her. She had given him her promise and then rejected him to satisfy her tyrannical mother and manipulative fiancé. Now her husband, he amended resentfully. On top of that, her actions had forced him to forsake his family and sink to the status of a wandering beggar, and there was no joy in recalling *that* agonising time.

Lost in his wretched memories, he did not realise that he was no longer alone in the orchard until he heard Lady Bewley say, 'Oliver, dear? Are you not feeling well?'

He came to himself and found that he was sitting on the stone bench, his elbows on his knees and his hands clenched tight in his hair. Knowing how disturbing this must appear, he jumped up and tried to arrange a smile onto his face.

'Aunt, you startled me.'

Her forehead furrowed into plump folds of anxiety. 'You are as white as a ghost. What is the matter?'

'Nothing at all,' he tried to assure her.

'That is not the truth. You looked like you were attempting to tear your hair out.'

'Did I?' he said with as much innocence as he could muster. 'I was preoccupied with inconsequential thoughts, that is all. There is no need to worry.'

'Please know that you can confide in me whenever you wish to. I am always here to share your burdens.'

'I do know that and I thank you for it.' He took her hand and held it affectionately in both of his own. 'I owe you and my uncle more than I can ever repay you.'

She relaxed, mollified. 'You are such a dear,' she said. 'Come, let us go inside.'

She slipped her arm through his and they walked through the garden back to the house.

\*\*\*

By the time two days had passed, Bridget had reached a high state of agitation. Having received no word from Cormac after the party, she could only assume he remained resolute in not wishing to meet. She had made some discreet enquiries about the Earl of Bewley but it seemed he was a legitimate peer; there wasn't a whisper of fraudulence in connection with the family, and all reports claimed that his heir was an estimable gentleman in every regard. Baffled and frustrated, she wondered what she ought to do. Did she dare seek Cormac out? It was unseemly for a lady to call upon an unmarried gentleman, but she could not tolerate the idea of encountering him at further social events and pretending to be strangers. There was a history between them which they needed to address, for good or for ill.

She was brooding over her dilemma at the breakfast table, while at the same time trying to persuade Emily to eat the last of her bacon, when Garrett spoke.

'So tell me about this Oliver Davenport.'

She gaped at him, nearly dropping Emily's fork. 'Pardon me?'

'I was talking to Newby at the club yesterday. He mentioned there was a new bachelor on the scene turning all the ladies' heads.'

'Oh, yes, that's right,' she said and gave a false laugh. 'Mr Davenport.'

Garrett sat back in his chair with a smirk. Was he recalling the days when it had been he who had set all the ladies swooning? 'What are his circumstances?'

How she wished she knew. 'There is not much to tell. I believe he is in the city for the season with his aunt and uncle. They have a sizeable estate in Bedfordshire. That is all I know about him.'

'Newby said he was quite the star of the party the other night.'

'I suppose he was. Lucy and Cassandra regard him as a perfect match for Alice.'

She held her breath, fearful that Lord Newby's loose tongue had also divulged her near-fainting episode, but Garrett made no mention of it. He sat forwards to eat again.

'I shall have to meet the fellow sometime. Newby had a fine conversation with him about horse racing.'

'Indeed,' she said placidly, even as her insides shrivelled. Garrett meeting Cormac was the least desirable event imaginable and she would have to do all in her power to prevent it from ever happening.

A few minutes later, the messages arrived, two for Garrett and one for Bridget. She opened hers and peered at the signature. A small gasp escaped her which she hastily converted into a cough. After glancing at Garrett to make sure he had not noticed her unusual reaction, she swept her gaze down the page.

Dear Lady Wyndham,

I trust this letter finds you well and that your injury has fully healed. I am writing to invite you to luncheon the day after tomorrow at Raynesworth House, where my uncle and aunt, Lord and Lady Bewley, are residing while in London. I mentioned to my aunt that you are engaged in charitable work in the city and she is most eager to discuss that subject with you as she too is involved in such efforts in Bedfordshire. She also asked me to request that your daughter accompany you for she adores children and has a little gift for her.

I look forward to your response.

Your servant,
Oliver Davenport

She admired the elegant script, a far cry from the stocky letters he used to scrape onto slate. He had worded it well too; to any eye, this was nothing more than polite correspondence between acquaintances. She supposed he had written it like that in case it happened to fall into the wrong hands.

She reread the message with a measure of apprehension. She was keen to accept on her own behalf but the invitation had also been extended to Emily. How wise would it be to allow Emily into his presence? There was so much she did not yet know about his unexplained past that she wondered whether it would be best to be cautious for now where Emily was concerned. Until she could trust him, perhaps she ought to keep the truth concealed.

In the end, she concluded that it would be discourteous not to bring Emily when Lady Bewley had made a particular request for her attendance but that she need not be so fretful over Cormac and Emily being in each other's company. He had no suspicions of fatherhood so why would he look too closely?

After breakfast, she penned her acceptance and instructed Peter to carry it to the Bewleys' residence. However, the day before the visit to Raynesworth House could come to pass, she came unexpectedly face to face with Cormac again.

She and Alice had decided to go to Regent's Park to enjoy a bout of skating on the ice-covered lake. The snow had retreated, a weak sun had emerged, and a hard frost the night before promised good skating conditions. Neither Lucy nor Cassandra accompanied them; Lucy had a prior arrangement at the milliner's, while Cassandra considered putting on a pair of skates a pursuit as agreeable as visiting the disease-ridden workhouse.

When Bridget and Alice arrived at the park, they found the lake already teeming with skaters. Men and women glided across its smooth surface, chattering and laughing, the ice sparkling beneath their boots. The gentlemen were being attentive in assisting the ladies to stay upright, their helpful hands clutching arms, elbows, and sometimes waists. Here and there, less experienced skaters lost their balance and tumbled to the ice, rising to their feet with embarrassed grins.

Bridget had debated the wisdom of skating so soon after she had injured her wrist, but she resolved to be cautious on the ice and stay well away from other skaters who might wobble into her path. She desired a spell outside in the bracing cold. Though it stung her nose and made her fingertips numb in spite of her gloves, the activity would be a welcome distraction from her chaotic thoughts.

Or so she had believed. She and Alice had been on the ice for scarcely a few minutes when a pair of gentlemen came skating towards them and she distinguished Cormac's familiar face below his fine hat. She teetered on her skates and it took all her effort to maintain her equilibrium, in every sense of the word. How could she ever become used to the idea of Cormac dressed in the best fashions of the day, socialising with the upper classes, and betraying not the barest hint of his lower class beginnings?

With Cormac was Cassandra's athletic husband, Lord Radcliffe. That gentleman was the exact opposite of his wife – he was most likely to be found where there was sport of some kind, preferably out of doors; the extravagant parties were all Cassandra's doing and he was merely obliged to suffer them. His lithe form glided with ease over the frozen lake, and he chuckled as Cormac made some sort of amusing joke alongside him.

There was a moment when Bridget thought they might all just skate by each other without interaction. She could identify the precise instant when Cormac spotted her by the sudden stiffening of his previously relaxed posture, but he made no move to acknowledge her. Flummoxed, she did not dare initiate the greeting herself.

But then, as the men drew nearer, Lord Radcliffe glanced their way. Recognition filled his features and he hailed them, causing all four skaters to skid to a halt.

'Greetings, ladies,' said Lord Radcliffe. 'Are you enjoying the skating?'

'Very much,' said Bridget. She could not rely upon Alice to make conversation; her friend was shrinking further inside her scarf.

'I hope you're being careful on the ice. It can be treacherous to the unwary skater. I saw one young fellow slip not ten minutes ago and achieve a painful twist of the knee in the process.'

'Thank you for your concern,' said Bridget. 'We are taking the utmost care.'

Lord Radcliffe turned his genial expression on Alice, offering her the opportunity to contribute.

The bit of Alice's face that was visible above her scarf went blotchy with self-consciousness. 'I do love to skate,' she said, her voice coming out in a squeak.

'It's an invigorating pastime, is it not?' said Cormac, casting her a kind smile of his own.

'Indeed, Mr Davenport. Do you' – Alice took a breath and plunged on as though she were asking a very personal secret – 'do you get much opportunity to skate during the winter in Bedfordshire?'

'There is a river that runs through my uncle's estate. When it freezes over, the greatest sport is partaking in skating races along it.'

'How exhilarating,' said Alice. Her chin started to emerge from her scarf, like a small animal nosing out of its burrow.

'It is a pity we cannot attempt such a challenge here,' said Lord Radcliffe ruefully, 'but circling around the lake is pleasurable too. Perhaps we may accompany you for a while?'

He held out his arm to Bridget, leaving Cormac to offer his to Alice. Bridget experienced a twinge of paranoia. Cassandra had known about the skating trip – had she persuaded her husband to instigate this encounter in order to further the matchmaking plans she had hatched with Lucy? The crisp air and the glimmering winter sun provided a romantic setting for the encouragement of an attachment.

She could say nothing as Alice shyly accepted Cormac's arm. They turned to skate away closer to the centre of the lake. Lord Radcliffe gestured to Bridget, indicating that they would follow, but she stopped him with a shake of her head.

'Thank you, but I am feeling tired from the exertion. I should like to take a rest, if you do not mind.'

With a courteous bow – all the more impressive for having been executed while wearing a pair of ice skates – he escorted her to the side of the lake and, after her repeated protestations that she would be fine by herself, he returned to the ice. Instead of rejoining Cormac and Alice, however, he sailed off on his own, making Bridget suspect even more that the meeting had been by design rather than by chance.

She sat on the bank of the lake. At first, she spent some time untying and retying the laces of her skating boots but, irresistibly, her gaze was drawn upwards and across the surface of the lake.

Even at a distance, she could tell that they were enjoying each other's company. As they skated along, Alice's gloved hand rested comfortably in the crook of Cormac's elbow and she looked up into his face with a beaming smile. Then she lurched on the ice and lost her footing. She clung to Cormac as she tottered, causing him to stagger too. They hovered on the cusp of falling but managed to regain their balance, his arms around her waist to keep her steady. Their laughter drifted over the lake, warm and genuine.

Bridget hated the black feeling this roused in her. Alice was so sweet and affectionate once she overcame her timidity; she deserved to have a good man fall in love with her. But Cormac...

She imagined how it might play out. They would encounter Cormac at more parties and balls. He would make sure to write his name in Alice's dance card, no doubt for the waltzes where the giddy speed, the close embrace, and the opportunity for uninterrupted eye contact afforded a more sensual, intimate experience. They would go riding along the popular Rotten Row in Hyde Park, and others would begin to comment on how much time the two young people were spending together. And then the announcement would be in the paper: an engagement, a perfect match, a very happy couple.

But the name of the groom-to-be would be Oliver Davenport. Who on earth was Cormac pretending to be? How was any of this even possible? And how would poor Alice feel if she ever learned how she had been deceived?

Bridget had promised Cormac she would keep her silence. But in knowing the truth about his past, she was now complicit in whatever unknown act he had committed to obtain his place of prominence in society. If only he would speak to her, explain how he had come to be here, help her to make sense of it all. She was adrift in ignorance.

At length, he and Alice came skating over to her. Alice was breathless and pink-cheeked, her eyes sparkling. Cormac's cheerful expression transformed into a controlled mask of detached civility as soon as he met Bridget's gaze. He held Alice's hand as she stepped carefully off the ice onto the bank.

'Until our next meeting, ladies,' he said and glided away from them.

# CHAPTER 22

Though it was no great distance from Berkeley Square to Park Lane, the weather was bitter and Emily's legs were short so she and Bridget travelled by carriage to the door of Raynesworth House, where the butler greeted them and escorted them to the drawing room. Bridget felt her nerves heighten at the prospect of seeing Cormac again but he was not present when she and Emily entered the room. Lady Bewley came forwards to receive them, her rotund body bobbing with pleasure.

'Lady Wyndham, you are most welcome! I am so pleased you could visit. And this adorable cherub must be your daughter! How do you do, little one?'

Once the initial exchanges of introduction were complete, Lady Bewley led them to a round table laid out for luncheon. As they sat, Bridget could not restrain herself from asking, 'Will Mr Davenport be joining us?'

Lady Bewley laughed. 'Oh, no, he has no interest in ladies' conversations. He and my husband have gone out for the afternoon. And now, my pet, what have I got for you?' she added, directing her words towards Emily, who was eyeing a small, wrapped package next to the sugar bowl. Lady Bewley handed it to her and Emily pulled back the layers of material to reveal a delicate, silver-handled hairbrush.

'My goodness, it is beautiful,' said Bridget. 'Emily, what do you say?'

'Thank you!' Emily said with delight, looking like she longed to pull down her neatly-arranged curls to prove the brush's efficacy at once.

Bridget sent her a suppressing glance and turned back to Lady Bewley. 'This is exceedingly generous of you, thank you very much.'

'Do not mention it. I gain the utmost content from witnessing a child's happy face. We were never fortunate enough to have children of our own. In all the years of our marriage, I believed only once that such joy might be within our grasp, but I was mistaken. However, I hope that one day Oliver will find a charming lady who will help him bring some little Davenports into the world. In the meantime, I have this enchanting vision to look upon. What wonderful hair and such blue eyes! She is a treasure to behold.'

Bridget expressed her gratitude again for the gift and for the lady's kind praise, privately wondering how Cormac felt about the lofty ambitions his 'aunt' held for him. Howsoever he had assumed the persona of Oliver Davenport, he had let himself in for an incalculable amount of strife in the process. The aristocracy retained high expectations of their class; was he going to be able to live up to them?

While they dined on a luncheon of dainty sandwiches, cakes and tea, Bridget and Lady Bewley talked about their involvement in charitable activities, particularly lamenting the egregious effects of the new Poor Law. Emily, having nibbled enough to satisfy her mother, grew bored of sitting still and hopped off her chair to wander around the drawing room. Lady Bewley made no objection when the little girl discovered the connecting door into the music room and encouraged her to thump away vigorously on the piano she found there, despite the fact that Emily knew nothing more of the instrument than where the high and low sounds were. Though the ladies winced at the discordant noises wafting in from the music room, it was better for Emily to be distracted for, in the course of their conversation, Bridget found herself revealing the details of her recent assault at St Swithun's. Lady Bewley sympathised most earnestly and then surprised her by confessing that she too had been a victim of such violence in the past.

'He was starving, the poor wretch,' she said. 'There were more holes than material in his clothing and his ribs protruded in the most appalling way. This was before the soup kitchens were shut down, but that winter was harsh and the demands of the needy outstripped our supplies. I was obliged to go outside and announce that there was no food left, which meant he must endeavour to last another day with an empty stomach. It was too much for him to endure. He became distraught and needed to release his anger, of which he deemed me to be the rightful recipient.'

'What did he do?' asked Bridget, horribly fascinated.

Lady Bewley's cheeks, red from eating and enthusiastic chatter, turned pale. 'He slapped me across the face so hard that I fell to the ground. I tried to crawl away but he grabbed me around the neck and started to strangle me.'

Bridget clasped her own throat in horror. Her twisted wrist now seemed utterly insignificant.

'Was there nobody to assist you?' she breathed.

'My fellow volunteers were inside the kitchen attempting to keep control over the desperate creatures who had already managed to gain entry. Those left outside were others who had also been turned away and, in their despair, they simply jeered and made no move to save me. I believe I would have died had Oliver not come to my rescue.'

'Cor—' Bridget began but caught herself. 'Mr Davenport was there?' she said quickly.

Lady Bewley's expression lifted with pride. 'After our nephew came to live with us, he always insisted on escorting me to and from the soup kitchen. I think he would have preferred for my own sake that I had no involvement at all but, as I remained adamant in that regard, he made every effort to ensure my safety. He was standing at a distance with our horses, waiting for me to finish my work, but he saw what was happening, thank the Lord, and dashed to my aid. He hauled the man off me just in time, for a moment later I would have been wholly out of breath. As it was, I suffered severe bruising around my face and neck, leaving me in acute pain for many days. Oliver tended me throughout my recovery.'

Bridget's eyes widened. 'It sounds like your nephew is a very caring person.'

'Oh, he is. He treats me with such devotion that anyone would think he was my own son. I do believe he misses his own mother dreadfully. But I am glad that I have been able to stand in as a sufficient substitute.'

Bridget felt compassion rise within her. Cormac had been very close to Maggie; it must have been unbearable for him when they had been torn asunder. Perhaps the severance of that maternal bond had driven him to fill the gaping hole left behind. It seemed he harboured a genuine fondness for Lady Bewley; was it possible that not everything about his new life was an act of falsehood?

Lady Bewley carried on, 'After that incident, he tried to convince me to cease all association with the soup kitchen. I comprehended that he pleaded only out of concern for my welfare but I refused. The benefits of this kind of work far outweigh the evils. Perhaps you will view your own regrettable episode in the same light? Even with the restrictions imposed by the new Poor Law, we do more good helping those unfortunate people as much as we can than sitting in our drawing rooms drinking tea.'

Bridget looked down guiltily at her cup.

'Everything in moderation, however,' Lady Bewley said with an understanding smile. 'It is important that we always return to our proper stations. We are gentlewomen, after all, and must adhere to the duties of our class.'

After a maid came to remove the luncheon plates, Bridget rose to take her leave; there was no polite way to wait any longer for Cormac to make an appearance and the cacophony from the music room had increased to a level beyond fortitude. Lady Bewley instructed for the Wyndhams' carriage to be brought around from the mews behind the house, where it had retreated upon arrival, while Emily obeyed her mother's call and skipped back to the table to seize her new hairbrush.

'Would you like to come meet our footman?' she asked Lady Bewley, as though she were offering a gift equal to the one she had received. 'His name is Peter and he sometimes slips me biscuits from the kitchens.'

She sent an alarmed glance in Bridget's direction, plainly suspecting that she had revealed too much, and Lady Bewley hastened to intervene.

'What a lovely suggestion, my pet. It would be a privilege to make his acquaintance.'

Once they were all clad in cloaks, she accompanied them to the door and down the front steps to the street. Peter was flummoxed to be gravely introduced to the countess by the little girl but regained his equanimity, bowing and apologising that he had not thought to bring any biscuits today.

'Perhaps next time,' Lady Bewley said, twinkling down at Emily. Turning to Bridget, she added, 'And I do hope there will be a next time. I would be very interested in making a visit to St Swithun's, if you were amenable to the idea?'

Bridget was just expressing her agreement to that venture when two figures came walking up the street towards them, their breath puffing out in the cold air: Cormac and a white-haired, older gentleman. She hiccupped and stumbled over her last few words to Lady Bewley.

'—shall write to y-you to arrange a d-date.'

'Thank you, my dear. And here are the men now! How fortunate. I know my husband will be charmed to meet Miss Lambourne.'

With a beaming salutation, Lord Bewley proved to be as jovial as his wife and, after Bridget and Emily had been presented to him, he said with frank disappointment, 'Are you leaving already?'

'Yes, they must return home before it gets dark.' Lady Bewley laid an affectionate hand on Emily's head. 'The night comes so early at this time of year.'

'Well, it was an honour to make your brief acquaintance,' he said, lifting his hat to Bridget and winking at Emily.

Cormac concurred with a similarly civil remark, though he did not spare a glance for Emily. Bridget examined him surreptitiously to see if he regretted having missed this opportunity to speak with her but his face was unreadable. She curtseyed to them all and stepped up to the carriage door, her heart heavy.

After she and Emily had settled themselves, Peter hopped onto the footboard at the back of the carriage and, up front, Sawyer clicked his tongue at the horses. As they jolted into movement, Lord and Lady Bewley ascended the steps with Cormac to their front door, Lady Bewley's voice carrying back faintly to Bridget.

'—delightful young lady. And her daughter, what an angel. Those eyes! The only other person I have seen with eyes as blue as hers is you, Oliver.'

She saw Cormac's head whip around after the carriage and then her view was obscured as they continued down the street. She sank back in her seat and let out a shaky breath. He knew. Or, at least, the idea had been put into his head. She put her arm around Emily who was twirling the silver hairbrush around and around.

What was he going to do next?

She did not have to wait long to find out. The evening sky was darkening to a deep navy and the lamps had been lit in Wyndham House when Thrussell entered the drawing room and informed Bridget that a gentleman had left his card.

She had been warming herself in front of the fireplace. With a tremulous hand, she took the card from the butler's silver tray and read the name.

'Shall I tell him you are not at home, my lady?'

She reached out to the mantelpiece to steady herself before replying, 'No, you may send him up.'

Once alone, she pressed her fingers to her lips in distress. What could have possessed Cormac to show up unannounced like this? It was improper on a number of levels. He should have been able to restrain himself until he could speak to her at a more appropriate time and venue.

One look at his face when he entered the room told her he was beyond that kind of self-control. His eyes were wide and frantic and his hair was untidy as though he had run his fingers through it many times. He wore no gloves or hat and he forgot to acknowledge Thrussell for showing him in or bow in greeting to Bridget. He stood rooted to the spot until Thrussell had departed, leaving the door ajar, and then he burst out, 'I'm sorry, I had to come!'

Her pulse thrummed in her ears. 'Why?'

'Why!' he said helplessly. 'I had to—find out...' He trailed off, unable to articulate anything further.

'You need to leave,' she said, her voice low and full of urgency. 'Garrett could arrive home at any time. Did you even consider the possibility that you might have come face to face with him just now?'

Finding his tongue again, he said, 'I asked the butler if his master was here. If he had answered in the affirmative, I would have handed in my card and left.'

'And what do you think Garrett will do if he returns in the meantime and discovers Cormac McGovern in his drawing room? He will be enraged and we shall all pay the price for your rashness.'

She had not meant to place emphasis on 'all' but it came out that way anyway and he picked up on it. They were not the only ones who would suffer the repercussions.

His eyes fixed upon hers. 'I am not going anywhere until you tell me the truth.'

She sagged. He was not going to be dissuaded and, in all honesty, she could not blame him. The truth he was searching for, the truth he suspected, was well-deserving of this kind of reaction.

Conscious of the open door, she sat down on the sofa nonetheless, her heart beating like mad. 'What do you wish to know?'

He crossed the room swiftly and knelt in front of her, clutching her hands with both of his own. His skin was soft and smooth to the touch, nothing like the roughened surface it used to have.

'Tell me,' he entreated, staring at her with such intensity that she found it difficult to hold his gaze. 'Please. Your Emily. Is she' – he swallowed – 'mine?'

'Yes,' she said and squeezed his hands.

He rocked back on his heels, total shock written across his face. It was several moments before he was able to speak again. 'How can you be so sure?'

'She was born just less than eight months after Garrett and I married. If she had been his, she would have been frail and underdeveloped. But she was a fine, healthy baby come to full term. Her birth took place almost exactly nine months after you and I...' She blushed at the memory, recalling the event in vivid detail with his fingers so tightly entwined in hers.

Understanding flickered in the blue irises. 'Does Garrett know?'

She nodded. 'It is obvious that she does not resemble him in her looks. There is some of me in her. And a lot of you.'

He let go of her and stood to pace back and forth. 'This is too much to take in,' he muttered. 'I have a child. A daughter. How does one process this kind of information?' He stopped abruptly. 'Can I meet her?'

Her teeth fastened on the tip of her tongue. 'I do not believe that would be a very good idea.'

'Why not? Why shouldn't a father see his own daughter?' he said, his voice rising.

'Shush, or you will alert the servants! As far as Emily is concerned, she sees her father every day. It would not be prudent to introduce you to her right now, as Mr Davenport or anyone else. She is not familiar with any of my other male acquaintances. It would arouse suspicion.'

'I beg you,' he said and knelt before her again. 'I just want to look at her. She does not have to know I am there.'

She considered his eager, desperate countenance. This revelation had wiped all the aloofness from him; the refined gentleman had vanished and been replaced by a young man ruled once again by his emotions. He was almost the Cormac she remembered from Oakleigh.

'Very well,' she said and his face lit up. 'But you must not let yourself be seen.'

They rose and she led him from the drawing room, up the stairs to the third floor, and along the landing to the nursery. Despite her warning, it was likely that Garrett would remain at his club for several more hours, therefore this action, while ill-advised, did not place them within too great a risk of discovery, so long as they were discreet.

The door to the nursery was open a few inches. Emily was visible painting at a small table and Miss Davison sat nearby reading a book. Both were absorbed in their occupations and did not notice that they were being quietly observed from the doorway. Bridget watched Cormac looking at Emily. He appeared to be drinking in every aspect of her: her hair, the exact same shade as his own; her eyes, as blue as Lady Bewley had described; her mouth, screwed up in concentration; her small hand, directing her paintbrush with precision across the page in front of her. Bridget knew she was biased but she could not imagine that there was a more beautiful child anywhere else in the world.

At length, she tugged on his arm and he reluctantly dragged himself away from his first proper look at his daughter. Neither of them spoke until they were alone in the drawing room once more, having avoided any servants on their way back down through the house.

'How do you feel?' she asked.

Breathless, he said, 'I just cannot fathom how perfect she is. Lady Bewley was right, she is a little angel. Everything about her seems so pure and sweet. And,' he went on, full of wonderment, 'we made her. Can you believe that? Out of all the tragedy of that summer, it amazes me that something so exquisite emerged.

She is the one good thing we ever accomplished together, Bridget.'

It was the first time he had spoken her name since he had shown up out of the blue; it sounded so familiar, so right to be coming from his mouth. He smiled at her and she felt her eyes brimming with emotion. Overwhelmed, she had to look away. In the next moment, his arms were around her, enfolding her in a tight embrace, and she sensed a pressure deep inside her ebbing away. She was relieved that he finally knew.

When at last they pulled apart, his expression had become serious. 'We have many things to talk about. Will you meet me tomorrow?'

'Yes,' she said without hesitation.

'The gardens across the street? At noon?'

'I shall be there,' she promised.

# CHAPTER 23

Cormac did not sleep that night. His mind was racing too fast to even contemplate rest. He sat before the fire in his bedchamber until the embers went dark and then he lay down on his bed, fully clothed and eyes wide open. He felt as though the world had upended itself, or else that the world was the same and he was upside down within it. It was impossible to adjust to the idea that he was a father, that he had been a father for more than six and a half years and had not known it.

Emily. His thoughts fluttered about like fallen leaves in the wind but they kept returning to her. His heart broke with the knowledge that he had missed so much of her childhood. He had not heard her say her first word or seen her take her first step. He had never had the opportunity to take a curl from her golden head in order to always keep her in his pocket with him. And she did not know that he even existed. She believed that smooth, selfish, manipulative Garrett was her true father. It was cruel and unfair.

Then there was the notion of fatherhood. Had he ever contemplated it before? Of course he had; every man desired progeny to strengthen his family tree. But that was a viewpoint he had taken when the prospective children were mere specks in the future, not yet conceived. Emily was real and living in the present and that made an enormous difference. He no longer possessed a vague urge to produce offspring; his awareness of Emily's existence had reduced that indistinct compulsion to a tangible purpose – to protect and cherish his daughter with every fibre of his being.

The most crucial thing now was to communicate this to Bridget.

The next morning dawned foggy and very cold. He suffered the slow passing of the hours in agitation until noon approached and he could head for Berkeley Square. He could not enter the private gardens without a resident to unlock the gate, so he lingered by the entrance, the tension of waiting burning deep into his bones. Barely three or four minutes had passed – though it felt like an hour – before Bridget emerged from Wyndham House and crossed the road towards him. His insides writhed with nerves.

When she reached him, he said, 'Does the weather bother you? If you feel too chilled...'

'No, this is fine,' she said. 'It is easier to breathe out of doors.'

He understood exactly what she meant.

They entered the gardens, which were deserted due to the freezing conditions. They began walking along the path beneath the plane trees but, now that she was beside him, he found himself tongue-tied.

After the silence stretched between them, she prompted, 'You said we had many things to talk about?'

'I did.' Which eloquent words would best convey what he was feeling? When he opened his mouth, the sentence came out in a clumsy rush. 'I want to be a part of her life.'

Her expression was tender. 'Of course you do, and I would not wish to prevent you from seeing your daughter.' He experienced a burst of optimism until she continued, looking torn, 'But at least one of us must think in realistic terms here.

212

There are so many impediments to such a venture. What would happen if Garrett saw you?'

'We could arrange to meet far from wherever he was likely to be,' he said, quick to quash her doubts. 'That could be managed without trouble.'

'What about Emily? Who would you be to her? How would we come up with a plausible explanation for your meetings?'

'I could simply be an acquaintance of her mother's whom she encounters every now and then. Perhaps you could say that I am a benefactor of the workhouse. If she let that slip, Garrett would not get suspicious and would have no reason to wonder why he has never met me.'

'And what if she did not want to see you?'

His chest tightened. 'Then I would leave her be. But I hope it will not come to that.' He shot her a hopeful look. 'Are those all the obstacles you can think of?'

'Not all,' she said cautiously. 'Will you not be returning to Bedfordshire after the season is over?'

He baulked. 'I refuse to consider the future responsibilities entailed to the persona of Oliver Davenport when the consequences of my true self are right before me.'

'That is all very well to say but you *are* Oliver Davenport now. I have conversed with Lady Bewley and know her expectations of you. You do not have the freedom to remain in London, where Emily is. You have promised to marry, to produce children, to inherit Lord Bewley's estate. Who will do that if not you?' She hesitated. 'Where is the real Oliver? Could he be prevailed upon to return to his own life, liberating you from it?'

'No,' Cormac answered. 'He could not.'

Accepting this, she did not press him for further details. He let her step ahead of him along the path and, staring after her, was struck by how affecting it was to be in her presence again. He had never been closer to anyone than this woman;

they had shared the innocence of childhood, they had shared the intimacy of a sexual embrace, and now they shared a child. That relationship required absolute trust. He took several quick strides to catch up to her.

'I will tell you everything,' he said, seizing her gloved hand and forcing her to stop and look into his eyes. Her dark brown ones stared back in surprise. 'I have concealed my past but I open it up to you now.'

She lowered her gaze and then looked up at him again. 'I confess that, when we were young, I prided myself on thinking I knew you better than anybody else. But now you are a mystery to me, a locked door.'

During the silence that followed this statement, Cormac was sure he could hear both of their hearts beating very fast.

'So unlock me,' he said.

He disengaged her hand and they started walking again. Neither of them made any acknowledgement of the sudden heat that had just risen between them despite the coldness of the day.

She was patient and did not push him; she seemed to recognise that this would be a difficult tale to tell, and indeed it was for it meant that she would learn the very worst parts of him. He gazed across the gardens, his view hampered by the encroaching fog, and gathered his memories from the past seven and a half years. When he spoke, his voice was low. He tried not to let the story of his poverty in Dublin become too grim but it was impossible to relate it without making some reference to the hardships he had endured. He chose not to mention his encounter with Thomasina, resolving that such a disclosure was irrelevant to the case. However, he did not hold anything back when he related his dealings with Cunningham and, later, Oliver Davenport – she had the right to know just what kind of man he had allowed himself to become. His recollection of the appalling incident with Oliver on that night-time sea crossing weighed heavily upon him; his voice became even fainter until he stopped speaking altogether.

He was shaken out of his despondency by the sensation of her arm slipping through his own.

'I am so sorry,' she whispered. 'Can you ever forgive me for the horrors I have caused you?'

'You played no part in my decision to work for a dirty money lender.'

'If I had not sent you away, you would never have had to make that decision.' Her eyes were full of tears.

'Please do not cry. We cannot change what happened and we gain nothing by holding on to remorse.' He realised that he meant what he was saying. He did not want to see her suffer, in spite of the fact that at least part of the guilt should rightfully be laid at her feet.

Her tears fell nonetheless. 'The things you have been through.' She gulped. 'The things you have been compelled to do.'

She was horrified, he could tell. He could not make her come to terms with it but he could at least offer some alleviation to her dismay.

'Some things in life are so complicated and have so many varied consequences that we cannot merely label them honourable or wicked deeds. I disposed of Oliver's body in a vile fashion. I took his identity and deceived everyone I became acquainted with over the past four and a half years. But I did it with his permission. And I am alive today because of it, as opposed to the very conceivable alternative. Not to mention the fact that it has also led me back to you. When I left Oakleigh I never dreamed it possible that we would meet again, but the ragged course of my life has served up this opportunity to see you once more and to learn of the existence of our daughter. I am very glad that we have been able to reunite in this way.'

Her cheeks flushed as she said, 'I am glad too.'

They followed the path's wide arc around the edge of the gardens yet another time.

'How did you adapt when you became Oliver?' she said after a while. 'I cannot imagine you slipped into the life of the upper classes entirely without mishap, did you?'

'No,' he confessed. 'It was challenging at first. I thought I had an adequate understanding of a gentleman's proper conduct but I did not know enough. When Lord and Lady Bewley took me into their home, I learned the graces and manners of the aristocracy and studied everything from philosophy to politics. I have quite the educated mind now,' he said with a hint of pride. To him it was one of the most valuable things he had gained from his new life.

'So they did not suspect anything? You were never in danger of exposure?'

'The closest I came to it was when an impoverished aunt of Oliver's expressed a worrying interest in visiting Bewley Hall. I sent money on several occasions to deter her and thankfully she never followed through on her scheme. As for Lord and Lady Bewley, I am certain they believe I am their nephew but I think they sensed there was something unusual about me when I came to them. Apart from my "coarse upbringing" as they called it, I used to get terrible nightmares about Oliver and I often woke them up as a result of shouting in my sleep.'

'Nightmares?' she repeated, her tone sympathetic.

He dipped his head. 'I still get them but not so often now.'

An elderly man emerged from the fog ahead of them, accompanied by an equally ancient dog. Bridget's arm was still linked through Cormac's; they detached inconspicuously and strolled forwards. Cormac nodded to the man and bent to pat the dog, and the old fellow ambled on without a single suspicious glance.

Even so, after he had disappeared behind them, they made their way without comment to the entrance of the gardens.

'We should part here,' she said, stopping outside the gate. 'Thank you for your confidence. I comprehend how hard it must have been for you to tell me all of this.'

'The burden is not so heavy now that someone else knows,' he said, feeling the truth of his words in the way he was able to hold his shoulders a little straighter. 'Can I hope to hear from you regarding Emily?'

'I promise to write to you.'

She locked the gate. Then she curtseyed and walked away from him.

***

Bridget maintained her composure while she crossed the street, entered Wyndham House, and climbed the stairs to her bedchamber. However, once she was behind the door and leaning up against it, she let out a shuddering breath that shook her from head to toe. Her hands trembled and not from the cold. Poor, dear, unfortunate Cormac, the awful existence he had been driven to lead.

His confession in the gardens had been outright shocking. He had carried out monstrous deeds which no principled human being could ever have the capacity to commit. He had threatened harm to deprived and desperate men, women and – her heart constricted in abhorrence – children. He had thrown another man's body into the sea like a common criminal. He was no longer the person he had been in his youth; those unspeakable acts did not belong to that honest, honourable boy.

And yet, look at what life had thrown at him. Starvation and loneliness and misery. Who would not have buckled under the hopelessness of it all? Who in the world would have had the strength to resist the opportunity that had presented itself in the form of Oliver's demise? A chance to live well and be valued by others once more. In many ways, he would have been a fool not to seize it.

There was also the undeniable fact that he would never have ended up in that dreadful position at all had she only stood up to her mother all those years ago and not let him be sent away. Her weakness was very much to blame for the path he had been forced to take following the events of that summer. So how could she censure him when it was by her actions that he had fallen into disgrace? Ought he to be held accountable for her mistakes?

Furthermore, since those murky times he had become a decent man again. She could tell by the way Lady Bewley spoke so fondly of him. Perhaps there was still a salvageable soul inside him, craving forgiveness and trying to make amends through kindness towards others.

And now he knew that he was Emily's true father. His reasonable request was that he be permitted to see his child, his own flesh and blood. It was within Bridget's power to prevent it, but was it her right or her will? Emily deserved the warmth of a father's love and, needless to say, Garrett was not forthcoming in that area. Allowing Cormac and Emily to spend time together would be a positive experience for them both.

But there were dangerous complications. Bridget and Emily were irrevocably tied to Garrett; there was no scenario in their future which did not include him. Where, then, could Cormac fit in?

She was startled by a smart rap on the door. She turned and pulled it open to find Garrett standing beyond the threshold.

Her first instinct was to pray that Cormac had departed Berkeley Square at once so that he would not be visible from the windows of the house. Her second was to wonder what Garrett was doing home at this time of the day.

'I came to collect a few personal items,' he said in response to her unspoken question. 'Brewer is packing them now. I intend to stay at the club tonight.'

She raised her eyes to his but he would not meet them, focusing instead on adjusting his cuffs.

'The other fellows and I have planned a lengthy card game, and it will be too late for me to return home afterwards.'

She felt a wry twist of black humour at the blatant lie. What pretty young thing had caught his eye this time? And how long would it last before the poor girl was put aside, her reputation ruined? Bridget did not know which was worse, to be the mistress who pleasured him for a time or the wife who could say not a word against it.

Did he feel any regard at all for the women he bedded, or was it nothing more than satisfaction of the flesh? He may have harboured some superficial attachment towards herself in the past, but she suspected that the only woman he had truly loved was the one to whom he had referred when he had tried to apologise to her by James's cradle. What had happened to that lady? Did he ever yearn for her the way she had yearned so long for Cormac?

As she recalled the heat of clasped hands and fast-beating hearts in the fog-enshrouded gardens, light footsteps came skipping down the stairs and Emily appeared on the landing. She faltered at the sight of Garrett and then stepped forwards shyly, holding out a sheet of paper.

'I brought this down to show Mama but I painted it for you, Papa.'

It was the shape of their house with a yellow circle above it.

Garrett looked impatient. 'Not now, Emily.'

He gave Bridget a curt nod and headed for the staircase.

She was reaching for her pen and notepaper before the front door had snapped shut.

# CHAPTER 24

'I wish the snow would come back,' said Emily, hopping along on one foot beside her mother.

They were in Berkeley Square's gardens, passing by sodden plane trees which dripped with rain that had fallen the night before. It was not raining at present but grey clouds loomed above and Bridget had an umbrella tucked under her arm.

Emily wobbled and flung out her arms to keep her balance. 'Snow is so much more fun than rain.'

'Indeed? Why do you think so?'

'You can't throw rain,' said the little girl emphatically, as though that ended the argument right there.

'But you can slip in the snow.'

'You can't build snowmen out of rain.'

Bridget chuckled. 'You win. Is your leg getting tired?'

Emily switched feet and continued to hop her way along the path. 'I'm exercising my ankles.'

Bridget smiled and cast a furtive glance towards the entrance of the gardens, where she had left the gate unlocked. She and Cormac had arranged by letter that his first meeting with Emily should take place here, because they could pass it off as a chance encounter. She expected him to appear at any moment.

As if he had read her mind, the gate opened and he came striding into view. At the sight of him, she felt an unusual sensation somewhere in the region of her stomach.

Trying to keep her voice steady, she said, 'That gentleman is a friend of mine. We met him outside Lady Bewley's house, do you remember? Shall we stop to speak to him?'

Emily nodded and placed both feet on the ground just as Cormac reached them, lifting his hat in greeting. He too carried an umbrella.

'Lady Wyndham, it is a pleasure to see you again,' he said, bowing.

'How do you do, Mr Davenport?' In her letter she had urged that they use his false identity, lest the name slip from Emily's mouth afterwards in Garrett's presence. 'Emily, what do you say?'

Emily dropped into a sweet curtsey. 'It is a pleasure to see you again, Mr Davenport.'

He grinned at her endearing manners. 'The pleasure is all mine.'

Emily frowned. 'No, some of it's mine too,' she insisted.

He laughed. 'Agreed,' he said, bowing to her as well. 'And what brings you to the gardens today?'

'I'm exercising my ankles. Mama is just walking the normal way.'

'And how does one exercise one's ankles?'

'Like this,' she answered and started hopping on one foot again. 'Miss Davison says jumping is good for making my bones and muscles strong.'

'Hmm,' he said, surveying her with barely-concealed delight. 'Do you think it would work for my bones or am I too old?'

She considered his question as she danced on the spot. 'I suppose it is never too late to start.'

He began hopping from one foot to the other, his arms waving like the vanes of a windmill. 'Am I doing it right?'

She erupted into peals of laughter. 'You look silly!'

He ceased his madcap antics. 'Perhaps it is not for me then,' he conceded and straightened his coat.

'Perhaps not,' Bridget said, endeavouring to keep a straight face. 'Would you care to walk with us, Mr Davenport?'

'I would be honoured. That is, if Miss Emily is happy to consent to that arrangement?'

'I am,' she said regally.

The three of them set off along the path. Emily chattered away about everything that came into her head, from painting pictures to the shapes of puddles on the ground, and did not seem to find it at all extraordinary that her mother's friend was so engrossed in what she was saying. After all, who wouldn't find it interesting to know what colour was made when blue and yellow were mixed together?

As it had threatened, the moisture-laden clouds opened above and poured down on them for ten minutes straight. They huddled under a plane tree, listening to the heavy drops fall onto their umbrellas. At first, Emily stood with Bridget, holding her hand, but after a minute or two she sidled under Cormac's umbrella, claiming that the drops did not sound so loud there. He glanced over her head at Bridget; his face was full of elation. She wondered if he had been worried that Emily might not warm to him. The small girl's guileless, engaging nature had eradicated the notion.

It was with a great deal of reluctance that he parted from them at the end of their walk. Bridget sensed that he wanted to say something to her in private so she suggested to Emily that she do one last ankle exercise before they left the gardens. The girl hopped off with her arms outstretched.

When Bridget looked back at Cormac, she found him staring at her with such a fervent expression that she felt breathless.

'Thank you,' he said, 'for raising this wonderful child and for allowing me the privilege of knowing her.'

'Oh, I—you're welcome. She seems to like you.'

'I am awestruck by her,' he murmured, his gaze now following Emily as she leapt one-footed over puddles.

Instead of turning to watch her too, Bridget continued to observe him. His blue eyes were bright and his cheeks glowed with exhilaration. There was no mistaking that his first proper contact with Emily had meant very much to him.

He dragged his gaze back to Bridget. 'Can I see her again tomorrow?'

She hesitated. 'It might seem unusual to meet two days in a row,' she said, but her objection was half-hearted. Though she wanted to exercise caution, she too was keen for another meeting.

'The day after tomorrow?' he pressed.

'Very well then,' she said, knowing she was giving in far too easily.

His smile was so brilliant that she found herself matching it with her own.

# CHAPTER 25

Bridget noted the blood on her undergarments with dispassion. Garrett's latest attempt to produce an heir had failed. Usually, she felt a small stab of regret at the sight of the red smear, for it reminded her that the possibility of having another baby had escaped her yet again, but today she had no room for sorrow. Today, her mind was occupied with only one prospect: she and Emily would be seeing Cormac.

They were to pay another visit to Raynesworth House. She had initially questioned the wisdom of such a visible encounter, but he had rationalised that meeting under circumstances so legitimate would raise no suspicion. She would call upon Lady Bewley to ostensibly continue their discourse on London's workhouses, bringing Emily again for the lady's doting pleasure, and he would just happen to be present this time.

Bridget's insides quavered as the carriage drew to a stop on Park Lane. She realised that she wanted very much to see him again, not just for Emily's sake, but for her own.

He delayed a while before making his appearance to further the impression of accidental meeting. She and Lady Bewley were deep in discussion at the luncheon table and Emily, having received the instruction to be seated and give the suffering piano a rest, was swinging her legs listlessly back and forth when he

225

entered the drawing room and gave a courteous bow. The little girl brightened at once.

After exchanging the necessary pleasantries with the ladies, he shot her a wink and said, 'And how are you today, Miss Emily?'

She glanced towards Bridget and Lady Bewley and then imparted in a carrying whisper, 'I'm a bit bored.'

He looked dismayed. 'Bored? We cannot allow such a lamentable state of affairs to persist. Lady Wyndham, would you permit me to steal your daughter for a time, to remedy this tragic situation?'

'That would be most kind of you, Mr Davenport. But only if she will not be a nuisance to you.'

'I am certain she will not. Miss Emily, are you fond of a game called hide-and-seek?'

She straightened her shoulders with glee. 'Yes! And I am very good at it.'

'I warn you, so am I. Who will be victorious?'

He darted out the drawing room door and she raced after him, her gaze fierce with determination.

Lady Bewley's face glowed. 'How natural he is with her. It is a joy to see him with children. How I do hope he will find a wife soon.'

Bridget's own pleasure at the image of father and daughter together diminished as Lady Bewley's innocent wish brutally reminded her of the transitory nature of the situation. What on earth were they doing? How could they sustain this, for where would it all end but with separation? Cormac had mired himself in obligations which he could not shun and, if Emily became too attached, his return to Bedfordshire would be a distressing blow to her.

And yet, Bridget could not resist granting her daughter this experience of fatherly love. The child deserved to know what it felt like to be cherished in such a way.

Knowing she was being cowardly, she shied away from any further contemplation of the dangerous consequences of their actions, and returned to her conversation with Lady Bewley. They spoke at length about measures they could take regarding the workhouse crisis – a renewed appeal to the Ladies of Compassion Association, a petition to Parliament, the recruitment of more volunteers – and, at the conclusion, established a date for Lady Bewley to visit St Swithun's.

'You do not think Miss Blythe will deem me an interference?'

'Not for one instant. Frances welcomes help from any quarter and is always grateful for it.'

They heard a few thumps and laughter from the floor above, which sounded as though the most recent hider had been found.

'I ought to release your nephew from my daughter's clutches,' Bridget said, eager to witness the merriment. 'I do believe he has been obliged to entertain her for long enough.'

'I doubt he minds but off you go. I shall remain here, if it please you. I try to avoid climbing stairs as much as possible.'

With a reassurance that Lady Bewley should stay behind for her own comfort, Bridget departed the room in search of the playmates. All had become quiet upstairs again. Ascending the staircase, she came upon Cormac at the top, eyes closed as he mouthed a silent countdown.

'Three, two, one,' he said aloud. 'Ready or not, here I come!'

He opened his eyes and grinned when he saw Bridget.

'She's winning,' he said.

'I'm confident that you are both savouring the triumph of the occasion,' she replied.

'Truer words were never spoken.' He marched along the corridor, making no attempt to subdue the noise of his footsteps. 'I will find you,' he called. 'You shall not elude me this time!'

He sidled through a door and she followed him. Aghast, she realised they were in a bedchamber. Her consternation was two-fold: she could not countenance the idea that Emily might be concealing herself in what must be Cormac's own bedchamber – judging by the shaving apparatus on the washstand and the stylish clothing his valet had already laid out for dinner – but she was also astounded by the wave of heat that swept through her body at the spectacle of the neatly-made bed and the sudden, unbidden vision of its covers in disarray.

'Please tell me she is not hiding in here,' she said faintly, thankful that his back was to her, for she didn't think she could control her flushed features in that moment.

'There is only one way to find out,' he said. 'I'll wager she has taken refuge in the wardrobe.'

He flung open the wardrobe door but only a tidy display of shirts and waistcoats greeted him.

'Perhaps she has hidden behind the curtain? Is that a toe I see peeping out?'

He swept back the material but all was empty behind it.

'She cannot be small enough to fit into the pitcher, can she? If I turn it upside down, shall I expose her or shall I just get very wet?'

A muffled giggle, swiftly stifled, came from beneath the bed.

'Ah, Miss Emily,' he said, sounding disappointed. 'How clumsy of you.'

He dropped to the floor and peered under the bed. A burst of hilarity bubbled out.

'I've found you!' he announced.

Emily wriggled into view, her dress and shoes dusty and her hair falling down in bedraggled coils. Bridget thought to berate her but stopped before the reprimand left her lips. She remembered when a young boy had taught her to climb a tree and she had descended from it in a similarly dishevelled shape. She would not detract from Emily's enjoyment now.

'I believe you have lost, *a stór*,' Cormac informed his daughter.

'Only because I laughed,' she said. 'Next time I will be so quiet you will never find me.'

'I accept your challenge,' he said gravely. 'Do your best.'

She ran for the door.

'Downstairs!' Bridget called after her. 'No more hiding in bedchambers!'

When she looked back at Cormac, he was leaning against the bed post, his face alight with jubilance.

'What was that you called her?' she asked.

His expression softened. '*A stór*. It means "my treasure".'

'Did she not wonder what you were saying?'

'When we went upstairs, I suggested that it could be a secret code of friendship between us. She doesn't know its translation.'

She bit her tongue. 'Don't you think it was risky to do such a thing?'

'It's too late to take it back now,' he said without repentance.

She understood his impulse; he desired a special connection with Emily, something that no one else – especially not Garrett – could have with her.

Moved, she said, 'I did speak Irish to her when she was very young. I wanted her to have some awareness of that part of her parentage, if obliquely. But Garrett put a stop to it.' Her heart squeezed at the memory of the burned wooden bird and how great that loss had been, and she marvelled yet again that its maker now stood before her. 'I whispered the prayers to her, over and over and over. Except I could not remember a section of the Hail Mary. What comes after *Sé do bheatha, a Mhuire, atá lán de ghrásta, tá an Tiarna leat*?'

He picked up the next line. '*Is beannaithe thú idir mná, agus is beannaithe toradh do bhroinne, Íosa.*'

As he carried on with the rest of the prayer, she let the lyrical words wash over her. They almost sounded like romantic verse the way he murmured them, with an intensity in his eyes that seemed to have nothing to do with devotion to the Blessed Virgin. She became conscious once more of the bed behind him and it occurred to her that it was quite wicked to have such thoughts with the Hail Mary echoing in her ears.

Silence bloomed between them after he finished the prayer.

Unwillingly, she said, 'Emily and I really ought to leave now.'

He pressed his lips together in resignation. 'Just one more game then.' He strode to the door and disappeared through it, calling, 'Ready or not, here I come!'

# CHAPTER 26

During the weeks that followed, Cormac continued to meet Emily in the guise of Oliver Davenport and the bond between them took root and strengthened as he gave her the attention and affection of a loving father which had been conspicuously absent in her life until now. With the arrival of February, the first traces of spring emerged and they went for more walks in the gardens, where he taught her the names of the birds starting to nest there and the flowers expected to blossom first. She introduced him to her favourite doll and presented him with countless painted pictures for his 'art collection' which he accepted with solemn gratitude. She and Bridget made several more visits to Raynesworth House, where the unsuspecting Lord and Lady Bewley were only too delighted to receive them, and all and sundry were pressed into playing games of hide-and-seek around the house and conducting tea parties with imaginary friends on the hearth rug. Once, Cormac took Emily into the library and had her read to him from her storybooks. Bridget's heart nearly overflowed with emotion as she observed their two fair heads bent together.

At home, it was impossible to prevent Emily from speaking about kind Mr Davenport in front of Garrett but the occasions were few; 'card games' had kept him away for many more nights.

It was these prolonged absences which gave Bridget the confidence to acquiesce when Cormac asked one day in late February if they could arrange a meeting at Wyndham House. He had something very special to give to Emily.

He arrived that afternoon with a mysterious package tucked under his arm. Emily jumped up and down when he told her it was for her but he said she could not have it until she sang a song for him. As musically deficient as she was artistically talented, she nevertheless sang an out-of-tune lullaby to which he applauded with enthusiasm. He then handed her the coveted package and she ripped off the paper to discover a gift like no other. It was a rectangular wooden box which, when she lifted its lid, revealed a sequence of compartments for storing watercolour cakes, two porcelain pans for mixing colours, and a drawer to hold brushes.

She let out a rapturous gasp. 'Oh, thank you, thank you, thank you! It's wonderful!'

'Let me see you paint something right away,' he urged, and she thrust the box into her mother's hands before running to fetch her paints and paper.

'Don't forget your smock,' Bridget called and heard Emily's groan of compliance. To Cormac she said, 'Let us go into the breakfast room. She can paint at the table there.'

In the breakfast room, she examined the interior of the box with admiration. The craftsmanship was immaculate. 'Did you make this?'

'Yes, apart from the porcelain pans. I am glad Emily likes it. I wanted her to have something from me.'

'She adores it,' she assured him. 'It is exquisite.'

'It might be somewhat sophisticated for her current abilities,' he said, taking it from her and touching one of the pans meditatively. 'But she will progress as she grows older.'

He closed the lid and her breath caught in her throat. She had not noticed when Emily had first unwrapped it, but now she could see an engraving on the top of the box. It was a stylised depiction of an oak tree. Her pulse quickened. There could be no mistaking its import; the oak tree in the centre of the orchard at Oakleigh had been a place of significance for her and Cormac throughout their relationship. It was where they had first met, where they had played as children, where they had kissed as lovers. What did he mean to imply by it?

She gathered the courage to look up at him, but his face was averted like he was listening for Emily's returning steps. Did she dare ask him about it? Before she could determine what to say, Emily dashed into the room, carrying her painting things and wearing a smock down to her knees.

'I've asked Lizzie to bring me a jar of water,' she announced, breathless. 'I'm going to paint a dog first.'

She spent a happy hour mixing colours from every watercolour cake she possessed and enjoying the praise from her admiring companions. After she completed a picture of a brown dog with a wagging tail, and another of two winged horses flying over rooftops, she painted a blurry woman in a blue dress holding an umbrella.

'This is Mama,' she said, lifting it up for Cormac to see. 'Isn't she pretty?'

He looked over her shoulder at Bridget. 'Beautiful,' he said before his gaze returned to the little girl.

Bridget's heart skipped at least two beats before resuming its normal tempo.

When Emily finished the next painting – one of two vague figures who were meant to be Lizzie and Peter – Bridget decided that the servants would get suspicious if Cormac was to stay any longer, and said, 'Gooseberry, I do believe Mr Davenport has to go now. What do you say to him before he leaves?'

Cormac's disappointment changed to astonishment and delight as Emily threw her arms around him. 'Thank you for my present. I love it!'

'Emily!' Bridget scolded when the girl drew back to reveal a blue smudge on his sleeve.

'It's no trouble,' he said, looking like he would gladly have had paint smeared on every item of clothing he owned in exchange for the hug he had just received from his daughter. 'You are very welcome, *a stór*. I hope you will get many years of enjoyment out of it.'

Bridget instructed Emily to pack up her paints into the watercolour box and bring her pictures to the nursery. Arms full, she bounced out of the room, exclaiming, 'I shall paint our birds from the gardens next time!'

Conscious that her next action ought to have been to ring the bell so that Cormac could be seen out of the house by a servant, Bridget said, 'I'll walk with you to the door.'

In the hall, he lifted his hat and coat from the stand, put them on, and grimaced theatrically.

'I must have paint on the inside of my coat now,' he said with a grin, but then his expression turned serious. 'Even though she does not know who I really am, that hug meant very much to me. *She* means very much to me.'

'I am in no doubt that the feeling is mutual,' said Bridget. 'She has become exceptionally fond of you.'

'Then I am the happiest man in the world today.'

With a smile, he turned to go.

'Wait,' she said, and put her hand over his to prevent him from pulling the door open.

He looked back at her. 'What is it?'

'I don't—' she began, and stopped. She had been about to say 'I don't know' but it wasn't true. She did know. Staring into his clear blue eyes, she recalled the taste of passion in a hay barn on a sweet September night. She remembered their declaration of love, and their physical need for each other. She could feel it bubbling inside her, heating her body to its core. She wanted him to kiss her.

She took a small step towards him so that their bodies were only inches apart. His fingers twitched beneath hers. She gazed up at him under her dark eyelashes and he inhaled sharply. Rising on her tiptoes, she tightened her grip on his hand. Their mouths were almost touching, her lips were parting...

Then they sprang apart as they heard the clatter of a door opening onto the hall, and Lizzie appeared clutching a bucket and a mop.

'Thank you very much for calling by, Mr Davenport,' Bridget said, dropping into a demure curtsey.

'Good day, Lady Wyndham,' he said with equal nonchalance. He bowed and exited through the front door.

She turned to Lizzie. How much could the maid guess from what she had just seen? Had she observed them standing as close as lovers? Furthermore, this was Mr Davenport's second visit without her master present in the house – would she find that suspect in itself?

But Lizzie betrayed no sign of what she might be privately speculating. She curtseyed and said, 'I was going to mop the hall, m'lady. If now ain't a good time, I can leave it until later?'

'Now is fine,' said Bridget. 'I shall step out of your way.'

She climbed the stairs to the nursery to check on Emily. That had been a most ill-timed end to Cormac's visit. Just one more second and her lips would have been pressed to his. With her own emotions in chaos, she wondered what he was thinking and feeling in the aftermath of their inappropriate intimacy.

# Chapter 27

Cormac prowled the streets. It was not long past daybreak; the only other people stirring at that hour were bakers and milkmen. A light mist hung above the houses and shops of London as he walked without noticing where he was going.

He had returned to Raynesworth House the previous evening but had shunned the company of Lord and Lady Bewley, retiring early to his bedchamber. Then he had been up at dawn with the servants and out of the house before the lord and lady had even woken. Unable to keep still, he had set off in no particular direction; his body just needed to be active while his brain worked so feverishly.

They had been about to kiss. If the maid had not interrupted, they would have kissed. Their lips had been so close that he had been able to feel Bridget's breath tickle his skin. Her fingers had been warm on his and her body had been very near; one more step and she would have been pushing up against him. It had been a dizzying moment, an intimate reminder of their passionate night in the hay barn so long ago.

He could not deny that he was aroused. The attraction he had felt towards her when they were younger had not diminished. Though time and heartache had taken their toll on her, he thought she was as beautiful now as she had been at nineteen, and her dark brown eyes drew him in with a magnetic force that made him yearn to lose himself in her.

So his body was being very persuasive. Still, he could not surrender to those impulses unthinkingly. Not when his brain shouted at him that it was too dangerous. The last time this had happened it had ended in disaster, and her betrayal had led him into the most dreadful period of his life.

This time it could be different, his heart whispered.

She had done a terrible thing to him but he believed she was truly remorseful about it. She could not change the past and he could not hold her tremendous error against her – it was not in his nature to keep a grudge like that. Besides, he was no saint himself; there were many people from whom he wished he could beg forgiveness, and he had no right to expect compassion if he was unwilling to bestow it.

And it was vital to remember that this was Bridget he was thinking of: his closest friend and deepest love of his youth. Could the heart ever forget an attachment as meaningful as that? Was their almost-kiss an inevitable consequence of their reunion, even though it seemed a lifetime had passed in between? In reality, could he ever be content with anyone other than her? She was also the mother of his cherished daughter; surely there could be no greater bond for two people than the creation of a child together.

In the depths of his soul, he knew what he wanted, but he was overcome with misgivings as he wondered where her own desires lay. How did she feel about the incident that had occurred in her hall yesterday afternoon? She was the one who had initiated it but perhaps she had begun to harbour doubts since it had happened. It was all too easy to get caught up in the excitement of a moment and then rethink one's actions in the sobriety of solitude and reflection.

He had to find out for certain. This was not something which he could let lie. He started to stride more purposefully as the weak springtime sun rose over the rooftops and burned off the lingering mist. The city was awake now and there were carriages rattling down the streets, men swamping the footpaths, and shops opening their front doors. He purchased a newspaper and made his way to Berkeley Square, where he lurked across the road a little way down from Wyndham House, ensuring that he had a view of its front door. He was willing to wait as long as it took.

Garrett was the first to leave the house. Cormac gave him a surreptitious glance over the top of his newspaper as he passed down the street on the opposite side. The last time he had seen this man was at Oakleigh Manor. He looked older – Cormac supposed he must be nearing his mid-thirties by now – but he had retained his good looks and he carried himself proudly as he disappeared around the corner.

Cormac resumed his waiting. His patience was rewarded when, after half an hour had passed, the front door opened again and Miss Davison emerged with Emily by her side; they made their way across the street and vanished into the gardens. This was what he had been hoping for. Now there was nobody left in the house but Bridget and her servants.

He tucked the newspaper inside his coat, crossed the street, and was approaching the building when the door opened once more and Bridget herself came out onto the top step. Anticipation mounted within him. Strangely, she was wearing a rather drab ensemble consisting of a plain bonnet, a weathered cloak and a dull-coloured dress. She pulled the door shut just as he reached the steps; looking around, she gasped to see him standing below her.

Glancing over his shoulder at a passerby, he said, 'May I come in?'

After the briefest of pauses, she nodded wordlessly.

He followed her into the hall, where he watched her remove her bonnet and cloak and drop them onto a dresser. Her back was to him but when she turned around he found it easy to read her expression. Though she was biting the end of her tongue in nervousness, her cheeks were pink with excitement.

That was all he needed to see. Perhaps he ought to have been tender but he was too exhilarated to think of such restraint. He strode across to her, pulled her to him roughly, and pressed his mouth upon hers. The kiss was fierce and almost painful with desire. She clutched at his neck, her grip ferocious, not allowing him to draw away for one second. They were starving for each other, craving the other's touch. Her back was only steps away from the dresser; he pushed her up against it, pressing the length of his body against her own. Something toppled off the dresser and made a tinkling noise as it shattered on the floor but neither of them paid any regard to it, even though they were in great danger of being discovered by one of the servants.

They remained locked in the embrace until they were forced to break apart for air. As he rubbed his face into her throat, inhaling her alluring lilac scent – how giddying it was to be able to breathe it in, breathe *her* in, at last – he heard her pant, 'Upstairs.'

They made it six steps up the staircase and then their passion overcame them again and they were kissing and clinging harder than ever, leaning against the banister for support. Compulsion made them grapple at their clothing, her fingers fumbling with the buttons on his coat, his hands groping at her skirts, but they could not carry on like this in the open spaces of the house. She grasped his wrist and tugged him up that flight of stairs and the next. They reached her bedchamber, where she ushered him in and locked the door behind them. The twist of the key and the snap of the lock into place seemed to herald their final commitment to this precarious course of action.

This time they came together more tenderly. The bruising force of their initial frenzy gentled into a slower, but no less thorough, exploration of each other's mouths. He savoured each sensation, the softness of her lips, the moist welcome of her tongue, and its insistent strokes that both gave and demanded pleasure.

She knocked off his hat to fondle his hair. They were both still wearing gloves – breaking the kiss, he loosened hers one finger at a time and plucked them off. Her hands, so often concealed, seemed almost like a private part of her body. He removed his own gloves and discarded them on the floor, then interlocked his fingers with hers in a gesture that felt as intimate as their caressing tongues. Raising their joined hands between them, he touched his lips to her knuckles. With a devilish ripple of need, he thought it might be his last gentlemanly act for quite some time.

He let go and hastened to undress her, to expose the feminine curves veiled by her plain dress. She too sought the buttons and knots of his clothing and the various layers, from his waistcoat to her petticoats, fell about their ankles. She jerked at his shirt, freeing it from the waist of his trousers, and thrust her hands up under the material, her fingertips running lightly over the planes of his back. It was a simple movement but it ignited the lower region of his body. She must have seen the fire in his eyes because she turned to lead him towards the bed, but he halted her at the bedside.

'Wait,' he said and, with a flick of his hand, indicated the fact that she still stood before him in shift and stays.

'These as well?' she said uncertainly.

'Yes,' he said firmly.

The stays would cause a delay but it had been over seven years since he had seen this woman naked and he had no intention of doing anything by halves. He turned her from him and began to unlace the back of the stays, each jerk of the cord through an eyelet like a whip against his groin. Her shoulders rose and fell as her breathing became more pronounced. He kissed her ear with the final tug and the stays dropped away from her. His anticipation climbing ever higher, he stripped off her ankle boots and the rest of her undergarments with swift movements.

He took a step back to admire the graceful line of her back and the round shape of her buttocks. He was in awe but she was self-conscious now; she crossed her arms and grasped her elbows, hunching slightly from his gaze. Alarmed at her insecurity, he moved closer again so that his shirt front pressed against her back, and enfolded his arms around hers. He clasped her wrists and coaxed her to let go of her elbows, guiding her hands to her sides. With her breasts now exposed, he could reach up and cup them both.

The air escaped her lungs in a breathy, 'Oh.'

While his previous acquaintance with them had been for just one brief night, he could tell that they had changed. Without the supportive boost of her stays, they sagged a little lower. But that by no means reduced their allure and she jumped as his body told her so.

With slow deliberation, he lowered one hand to the cluster of curls below. He stroked experimentally, shifting position and pressure until he located a spot that drew a patent physical reaction from her. She squirmed and moaned and he persevered, feeling her reserve dissolve within his embrace. Her limbs tautened as she emitted a high-pitched whimper and shuddered, then went limp. He held her, his face buried in her chestnut hair.

After a few moments, she turned and kissed him as though he were the air she needed to survive. He could feel her trembling from head to toe. She detached her lips from his to wrench off his shirt and, between them, they removed his boots and the remainder of his clothing and fell onto the bed at last. He lay over her and extended his own body along hers, their legs entwined, the hair on his chest grazing her breasts.

Her hand slipped down between them to guide him into place and he buried himself inside her as far as he could go. The idea of proceeding slowly, of any further delay, was impossible. He rushed to his release with her arms wrapped tight across his back.

Afterwards, they lay beside each other, panting with exertion. As his breathing slowed, he turned his head and found her staring at the underside of the bed's canopy, her face full of apprehension.

'What is the matter?' he asked. Considering the act they had just engaged in, there were several valid responses to his question.

'It's just—' she said, not looking at him, 'when Garrett and I...he does not...we never fully...he just pushes up my nightdress and I pull it down when he is done.'

Anger surged in him that Garrett could treat this heavenly woman so cheaply but he phrased his response with delicacy.

'I could not imagine being clothed during an experience such as this,' he said, his voice tender. 'When I was holding you, I wanted every part of my skin to touch every part of your skin. We just shared the deepest kind of intimacy there is and we had to share it completely.'

Her body was stiff; now that their fervour had subsided, she looked like she very much wanted to screen herself from him.

'I know I am not very desirable anymore,' she muttered. 'It might have been preferable to keep me covered up.'

Raising himself up on one elbow, he stared at her, speechless. She waved an impatient hand down her torso in explanation and looked away. His gaze dropped to her breasts, which did not sit so high as they had when she was nineteen, and to her abdomen, which was slightly rounded instead of flat and had silvery-white streaks across it.

'Pregnancy and breastfeeding are not without their drawbacks,' she mumbled.

'Look at me,' he said.

When she didn't respond, he tucked a finger under her chin and eased it towards him. She met his gaze reluctantly.

Summoning every ounce of earnestness, he said, 'These marks show that you brought a child into this world and nurtured her at your breast. They are nothing to be ashamed of. On the contrary, they are a badge of motherhood and you should wear them proudly.'

He caressed her shoulder, traced the line of her collar bone, and trailed a fingertip under the curve of one breast, feeling her shiver at the stimulation. His hand drifted down to her stomach where her muscles were taut with anxiety. He massaged the stretch marks on her belly over and over until at last she began to relax. Only then did he sense he had her permission to reach down to that most private place. His touch wasn't sexual but reverential.

'You are sensational,' he murmured, 'and do not ever doubt it.'

He had not taken his eyes from her face. As he watched, the tension drained from her expression, to be replaced with a breathless joy. She pulled him to her and they kissed, less frantically than before. In the calm that followed, he held her in his arms and she nestled into his side. He knew he should leave before they got caught – Miss Davison and Emily would likely be back soon – but the bedchamber door was locked and there had been no sound from the servants so he reasoned that they had a few more moments' grace to enjoy first.

Her hair, so neat when she had removed her bonnet, had come undone during their vigorous activities, and the curls now draped in disarray over his shoulder and chest. He plucked out a loose pin that was digging into him and twisted a long curl around his thumb, marvelling at the rich shade of chestnut.

'Why were you wearing such plain attire?' he said, glancing at the clothes scattered around the floor. 'It seems rather incongruous with your position.'

He felt rather than heard her chuckle. 'I was on my way to St Swithun's. Drab garments are more suitable for the workhouse. Fortunately, I have instructed the servants to neglect their usual duties as part of that routine, or else Thrussell would have been at the door to see me out. I can't imagine what he might have thought of the entrance you made.'

Cormac stroked his fingers through her tousled hair and said, 'Do you feel guilty?'

Her amusement faded. 'Yes, though I do not know why, for Garrett has done this to me many times since we married, and even before that when we were courting. But then, it is far less scandalous for a gentleman to engage in an affair than it is for a lady to do so.'

'Do you still love him?' he asked, dreading the answer he might hear.

'No, I do not,' she replied, and he let out a silent breath of relief. 'We are miserable together. He has given me a title and wealth, but neither happiness nor love. He did give me a son but sadly he left us too soon.'

Cormac started. 'What? You had another child?'

She nodded. 'Four years ago. His name was James. He was only three months old when he died.'

She sounded like she was trying very hard to keep her voice steady. He was shocked; he had had no inkling that she had borne a second child.

'I am so sorry.' He shuddered at the very notion of any harm coming to Emily and could not begin to conceive the anguish that Bridget had suffered. 'That must have been a terrible loss for you.'

Peering down at her, he saw that her eyes had lost their sparkle and one thing became much clearer to him.

'Forgive me for saying this,' he said, pressing a compassionate kiss to her temple, 'but I knew that something grievous had happened to you during our years apart. I could tell that it had changed you at a profound level. Your spirits are not the same as they once were.'

She gave him a sad smile. 'It pains me to say that there are several causes for the alteration you see in me, not least my devastation in losing you and ending up in a loveless marriage. But yes, there is very little that can compare to the desolation of losing a beloved child. He was such a dear boy.'

She was about to say something else when noises drifted up from downstairs and she jerked away from him to listen.

'Miss Davison and Emily are back. We must hurry!'

He slid off the bed and hastened to don his clothes. There was no time to undertake the intricate and time-consuming process of lacing up Bridget's stays, so she fished a dressing gown from the wardrobe and wrapped it around herself. Creeping to the door, she unlocked it and opened it a crack.

'They are climbing the stairs,' she whispered as he looped his cravat around his neck and knotted it. 'They will continue on up to the nursery and that will be your chance to slip past.'

He shrugged into his coat and came to the door. Unable to resist, he gathered her hair in one hand, drew it back to expose the nape of her neck, and bent his head to kiss the bare skin.

She stifled her gasp as Emily's voice floated to them from the landing.

'I can't wait to show Mama my daffodils!'

They heard Miss Davison reply, 'She will be very pleased to see them. Let us take off our cloaks and gloves and then we shall find a jar for your flowers.'

Their footsteps grew fainter as they ascended the next flight of stairs.

Bridget turned to him. 'Quick, you should go now.'

He kissed her fully on the mouth, feeling the passion rise in him again. With great reluctance, he pulled away, checked that the landing was clear, and stole out of the bedchamber. He met no one on his way down the stairs but as he reached the bottom step he noticed that the little ornament they had smashed in their earlier tumult had been swept away and Bridget's bonnet and cloak hung tidily on the coat stand.

Discomfited that their actions had not gone unnoticed by the servants and heartily grateful for their discretion, he slipped out the front door.

# CHAPTER 28

Bridget's thoughts were in a whirl. She and Cormac had fallen as helplessly into her bed as they had fallen into each other's arms at Oakleigh. It was glorious but it left her with no small measure of anxiety. What did this make her? What was he thinking now? What might it mean for Emily? What would happen next?

It was fortunate that he sent her a note later that day, or she would have gone wild in her agitation. Naturally, he phrased it in the most reserved language but it conveyed an invitation to Raynesworth House the next day with the veiled suggestion that only her own presence would be necessary. If he wanted her to leave Emily behind, then that implied his intention for them to...what? Talk about what had happened? Repeat the event? Neither would be possible with Lord and Lady Bewley in attendance, that was certain.

She entered the drawing room at Raynesworth House an interminable twenty-four hours later to find Lady Bewley in a huff.

'My silly nephew,' she said, 'has mixed up the date of your visit. He told me it was Wednesday and so I arranged to call upon an acquaintance on Tuesday. But now here you are on Tuesday and it is too late for me to postpone my other engagement now.'

She bestowed a withering look upon Cormac who acted sheepish.

'I apologise once again, Aunt,' he said. 'I honestly thought I had told you Tuesday.'

'Be that as it may, I am obliged to take my leave without delay for I am already running late. You must take some refreshment before you depart, Lady Wyndham. Make sure you look after her,' she added in a stern voice to Cormac.

'Oh, I will.'

Bridget curtseyed to Lady Bewley. 'I am very sorry that we have missed each other. I look forward to the next time we meet.'

From the drawing room window, they watched the lady waddle out of the house and into her waiting carriage, which lurched away down the street.

'Where is Lord Bewley?' Bridget asked.

'Occupying his seat at a parliamentary session,' Cormac answered in a relaxed manner. 'The House of Lords doesn't often meet on a Wednesday but Tuesday is a reliable day to find him there.'

He winked. His untroubled expression made her a little easier. She trusted him. And she felt a flicker of heat stir down below.

For the benefit of Lord and Lady Bewley's servants, they sat in the drawing room for a time and drank tea in grave decorum. When the housekeeper came in to check that their comforts were being met, Cormac said to the woman, 'Do you remember that object I found in the storage room? I am going to bring Lady Wyndham there next, for she studied it in the past and might be in a position to let us know whether it can be salvaged.'

This statement baffled Bridget but the housekeeper accepted it without demur. Offering his hand but no explanation, Cormac led Bridget up through the house until they reached the top floor, which consisted of a long, deserted corridor flanked by several closed doors. Opening the last one, he gestured her inside.

'Oh, my goodness,' she said as she walked in.

The room was packed to the ceiling with every kind of domestic detritus imaginable: a wardrobe with its doors falling off its hinges, several chairs and a sofa with their stuffing spilling out, cracked mirrors, faded cushions, even an upright piano missing some of its keys. There was an air of utter abandonment about the room; it was easy to tell that nobody came in here except to deposit another item no longer regarded as having any value.

Cormac shut the door as Bridget crossed the room with difficulty, navigating her way around the clutter in order to examine the broken piano.

'How very sad,' she said, playing some of the keys which were still attached. It was woefully out of tune. 'Somebody used to love this instrument.'

'At least today it can serve a purpose again,' he said. 'When we go back downstairs, you must appraise its worth, or lack thereof, very loudly in the housekeeper's hearing.'

A thrill ran down her spine. Keeping her gaze on the keys, she said, 'You do not expect us to be disturbed here then?'

'The other rooms on this floor are sleeping quarters for the servants, who are all about their daily duties right now.' He came up behind her and slipped his arms around her waist. 'Do you still play?'

'Not very often. Music somehow lost its charm for me over the years. I think I should like Emily to learn though.'

He squeezed her at the mention of their daughter's name. 'If you can get her to put down her paints for more than two minutes.'

'Very true.'

She played a soft, two-note chord on the piano and let the sound die away. Then she turned within his arms. After just the barest hesitation, he eased her lips apart and their tongues met in a sensual dance, weaving and caressing. His body was warm, his hands light on her back. She touched his chest and felt the rapid beating of his heart beneath her fingers.

When they broke apart, it was as gently as they had come together. He kissed the tip of her nose.

'Did you ever imagine that we would be together again?' he said.

She shook her head. 'The idea was so fantastic that I never dreamed it to be possible. I think part of me doubts even now that you are here.'

He tightened his embrace so that she was flush against his body, able to feel every part of him.

'Do you still doubt?' he said with a mischievous smile.

She blushed. 'Not anymore.'

The playfulness faded from his face as he regarded her. 'We are treading a dangerous path. We ought to ask ourselves if we are prepared to continue down it, taking into account the significant risks involved. I know what my answer is, but what is yours?'

As she considered his words, her whirling thoughts over the past day coalesced into one unshakeable conviction. Taking a deep breath, she said, 'For many years, I treasured our night in the hay barn as the pinnacle of my earthly happiness. Reuniting our bodies and souls once more has made me realise that my memory of the experience did not do it justice. I am willing to accept any risk to feel such completion. With you, I am whole again.'

She supposed she ought to be embarrassed; it was unseemly for a woman to speak of such matters. But his look was full of appreciation.

'I would like to think that this is abundantly obvious by now,' he said, 'but I want to declare it in unmistakable terms: I am still very much in love with you.'

To hear those words was to soar high above the clouds. 'And I with you,' she said with a giddy joy.

Their lips joined in a chaste kiss, so sweet and pure that it was almost as if their tragic separation at Oakleigh had never transpired.

'I cannot believe this is really happening,' she breathed.

'Believe it,' he said and kissed her again, harder than before.

She realised she did not feel so apprehensive this time. Yesterday, she had been mortified when he had stripped her to her bare skin – how could a man find such physical flaws attractive? But he had made her feel perfect, despite her imperfections. Now, as he drew her down to the sofa, its insides bursting from its seams, his face and body language told her she was all he desired. He pulled her to him and she embraced him eagerly, recognising the hunger in his eyes as her own.

They sprawled awkwardly on the narrow sofa; it was not long enough to lie lengthways. Feeling wanton, she encouraged him into a sitting position and hauled at her skirts to straddle him with her knees on either side of his hips. A strange shadow passed over his expression but it was gone so fast that she wondered if it had been only a trick of the light. He stroked her legs from ankle to thigh and fingered the tops of her stockings with a hint of regret.

'God, I wish I could look at you naked again,' he said. 'But neither time nor circumstances will allow me to undress you fully this time.'

She caressed the outline of his strong jaw. 'In that case, we shall have to rely more on our other senses.'

Her lips hovered over his in invitation. He tasted her with exquisite attention to detail, addressing not only her mouth, but also her throat and the soft curves of her breasts above the neckline of her dress. She inhaled, relishing the smell of his skin. The faint trace of cologne was quite in opposition to the tang of horses that had clung to him in the past, and yet underneath it was a scent that remained unchanged, something familiar and masculine and indescribably *him*. Intoxicated by his nearness, she pressed closer, aching for the physical bond they had forged yesterday but unsure how to ask for it.

He understood nevertheless. He reached down to unbutton his fall front and adjusted her masses of skirts around them, bunching them high at her waist.

'Let's see,' he murmured. 'Which senses have we not tried yet?'

Her wits were growing muddled with yearning. 'S-sound?' she tried.

He smiled; evidently he had not expected her to offer a rational answer. 'Hmm,' he said. 'Shall I whisper sweet nothings in your ear?'

Suddenly more alert, she said, 'Anything but "darling".' He cocked an eyebrow and she cringed. 'I'm sorry, I shouldn't have said that. It's just...'

'It's what Garrett says?' he said perceptively.

'What he used to say. He hasn't for a long time.' She squirmed, appalled that she had mentioned her husband in her current position, but felt she ought to finish now. 'To me, it is an endearment empty of any true feeling.'

He didn't look offended. 'Duly noted,' he said with a solemn nod.

He took her hand and kissed the inside of her wrist, his lips locating her pulse. Its rapid throb echoed in her sensitive place below which strained against his open fall front. She rose up and settled herself upon him, sliding down with a torturous slowness that dragged groans from them both. He held her there, his face pressed to her breast, and murmured something inaudible.

'What?' she said, her breath coming shorter.

He lifted his head, his blue eyes hazy with devotion. 'I said I love you, *a rún mo chroí*.'

Clasping her hips, he urged her to take charge. She obeyed, cautious at first and then, finding a rhythm, moving with more abandon.

Panting, she asked, 'What does it mean?'

He didn't reply, leaving her to focus only on the sense of touch: the gliding friction, their sweat-drenched skin, the clench and stroke of muscles. She gasped as he spilled himself inside her at last with a ragged sound of repletion.

'Secret of my heart,' he said and sighed.

# CHAPTER 29

'We have excellent news to impart, dearest!'

Lucy and Alice had come to call upon Bridget at Wyndham House and Lucy was brimming with enthusiasm. 'As you know, Cassandra is hosting a ball on the fifth of March. Having speculated at length on the subject, we can finally confirm that the delightful Mr Davenport is to be in attendance!'

Apart from the ice skating incident at Regent's Park – of which Cassandra had never claimed orchestration, though she always adopted a secretive smile whenever they referred to it – Bridget's companions had encountered Cormac on just two other occasions since the first party. Both had been dull gatherings with no music or dancing and therefore little opportunity to ignite a stronger attraction. However, a ball meant that dancing would be the main agenda of the evening.

'We must therefore get Alice partnered with Mr Davenport as often as we can,' said Lucy. 'For he is bound to fall in love with her by the third dance.'

Alice coloured. 'Oh, Lucy, you know it is improper to partake in three dances with the same gentleman. How I do wish you would not say such things.'

'Why so? Do you not desire him to fall in love with you? Can you deny that you feel a particular regard for him?'

Alice's protesting squeak was reply enough.

Bridget experienced a dart of discomfort. Though reuniting with Cormac in such a meaningful way gave her the greatest joy, she now suffered the deepest guilt that she was depriving her dear friend of a romantic association. Alice did not deserve to be a spinster; she would make a good wife for any gentleman. But the very idea of Cormac being with another woman tore at Bridget's heart. And she could not dictate how he felt; it was Alice's grievous misfortune that the recipient of her affections had given himself to another.

The rest of the conversation consisted of Lucy determining ways to keep Miss Norwell as far away from Mr Davenport as possible. When she and Alice rose to leave, Bridget stood with them as she would be departing for St Swithun's shortly in the company of Lady Bewley. The lady had visited the workhouse three times already over the past few weeks and she and Frances had connected so well that they intended to keep up a correspondence even when she returned to Bedfordshire. Whether her nephew would be returning with her was something Bridget decided not to contemplate.

The three of them went out to the hall where Thrussell appeared to open the front door, just as Emily came bounding down the stairs, Miss Davison trying to keep up behind her.

Alice beamed at her. 'How lovely to see you, Emily. Good gracious, you have grown so much!'

Emily dropped into a little curtsey and then turned to her mother. 'Mama, will we be going to see Mr Davenport today? I have a new painting for him of the bird's nest we found in the gardens!'

'Mr Davenport?' said Lucy, looking at Bridget in puzzlement. 'He has met Emily?'

Bridget endeavoured to keep her countenance calm. 'Quite by chance. I have become acquainted with his aunt, Lady Bewley, as she too takes an interest in charitable activities. She is very fond of children so Emily has accompanied me on some of my visits to Raynesworth House.'

'How nice,' said Alice with a smile.

'Indeed,' said Lucy. 'We shall take our leave of you. Let us begin counting down the days to Cassandra's ball!'

As Thrussell saw Lucy and Alice out the door, Bridget gave silent thanks that Emily had not blurted anything else. She considered the growing number of people who could reveal the extent of her and Cormac's connection – Lord and Lady Bewley, Lizzie, Miss Davison through Emily's endless chatter, and now the butler and Bridget's closest friends – and realised that they would need to exercise more vigilance.

On the night of the ball, Bridget entered Radcliffe House with a mixture of apprehension and anticipation. The merriment was in full swing and the ballroom was crowded with people dancing, mingling and gossiping. She searched for Cormac and spotted him in a set, partnered with Alice. Almost as if he sensed her presence, he glanced around and made eye contact with her. His shining gaze was enough to set her nerves tingling everywhere. She stood to the side of the dancing floor and hoped no one would notice her flaming cheeks.

At the end of the dance, it became apparent that Alice had promised the next one to Lord Newby and Cormac was swift to take Bridget for his own partner. He led her into the group of dancers and they took their places in the formation.

There was a pause before the dance started and, wondering whether he and Alice had just engaged in their crucial third dance, she said casually, 'Are you having an enjoyable evening so far?'

He chuckled. In a low voice that nobody else could hear, he said, 'Passable, with a substantial improvement upon your arrival. Alice is very amiable but she does not compare to the incredible woman next to me right now.'

She found herself reddening again. How could she do anything but melt when he spoke to her like that? The dance began and, despite the modest nature of the steps, it became extraordinarily sensual between them. Every touch, every look, was loaded with heat, reminding them of their recent clandestine encounters...

It was an effort to drag her concentration back to a more lucid train of thought. She had to tell him about Emily's injudicious comment in front of Lucy and Alice.

'We need to talk in private,' she said, peeking over his shoulder at Alice who was having difficulty maintaining rhythm with Lucy's uncoordinated husband. 'Will you meet me after this dance?'

'I am at your service,' he replied, though the mischief in his eyes rather negated the formal address.

They could not retreat to the terrace for it was a far more welcoming place in early March than it had been in the heart of January and, through the open French doors, she could see that it was teeming with guests seeking a breath of air.

'There is a door at the back of the room,' she said, familiar with the layout of Radcliffe House from so many visits over the years. 'It is not the main access to the ballroom so, with any luck, there will be nobody lingering out there. I shall go first. Delay a little while and then follow.'

He nodded with detached civility for the dance was ending and Cassandra was approaching. As usual, her attire was unforgettable; tonight her gown was lavish with lace and she wore an elaborate display of feathers in her hair.

'Mr Davenport!' she exclaimed. 'I wonder if you could assist Alice and me? We are trying to determine whether the punch has been soured by too much lemon.'

Bridget slipped away from them. She stepped out into the hallway; it was indeed deserted, lit only by a lamp mounted on a bracket by the ballroom door and a stream of moonlight which fell through an uncurtained window at the end of the corridor. There was an alcove halfway down towards the window – it may have been intended as an exhibition space for a piece of sculpture but it was vacant at present. She hid in its shadows and waited.

Several minutes passed before Cormac made his appearance. When he shut the door of the ballroom behind him, she emerged from the alcove and called his name softly. He glimpsed her hovering at the edge of the patch of moonlight and strode towards her.

'I'm sorry you had to wait so long,' he said as he approached. 'Lady Radcliffe is the most persistent woman I have ever met.'

She meant to tell him what Emily had said in Lucy and Alice's presence. But when he reached her, she discerned the undisguised lust burning in his eyes. He pulled her into the alcove and crushed his mouth upon hers. Urgency and desire overwhelmed them, so powerful that it compelled them to abandon the caution of which she had intended to warn him – a mere wall separated them from discovery. His hands roamed all over her, caressing the tops of her breasts and stroking her waist and hips, while hers roved over him in turn, skimming across his solid chest and gripping his backside in shameless gratification. He scrabbled at her skirts.

'Why do there have to be so many layers?' he complained, his voice muffled against her lips.

She began to laugh but stifled herself when the ballroom door opened, and light, music and chatter spilled out into the hallway. The door closed again, leaving the hall dim and quiet once more, but they knew they were no longer alone.

'Where is he?' came Cassandra's ringing tones. 'I'm certain I saw him slip out here.'

'I thought I saw him too,' said another female voice which Bridget recognised as Lucy's.

Cormac released her from his embrace and they stood motionless.

'Perhaps he went this way,' Lucy suggested and, horror-struck, Bridget heard her footsteps coming down the corridor in the direction of their alcove. There was nothing whatsoever to hide behind; if she came near, she would not fail to discover them.

'No,' said Cassandra dismissively. 'There is nothing down there but a door to the servants' staircase.'

Lucy's footsteps retreated but they did not dare breathe a sigh of relief just yet. As long as Cassandra and Lucy remained in the corridor, they were trapped. If the ladies chose to wait for Cormac to reappear, they would be obliged to stay concealed and suspicion would mount ever higher with regard to Mr Davenport's mysterious absence.

But then Cassandra said, 'He could be gone to the smoking room. Henry escaped there a while ago so it is likely he will embroil Mr Davenport in a conversation about some kind of sport. The man thinks of nothing else,' she added, disgruntled.

'It may be a while before he returns then. Shall we go back in?'

'I suppose so. I do wish he would not waste his time with my husband though. I promised Alice I would have her married to Mr Davenport by midsummer and I intend to follow through on that. It would be helpful if he made more of a contribution to my efforts.'

With that, the ballroom door opened and closed once more and silence descended in the hallway.

Bridget looked at Cormac. His face was strained in the pale light of the moon. He leaned his head back against the wall of the alcove and shut his eyes.

'I cannot take much more of this,' he said. 'They are vultures. They see me as a piece of meat, not a human being.'

Her tone was sympathetic as she replied, 'That is the unfortunate lot of a handsome young man who is to inherit a fortune and estate.'

The ghost of the true Oliver floated in the wake of her words.

Cormac opened his eyes and stared straight at her. 'I can't stand it anymore. When I look over my shoulder, all I see is those women dogging my heels or potential scenarios where our connection could be discovered. I want to get out of London, and out of this life. Let's run away, you and Emily and I.'

Her breath left her body in a rush.

'Think about it,' he urged. 'The prospect of going somewhere where we could be ourselves rather than pretending to be other people. Where the three of us could be a family. Where you and I could be a couple overtly in love instead of hiding behind locked doors. I hate this duplicity, I have lived with it for too long now. I want to be me again and I want to be with you, without the disgust of deceit and the constraints of high society restricting us at every turn. Don't you crave it too?'

She was forcibly reminded of their night in the hay barn and his similarly impassioned plea back then. They were older now, but were they any wiser?

Hesitant, she said, 'I crave the simplicity of what you describe. But we are not two people alone. We have Emily and she is the most important person of all. I could not bear to bring any hardship or unhappiness upon her.'

'You would not be doing that if you came with me. I would look after you both and ensure no harm came to either of you. Listen,' he said, clutching her hands. 'We could slip away, flee on a ship before anyone realised we were missing, and go home, back to my mother and sisters and nephew. If they were willing to leave Oakleigh, they could come with us and we could all be a family together somewhere else, living the life we really want to live.'

Her jaw dropped. She had taken in every glorious thing he had just said but her mind had caught on one essential flaw. His mother, sisters and nephew. He did not know what had happened to them, that they had been driven from Oakleigh too, that there was very little hope any of them had survived. How had she been so remiss as to not realise this? And how on earth could she tell him that his family was not safe at home as he believed and that – her heart constricted horribly – it was her fault?

'Cormac—' she began in a cracked voice.

'Do not give me your answer now,' he cut in. 'I want you to take the time to consider it first. Just know this: I love you and I love Emily and I want to do everything I can to make you both happy.' He glanced out into the empty corridor. 'I am going to return to the ball now. I'll tell the ladies I went to seek a quieter spot than the terrace for some air. I cannot use the smoking room as an alibi as there is no smell of smoke on me. It's best if you wait a few minutes before following.'

He kissed her forehead and left her alone in the alcove. She gazed unseeingly at the wall, her mind blank with shock. What in the world was she going to do?

Feeling shaky, she gathered her wits and returned to the ballroom. She caught Lucy's eye as she entered; Lucy glanced over to where Cormac was conversing with Alice and then looked back at Bridget with a frown.

# CHAPTER 30

Bridget woke with a start the following morning, wondering why she had such a sick feeling in her stomach. Then the memory of the previous night crashed over her and the nausea intensified to a severity that had her reaching for the chamber pot.

Cormac was unaware that his family had been rendered homeless just like him. She saw now how obvious this was, for he had been banished from the estate before her mother had delivered that devastating blow. So he had lived these many years believing they still dwelled safely in the cottage that had been his childhood home. And it fell to Bridget to shatter that illusion.

She had had no other private moment with him for the remainder of the ball to divulge the terrible reality to him. But a visit to Raynesworth House had been prearranged for that afternoon – Lady Bewley wished to discuss the possibility of speaking to the Ladies of Compassion Association herself – so Bridget would be obliged to face him then.

What would he say? What would he think of her? He would never be able to look at her the same way again, forevermore seeing her as the person who had allowed ruin to come upon his beloved family. He might have been able to find it in himself to forgive her for the pain she had caused him personally, but surely he could never absolve her for inflicting such agony upon a dear mother who had already suffered far too much.

Would he terminate their relationship, rescinding his offer of the wonderful future he had just proposed to her? She despaired at the thought. She had no clear concept of the practicalities of running away; she only knew that it would be unbearable if he left her now. Their separation seven and a half years ago would be nothing compared to losing him this time, when the reason would not be the cruel manipulation of her mother but the fact that he could no longer feel any regard for her. That would be desolation beyond endurance.

Nevertheless, he must be told, of that she was in no doubt. She could not let him go one day further without knowing the unfortunate fate of his beloved mother and sweet sisters and that innocent baby. He needed to learn the horrendous truth.

But it would take all the courage she had.

The wretched hours trickled away and soon she was sitting in silent misery at Raynesworth House in the company of Lord and Lady Bewley and their 'nephew'. The elderly couple were delighted to see her, though their faces fell when they found that Emily was not in attendance. Bridget's excuse was that Emily had a cold and must remain at home to rest, which was for the most part true. The little girl did indeed have the sniffles but she was not quite as poorly as Bridget described to Lord and Lady Bewley, who clucked and fussed and pressed a variety of medicinal remedies upon her to take back to her daughter and help nurse her back to health. Cormac, too, looked alarmed but she dispelled his worries with a slight shake of her head when the lord and lady were not looking. She had decided that it was simply better for their daughter not to be present today, bearing in mind the confrontation that she knew was about to take place.

Awash with anxiety, she could scarcely keep track of the cheerful conversation around her. She was tormented by her thoughts, imagining Cormac's face when she laid bare the true state of affairs, the way he would turn his back in fury and walk away from her. It was going to be the end of all the joy of her existence. Yes, she would still have Emily and she would still love her with all her heart, but how could she ever look upon her again and not see Cormac in her mind's eye? She was sure that twenty lonely years from now the image would still feel as sharp and piercing as a dagger thrust into her side.

'Lady Wyndham, my dear? Are you quite well?'

She looked up to find four pairs of eyes staring at her, for even the maid serving the tea had paused to gape. It was plain that someone in the room had posed a question to her and she had been too preoccupied to either hear or respond.

'Pardon me,' she said weakly. 'What did you say?'

'You look rather ill,' said Lady Bewley, her brows drawn together in concern. 'It is possible you have contracted the cold that is vexing poor Emily. Shall we call for your carriage to take you home? Or, indeed, ought we to send for the physician?'

'Thank you, no, it is not so serious as that. But I believe I am in need of some fresh air. Would you mind if I took a turn about your garden?'

'Of course, that may well revive you. Perhaps Oliver could accompany you, in case you become faint?'

Cormac was on his feet before she had even bowed her head in acquiescence. He led her slowly from the drawing room for she was in fact beginning to feel lightheaded. As she stepped over the threshold at the back of the house, she thought for an instant that she was going to pass out, but then a refreshing gust of wind blew across her face and rejuvenated her. The wave of dizziness receded to be replaced by her former apprehension, multiplied tenfold now that the moment she had been dreading was fast approaching. She hastened into the garden to avoid eye contact with Cormac and heard his footsteps following her.

It was a typical March day, cool and blustery with intermittent patches of sunlight breaking through the clouds. The breeze caught at her hair and whipped loose strands into her face. She brushed them away impatiently as she hurried deeper into the garden, heading for the small, walled orchard. The irony did not escape her but inside it they would be beyond the view of any prying eyes from the house. She slipped through the door and made for the stone bench as he entered the orchard behind her.

'What is the hurry?' he said, startled by her agitated manner.

She did not reply and she did not sit down on the bench, instead wringing her hands and gulping as she tried to force air into her lungs.

He came over to her and clutched her shoulders. 'Tell me what is the matter.'

She burst into tears.

He looked aghast. 'My God, what has happened?'

She shook her head as heart-rending sobs wracked her body. She couldn't do this, she couldn't. It would be like tearing herself in half.

Understanding seemed to dawn on his face. His eyes widened and filled with horror.

'Please do not do this to me again,' he choked out, his hands dropping to his sides.

Through her tears, she gazed up at him without comprehension. 'Do what?'

His voice did not sound like his own as he said, 'Please do not say you are going to stay with him.'

She stopped sobbing out of sheer surprise; his fear could not have been further from the truth. 'I'm not going to say that. I do not want to stay with Garrett. I want to go away with you.'

In a split second, his features changed from dismay to absolute elation and he laughed in relief. 'Then why are you so upset?'

'Because you will not want to go away with me,' she said and started to weep again.

He looked bewildered. 'Why on earth not?'

With a great effort, she tried to stem her flow of grief. 'I have something awful to tell you. And after you hear it you will detest me and you will never want to see me again.'

He frowned. 'I cannot imagine that there is anything in this world that would make me feel like that towards you.'

'That is because it is too horrible to imagine,' she said hollowly.

She took a deep, shuddering breath and sat on the stone bench. The moment had come. Her next words would mark the immediate end of their snatched, sunlit time together.

'There is something you do not know,' she began, staring down at her lap, 'and it was only at the ball last night that I realised you were not aware of it. You said you wanted to go back to your family on the Oakleigh Estate, back to your mother and sisters and nephew. But this is not possible for they are no longer there.'

He tried to interrupt but she talked over him; it was easier to keep going now that she had started. 'At the end of that summer at Oakleigh, my mother ordered you to leave the estate and you did so. What you do not know is that the following morning she did the same to your whole family. She had already threatened to do it but promised she would not if I let you go and married Garrett. I made an unspeakable choice, believing I was at least saving Maggie and the others. But then she threw them off the land anyway, leaving them with no home, no money, no means of obtaining help from anyone. You know firsthand the bleak reality they must have faced. I think' – her voice splintered and she swallowed – 'I think there can be no hope for any of them.'

She forced herself to look up at him. He stood unmoving, his face white and his hands balled into fists. She waited for the onslaught of his rage but he remained immobile. This mute statue was almost more frightening than the exclamations of hatred she had been anticipating and she felt compelled to fill the agonising silence.

'I am so, so sorry,' she said thickly. 'I shall never be able to forgive myself for this and I do not expect you to either. You have every right to blame me.'

This stirred him from his trance. He blinked. 'What did you say?'

'You have every right to blame me.' Heart heavy, she shut her eyes as the tears squeezed out again.

'I do not blame you!' she heard him say in an incredulous tone and her eyes snapped open.

'What?'

'I do not blame you,' he said again and went on caustically, 'I blame your conniving *bitch* of a mother. To condemn an innocent family like that, she either has a heart of stone or no heart at all. If she were in front of me right now, I would murder her with the greatest pleasure.'

He did not look at all apologetic at his coarse language but she barely registered this. She was trying to process the fact that his loathing was not directed at her.

'I d-don't understand. You do not think it was my fault?'

'Of course not. You believed she would allow them to stay, didn't you?'

'Yes...'

'Then you were as much deceived as anyone.'

'But it was because of me that she did it.' She did not know why she was arguing, only that it was important for him to fully understand the depth of her culpability. 'Because of what I did with you.'

'If that is the case, then we are both to blame. But our only crime is that we were in love. Lady Courcey is the root of this monstrous act of cruelty. I in no way hold you responsible for her unspeakable actions.'

She felt hope rise within her. 'So you—you still want to be with me?'

'More than anything else in this world.'

This was too much. Once again, she broke down in tears. Burying her face in her hands, she found herself laughing and crying at the same time. All that fear and dread had been for nothing. He still loved her and he did not see her as the person who had destroyed his family. The sun continued to shine in her life after all.

She felt a pressure along the side of her body as he sat on the bench beside her. He tugged at her hands until she let them fall away from her face.

'Did you think I was going to leave you?' he murmured.

She nodded jerkily. He leaned forwards and kissed each of her cheeks where the tracks of her tears still glistened.

'Impossible,' he whispered in her ear. 'Unthinkable. Unendurable. I am not going anywhere without you.'

She threw her arms around him and they hugged as if they had just saved each other from a sinking ship. All uncertainty was gone. Without consciously thinking about it, she had made her decision to run away with him. The prospect of parting had been so distressing that it had driven home the stark realisation that she could not live without him; it was absurd to even entertain the notion of separation when her happiness could only exist wherever he was. And he had already proved that he reciprocated those feelings without reservation. They needed no more words to confirm their wholehearted love and commitment to one another and to their treasured daughter.

When they broke apart, she was smiling with joy but his face was set in an expression of steely determination.

'We cannot delay,' he said in a fierce voice. 'You say there is no hope for my family but I do not accept that. I want to return to Ireland and find them. There is a possibility that they may have perished but there is also every chance that they survived. I won't be able to rest until I have uncovered the truth.'

She cupped his cheek tenderly. 'Emily and I shall be with you every step of the way.'

He turned his head to the side and kissed her fingers. Then he stood and began to pace back and forth, the bare branches of the apple trees waving above his head.

'We need to make a plan. I have already been thinking about this. We must depart without telling a soul, because that was our fatal mistake at Oakleigh. And we ought to leave during the daytime. First of all, Garrett will not realise you and Emily are missing until he returns home late in the evening. If we are lucky and he stays away for the night then it might even be the next day. Second, Lord and Lady Bewley will not become suspicious of my absence until well past nightfall. And third, it will be easier to lose ourselves in a crowd if we are pursued.'

'You are expecting us to be pursued?' she said, her elation of the previous minute diluted now with a stab of uneasiness.

'The probability is only slight. I anticipate that we shall be safely away by the time our absence is noted and the alarm is raised. But we ought to prepare for every eventuality and ensure that we depart without drawing attention to ourselves.'

'How shall we do that?'

'We must use different names. We shall be Mr and Mrs Marsh and our daughter Lizzie until we are out of harm's way. That will be an easy name for Emily to remember. I'll buy three tickets on the next ship departing for Ireland and send you word with the date and time. You and Emily will need to be ready when I come for you.'

'We will be.'

He looked at her. 'We should tell Emily who I am.'

'Yes,' she agreed at once. 'I shall tell her just before we leave. Any sooner and she might let something slip to Garrett. This will be very confusing for her, poor thing.'

'She is a bright girl and she has two parents who love her very much. She will be fine.'

He held out his hand to her; she stood and they embraced beneath the trees.

'We are really doing this,' she said, full of nerves and excitement.

'We are,' he replied.

# CHAPTER 31

Over the next few days, Bridget made her preparations. She surreptitiously packed a valise for herself and Emily with ruthless discrimination, selecting the plainest dresses and most sensible boots and omitting elegant mantles and decorative jewellery. One bonnet and one cloak each would be sufficient. Among a small number of personal items, she packed the silver-handled hairbrush Lady Bewley had given Emily, for both its practical use and sentimental value, and left enough space for the watercolour box, which there could be no question of leaving behind. She tried to keep the valise as light as she could for she knew there would be long days of travel ahead and the last thing they wanted was to be hauling a heavy burden along with them.

A harder challenge was the letters she must write. She and Emily could not disappear without a trace; there would be the assumption that they had been abducted and a citywide search would ensue. She needed to relay a message that it was their own choice to leave. She also wanted to attempt to say goodbye in writing as she could not do so to anyone in person. She therefore wrote separate letters to Lucy, Alice and Cassandra to apologise for the abrupt ending of her acquaintance with them, to assure them that this was what she wanted, and to wish them well with their own families and futures. She tried not to imagine the outrage and upset the letters would cause and sincerely hoped that Alice's heart would not be broken by the departure of Mr Davenport.

She wrote to Frances too, with a sadness that extended both to her dear friend and to St Swithun's itself. The place was gloomy and inhospitable and had been the site of her frightening assault by a desperate man, and yet she believed she would be sorry to bid farewell to it. Her efforts there had given her a sense of purpose in some of the bleakest hours of her existence and it would be the part of her life in London she would miss most of all when she left. She wished she could make a final substantial donation but that was impossible without Garrett's signature on the cheque, so she confined herself to infusing her letter with fervent expressions of hope for Frances's good health and the advancement of St Swithun's. She would give it and the others to Lizzie before she left; the loyal maid would ensure that the notes reached the right hands at the appropriate time.

Most difficult of all was her letter to Garrett. The desertion of his wife and child would expose him to widespread scandal which he would find excruciating to bear. But he had been unfaithful to her too and, worse, he had been hardhearted towards Emily. There was nothing to salvage from such a loveless situation, and she kept this point fixed in her mind as she penned her note.


Garrett,

Emily and I are gone. We have run away with Cormac. I am sure you have not forgotten who that is. I shall give you no details as to how he has come back into my life, nor shall I tell you where we are going. It will be futile to search for us so do not waste your time.

You and I must admit to ourselves that our marriage was a failure. You were never in love with me and I was always in love with somebody else. Our greatest triumph was bringing our beloved James into this world, and I thank you for that fleeting period of joyfulness. I know you will always feel his loss as keenly as I.

I wish to part on amicable terms so please understand that I hold no grudge against you. I do hope that, in time, you might come to feel the same towards me, recognising that this is the best for all concerned.

Farewell,
Bridget

It was perhaps a little brief for the termination of a relationship that had lasted nine years but it was all she could manage. She intended to return her engagement ring with the letter too but that could not be done until the last moment.

And so she waited.

On Thursday, she, Garrett and Emily were seated at the breakfast table when the morning messages arrived and with them Cormac's letter of deliverance.

Friday morning. I will come for you.

C.

He had initialled it with his true name which must mean he was convinced of their escape. She could hardly conceal her excitement and almost knocked the milk jug out of Peter's hand as the footman leaned in to place it on the table. She glanced up to find Garrett staring at her.

'Good news, my darling?' he enquired with raised eyebrows and a rather twisted smile.

'Another gathering at Cassandra's,' she said, hastily doubling over the note. She strove to keep her gaze from alighting upon Emily, fearing that her expression would reveal too much of her elation. 'I did so enjoy the last one. I am certain this next occasion will be just as entertaining.'

He folded the letter in his own hand.

'Perhaps I shall attend this time,' he said, draining his coffee cup. 'I am long overdue a visit to Radcliffe House.'

'Cassandra will be delighted,' she said with a mechanical smile.

That evening, she unpacked and repacked the secret valise three times, anxious that she was either forgetting something essential or including something that ought to be left out. When at last she was satisfied that all was in order, she wandered around her bedchamber, touching her possessions for the final time. She stroked the fur trim of her favourite mantle, trailed her fingers through the glittering pieces in her jewellery box, and said a wistful goodbye to the embroidered pillowcase that had belonged to James. The pouch containing his dark lock of hair was the only memory of her baby boy she had allowed herself to tuck into the valise.

After that, there was nothing to do but wait for the evening to end. She had eaten her last solitary dinner at the enormous dining table. She had sent Emily to bed with a special hug and kiss, knowing the upheaval that was in store for her tomorrow. She had tried reading but found it impossible to concentrate.

Every minute crawled by. She wondered how Cormac was whiling away this final night alone and longed for him with a physical ache. If only Friday would come more quickly.

She had expected that she would not see Garrett again until the next morning at breakfast, but she was not long in bed when she heard him enter the hall below, quite a bit earlier than usual. His footsteps came directly up the stairs to her door and his knock was firm.

Instinct made her wary. She wished she had blown out her candle so that he would have noted the absence of light under the door and believed she was already asleep. Her teeth fastened on the tip of her tongue.

'Come in,' she said unenthusiastically.

He entered the bedchamber and closed the door behind him. His hair was tousled and his hazel eyes held a wild gleam. He stared at her for a long time without saying anything.

She grew impatient under his silent appraisal and, with all the politeness she could muster, said, 'Is there something I can do for you?'

He shrugged and his gaze roamed restlessly around the chamber before landing on her again.

'Are you with child?' he asked without warning.

Her mouth fell open in mute shock. For one panicked moment, she thought he had somehow learned of her love affair with Cormac, but then she came to her senses. The last time she and Garrett had shared a bed, the night of James's birthday in January, he had demanded a son of her. He wanted to know if there had been a product of that union.

'I—no,' she said faintly.

'We will have to try again then,' he said and approached the bed. He smelled of smoke and brandy.

She blanched. He must have tired of whichever young mistress had been diverting him these past weeks and now here he was, intending to bed his wife on the very eve of her running away from him. The timing could not be worse. She felt nauseated at the idea of betraying Cormac at this eleventh hour – her body belonged to him now, not to the man in front of her. She had to prevent this act of unfaithfulness or she would not be able to face Cormac in the morning.

He was already pulling back the bedcovers; he had not even tried to kiss her. She pressed down on the skirt of her nightdress, blocking his access.

'No, we cannot.'

His gaze whipped up to hers. 'You shall not deny your husband.'

She shivered at the frost in his tone but tried to keep the tremble from her voice as she lied, 'I have my courses. It is not possible tonight.'

He glared at her with such mistrust that she feared he might rip off her clothing to check. Then his shoulders sagged. He smoothed the bedcovers back over her and placed a detached kiss on her cheek.

'A pity,' he said and stalked from the room.

# CHAPTER 32

Friday morning dawned with Bridget standing at her bedchamber window, watching as the dark gardens of Berkeley Square became visible with the rising sun. Though she had tried, she had not shut her eyes all night; sleep had been unattainable with such a momentous and perilous day ahead of her. In just a few short hours she would be unshackled from the charade she had perpetuated for so long, and she, Cormac and Emily would be at liberty to live as a true family at long last. Her whole body was taut with anticipation.

One more duty remained and that was to endure the final breakfast that she and Garrett would share in this house. It was an almost silent meal. He was out of sorts, no doubt injured by her rebuff the previous night. He frowned at the bacon on his plate as though it offended him and did not even open his newspaper, something which he had never failed to do in seven and a half years.

Judging this to be a rather disproportional reaction – her excuse had been a reasonable one, after all – she said tentatively, 'Is something troubling you, Garrett?'

He looked up with a glower. 'I am just mulling over some business dealings I must see to this morning,' he said and relapsed into silence.

She said nothing further. So long as his business dealings took him out of the house, that was all that mattered. She was taken aback, however, when he rose from the table soon afterwards and left the room without even a glance in her direction. He must be even more vexed than she had realised to snub her in such a way. It was the last time she would ever see her husband and the moment felt very unfinished, but there was nothing she could do about it now. He was gone.

Once he had left the house, she was able to complete her preparations for departure. She summoned Lizzie, gave her the letters addressed to her friends, and instructed her to make sure they were not delivered until the following day; the maid took the sealed notes without question. Then she sent a request down to Monsieur Lévêque in the kitchens to put together a parcel of food as she and Emily wished to have a picnic in the gardens. After that, she informed Miss Davison that she desired Emily's company for the day and the governess was therefore free to spend it as she pleased. She found it difficult to mask the guilt she felt; their flight would have many ramifications, and one of them was that this young woman would be without employment on the morrow.

Suppressing her conscience as well as she could, she made her way to Garrett's bedchamber and slipped inside. She could smell his cologne in the air, a scent which she had never been able to separate from that of charred wood since the day he had burned the wooden bird. Going over to the bedside, she slid the engagement ring off her finger and placed it on the pillow along with her farewell letter. All at once she felt lighter, as though the ring had been exerting a heavy pressure on her hand. The tie between her and Garrett was cut; he was no longer her keeper.

Next, she went to the chest of drawers. It took only a minute or two of searching to locate her dear father's pocket watch among Garrett's clothing and possessions. She retrieved the precious item and left the room without looking back.

Her last and most vital duty was to tell Emily the truth. Heart beating in her mouth, she brought her daughter into the drawing room and closed the door. This was the decisive act that would make it all undeniably real.

'Gooseberry, come sit beside me,' she said, sitting on the sofa and drawing Emily to her. 'I have something very important I need to tell you.'

Emily looked up at her with wide blue eyes, exact replicas of Cormac's own. Bridget took a steadying breath.

'Mr Davenport is coming to visit us this morning,' she began and Emily's face lit up. 'There is something I have not told you about him. Oliver Davenport is not his real name. He is actually called Cormac McGovern.'

Emily frowned. 'Why does he need two names?'

'That is hard to explain. He used to be Cormac and then he had to be Oliver for a little while, but now he wants to be Cormac again.'

'Can everybody have two names if they want to?'

'No, it is unusual for a person to change their name. But that is not the important thing I have to tell you. The important thing is that he is your real papa.'

She scrutinised the girl's face for her reaction. Emily stared back unblinkingly.

'Do you understand? The man you know as your papa is not your father. Your father is the man you have known as Mr Davenport but who I have just told you is really called Cormac McGovern.'

She cringed. The poor thing, how on earth could she comprehend it? It was far too confusing.

But Emily, brow furrowed, was trying to repeat what her mother had said. 'Papa is not my papa. Mr Davenport is my papa. Mr Davenport is Cormac McGovern. So Cormac McGovern is my papa.'

She cast an enquiring look at her mother for confirmation.

'Yes, that is correct. Does it make sense to you? Cormac is a friend of mine from a long time ago. We knew each other before you were born. I cannot explain it fully to you now but you will understand when you are older. All you need to know at present is that he is your true father.'

'So is Mr Davenport coming to live here with us?' asked Emily with interest.

'His name is Cormac,' Bridget reminded her gently. 'He is not coming to live here. We are going to go away with him. It is essential that you listen to this part, Emily. We are leaving this house today and we are not coming back. We are going to take a ship to Ireland, the country where your father and I grew up.'

'A ship! I've never been on a ship before. Will my first papa be going on the ship too?'

'No, he will be staying here. I am afraid you won't be able to say goodbye to him for he has left the house for the day and will not be home again until after we are gone. But I have written him a note that says farewell from both of us.'

Emily nodded, betraying no sign of distress at the prospect of never again being in the presence of the man she had believed her whole life to be her father. 'Will Lizzie and Peter be coming with us?'

'No,' Bridget said again and was saddened to perceive that this was a much greater disappointment for the little girl. How significant it was that she had built a stronger emotional connection with the servants than with Garrett. He had utterly failed her as a father figure.

'We won't be taking any servants with us,' Bridget went on. 'And very few possessions. I have already packed a valise with all of the necessary things. However, I shall allow you to bring one plaything with you. Bear in mind you will have to leave the rest behind, so choose wisely.'

'My watercolour box,' said Emily straight away.

Bridget smiled. 'I thought as much.'

She was about to suggest that Emily go and fetch it when there was a quiet knock on the door and Thrussell entered.

'You have a visitor, my lady. Mr Davenport. Shall I tell him you are not at home?'

Her heart leapt. 'You may send him up,' she said, disregarding the fact that the usually unflappable butler looked quite perturbed. It was too early for callers, and a gentleman caller at that. But the time for concealment was past.

Keeping his reservations to himself, Thrussell bowed and exited, and a minute later Cormac appeared in the doorway. He was wearing a nondescript overcoat and he carried a flat cap in one hand and a valise in the other.

'That is the last time I use that name,' he said in a low voice once Thrussell had departed. Setting down the valise and depositing his cap on top of it, he looked across the room at Bridget and their eyes met in identical expressions of joy and hope. The day was here at last to seize their future and be happy together, as they had been prevented from doing for so long.

Of her own volition, Emily got up from the sofa, went over to Cormac and gazed up at him. After a beat of silence, she said, clear and steady, 'Good morning, Papa.'

Stunned, he glanced from Emily to Bridget and back again.

'Good morning, Emily,' he answered and continued hesitantly, 'You know who I am?'

'Yes, Mama has just told me. She said that you and her were friends before I was born and that you're my real papa and that we're all going away on a ship together.'

'And how do you feel about that?'

'I'm excited about going on the ship.' It seemed she was not going to say anything else until her face broke into a brilliant smile and she exclaimed, 'And I'm glad you are my papa!'

She flung her arms around his waist and hugged him. He was so astonished that it took him a second to respond, but then he wrapped his arms around her and bent to kiss the top of her head. It was a beautifully sweet moment. Bridget felt tears come to her eyes as she saw them come to his.

When they separated, he knelt in front of his daughter and grasped her two small hands in his own.

'We have a long journey ahead of us,' he told her seriously. 'At times you might find it hard to bear. Sometimes you might even wish you were back here in this house and had never left. Just know that when you are feeling tired or upset, I'll be there to look after you. I promise to care for you and your mother every step of the way. And after the journey is over, we are going to make a home and be very happy together. Maybe we shall get some chickens for you to look after. Would you like that?'

'I would!' She beamed at the idea of being mistress of a brood of chickens.

He kissed her forehead and stood again. 'Are you ready to go?' he asked Bridget.

'We are. Emily just needs to fetch her watercolour box. I have everything else packed.'

He looked down at Emily. 'Will you go and get the box now?'

'Yes, Papa,' she said and ran from the drawing room.

As soon as she was gone, Bridget and Cormac met in the middle of the room in an emotional embrace. The pressure of his arms around her told her more than any words could say; he was ecstatic.

'I can't believe it,' he murmured into her hair. 'I just cannot believe it.'

They broke apart and at the same time burst into giddy laughter. The distant sound of the front door opening and closing a floor below halted them, but she shook her head at his alarmed expression.

'That will have been Miss Davison,' she reassured him. 'I released her from her duties for the day. She must be gone to call upon an acquaintance.'

He let out a breath, relaxing again.

'I have everything arranged,' he said, pulling three slips of paper out of his pocket. 'These are our tickets for the ship. We shall board it at the river docks and it will take us down around the south coast of England and into the port of Cork in Ireland. From there, we shall travel to Oakleigh. It was the last place my family was seen for certain, so that is where we shall begin our search. Seven and a half years is a long time but the folk there might be able to remember something. Any tiny detail will help us.'

She noticed he made no reference to the fact that they would be within range of the manor house and Lady Courcey, but she said nothing about that for now.

Instead, she said, 'And Raynesworth House? How did you depart without suspicion?'

'At breakfast, I told Lord and Lady Bewley I would be away for the whole day and they should not expect me for dinner this evening. With any luck, it will be late tonight or even tomorrow morning before they grow worried. Once my absence becomes prolonged, they will eventually search my bedchamber and that is when they will discover the letter I have left for them in my writing desk, along with a notebook of poems composed by Oliver.' He sighed. 'I wrote the entire truth. It pains me to imagine how hurt and angry they will be. They have treated me like their own son and I have returned their kindness by robbing them of the bright future they had envisioned: a thriving estate

283

and a new generation on the Bewley family tree. I am leaving them without an heir. My betrayal is deplorable.'

She squeezed his hand. 'But you need to make your own future,' she said. 'Try not to be too regretful. You are doing the right thing.'

He squeezed back. 'I know. But I shall miss them.'

Emily came dashing back into the room then, clutching her watercolour box. 'I'm ready to leave!'

Within minutes, Cormac had retrieved Bridget and Emily's valise from its hiding place beneath Bridget's bed, the watercolour box had been packed into it, and both mother and daughter stood with bonnets on their heads and cloaks fastened around their necks.

Cormac placed his own cap over his fair hair, picked up the two valises, and said simply, 'Let's go.'

Bridget led the way to the staircase. She had taken three steps down before she realised that the hall below was not empty. She froze, gasping in horror.

Garrett stood at the bottom of the stairs, staring up at her with his hands clasped behind his back.

# CHAPTER 33

A flood of dread swept over Bridget. Garrett's countenance was calm, as though it were not an uncommon occurrence for him to catch his wife in the act of running away with another man. Cormac appeared at Bridget's side and she sensed Emily's presence on the step behind them. As Cormac set down the two valises, his face was alight with unflinching determination. He would not give them up without a fight.

Bridget felt the blood pulsing in her ears, her nerves thrilling with fear. Their hope of escape had relied upon leaving without detection, on being gone before anyone realised they were missing. Now Garrett barred the way and he had every power to prevent them from getting past the door. Her shining image of a life with Cormac and Emily flickered like a candle flame in a draught. Don't blow out, she begged it. Please don't blow out.

Garrett spoke, his tone light and conversational. 'Going somewhere?'

'Yes,' said Cormac. 'And you're not going to stop us.'

'I think you will find yourself very much mistaken in that regard. It has been a long time since we were last face to face, Cormac. Or should I call you Mr Davenport now?'

Bridget grimaced. How could he possibly have found out? They had told no one of their plans. Could Lizzie have betrayed them, based on the questionable conduct she had witnessed between her mistress and Mr Davenport?

Trying to keep the shake out of her voice, Bridget asked, 'How did you learn of our secret?'

To her shock, Garrett said, 'Lady Newby. In the strictest confidence of the bedchamber, she imparted to her husband her concern that the relationship between her friend Lady Wyndham and their new acquaintance Mr Davenport might not be altogether proper. Of course, Newby disregarded his vow not to speak of it and came straight to me about the suspicion. A description of Mr Davenport removed all doubt as to who was involved. It appears my wife has not improved her vulgar tastes over the years.'

His lip curled as her heart sank. Lucy had been observing the tiniest clues all this time – if only she had not divulged her misgivings just as they were about to flee. Distressed, Bridget willed her tiny flame to stay alive.

Next to her, Cormac clenched his jaw. 'How did you know we would be leaving this morning?'

'I had Brewer tail you. He watched you purchase sailing tickets and bribed the clerk to tell him the date of departure. Then I was informed as soon as you entered the house a short while ago. That was all that was necessary to bring me to this juncture.' He looked amused. 'You did not genuinely believe you would get away with this, did you?'

'We have every intention of doing so,' said Cormac. 'We will be fleeing this city today as planned.'

'You shall not make it out of Berkeley Square, let alone out of the city. I have done my research on Oliver Davenport. By all accounts, he is the devoted nephew of the esteemed Lord and Lady Bewley, who at present reside at Raynesworth House. Knowing who you really are allows me to lay several charges at your feet: posing under a false identity, stealing the lord and lady's wealth, and now caught in the act of attempted kidnapping. Who knows, perhaps you murdered someone along the way as well. You are a criminal of the lowest degree and there is no chance that the law enforcement will let you sail away without capture. Your appointment with the hangman is inevitable.'

He seemed so steady in his conviction that Bridget too felt persuaded of that horrific outcome. She clutched Cormac's arm as though a constable were already standing below them, ready to drag her lover away from her.

But then Cormac said, 'You think you have halted our escape but you don't bring the power of the law with you. I do not consider you a threat. We'll be walking through that front door whether you stand in our way or not.'

The first sign of anger crossed Garrett's features. 'How dare you presume to thieve from me?' he hissed. 'Bridget and Emily are mine. You cannot just snatch them away.'

'I'm no thief. They are human beings and they are choosing to leave with me.'

'Oh, indeed? Has Emily made her own choice or is she just doing as she is told?'

'She wants to go too,' Cormac said and added boldly, 'She knows who her real father is.'

Garrett's eyes flashed. 'You have been filling her head with nonsense, I see. Emily,' he said in an authoritative manner. 'I am your father. Come down here to me.'

Emily looked uncertainly from Garrett to Cormac. After a long pause, she took a step down to squeeze between Bridget and Cormac on the stairs. Then she slipped her hand into Cormac's. Bridget could have sang with relief at the girl's innocent gesture; she had no inkling of how much it solidified Cormac's position and weakened Garrett's.

Garrett narrowed his gaze. 'That proves nothing except that you have hoodwinked her into believing a lie.'

'It is the truth and you know it,' said Bridget. 'You have known it ever since you first saw her. That is why you have never treated her as your own daughter, why you have always been so cold towards her. She has scarcely received a scrap of affection from you, which just made it all the easier for her to believe the truth. Cormac has been more of a father to her in a few short weeks than you have been in almost seven years of her life.'

'So you are content for her to be branded a bastard?' he said, incredulous. 'An outcast of society? She does not understand now, but in ten years she will hate you for it. Far better for her to remain here where she will grow up to be esteemed rather than shunned.'

Mystified by his persistence, she said, 'Why are you trying to cling on? You have never loved Emily and there is certainly no love between you and me. Why can't you just let us go?'

'It is not a question of love, it is a question of ownership. You and Emily are my wife and child as recognised by the law and I am exercising my rights as the head of this house.'

'Listen to yourself!' Cormac exploded. 'You speak as though they are inanimate objects under your control. They are individuals with real feelings. Why would they contemplate staying with you when you place such little value upon their own wishes?'

'Women and children are not entitled to such considerations.' Garrett dismissed the notion with an impatient jerk of his head. 'That is no argument in support of this ludicrous behaviour.'

'It is the strongest argument,' Bridget countered. 'You care nothing for us and that causes us to feel worthless. Why should we tolerate that anymore when Cormac makes us feel the exact opposite?'

'They deserve to be with someone who will treat them with love and respect,' said Cormac.

Garrett abandoned any further pretence at calmness as he retorted, 'You are just like Mary. You see yourself as equal to us but you're not. You are so far below our social status that the concept is laughable. The sooner you grasp that, the sooner we can put an end to this fiasco.'

Cormac stood as immobile as a block of ice. 'What did you say?'

Garrett fell silent.

Cormac released Emily's hand and took a step down the stairs. 'What did you say?' he repeated. 'What did you say about my sister?'

Bridget sensed the already-tense atmosphere heightening around them. She stared down at her sullen husband and her pale-faced lover. Cormac continued to descend the staircase, approaching Garrett one menacing step at a time.

'Did you know my sister Mary?'

'No, of course not,' Garrett said unconvincingly.

Bridget felt a tug at her arm.

'Mama, what is happening?' Emily whispered.

She shook her head, her gaze still trained on the two men. This confrontation had become about something else entirely but she had no notion what it was. What did Mary have to do with anything?

Cormac clutched the banister so tightly that his knuckles stood out stark white against the smooth, dark wood.

'How did I not realise it before?' he said, fury bubbling in his voice. 'She saw you the day she died. I was there when she saw you on the road. How could I have been so blind?'

'I have no idea what you are talking about,' said Garrett in an attempt at scorn.

'I am talking about *Mary McGovern*. The girl you exploited and then discarded once you lost interest in her!'

Bridget heard this accusation with astonishment and confusion. Garrett had never met Mary in all his time at Oakleigh Manor. 'Cormac, what—'

'Your husband is a hypocrite,' Cormac spat, glancing over his shoulder at her. His eyes were wild with rage. 'He slanders us for producing an illegitimate child when in actual fact he has one of his own.'

Her stomach twisted. The pieces fell sickeningly into place. 'Patrick?'

His livid expression confirmed it. He turned back to Garrett. He was almost at the foot of the stairs now. 'My nephew, Patrick,' he declared, 'is the forsaken son of Lord Wyndham.'

'I do not need to hear any more of this,' said Garrett. 'These lies are irrelevant to the matter at hand. I am going to send the footman to fetch a constable, who will come at once when he learns that I have apprehended a criminal in my own house.'

He looked like he was about to make a hasty retreat from the hall but Cormac was quicker. He launched himself from the last step of the stairs, grabbed Garrett by the front of his coat, and shoved him against the wall. Garrett tried to throw him off but he was unused to physical violence and struggled fruitlessly in Cormac's iron grip. Emily pressed into Bridget's side, frightened. She wrapped her arms around the girl's shoulders to comfort her and watched in alarm as Cormac pinned Garrett in place.

'You are vile!' he snarled. 'You took advantage of my sister, used her for your own pleasure, and then deserted her. She was in love with you but you cast her and your son aside. And when she killed herself, you were the only one on the whole estate who knew why. She died in despair, she died because of *you*.' He was shouting now, his hands twisted in Garrett's tailored clothes.

'Admit what you did! Admit you are the reason my sister is no longer alive!'

At that moment, the inner door into the hall opened and Lizzie came through, looking terrified. When she saw her master pinioned against the wall, she turned as though to run for help.

'Stay where you are, Lizzie,' Bridget said from the top of the stairs, her speech much steadier than she had expected. 'We do not want to involve anyone else in this.'

Lizzie stood still, wide-eyed at the entangled men before her. Cormac did not acknowledge her presence. Blue eyes locked upon hazel ones, scorching with condemnation.

'Admit it,' he growled.

Garrett sagged in his grasp. 'Yes, it was me.'

Cormac drew back an arm and punched Garrett in the face. Then he let go of him and Garrett slid to the floor, blood dripping from his nose down his chin.

'She did not understand,' he said thickly as Cormac stood over him, chest heaving. 'She thought we could be together but we came from conflicting backgrounds too disparate to reconcile. It didn't matter how I felt. My father would never have accepted her or the boy. I hurt her to drive her away. There was no other option. But I never dreamed she would take such drastic measures…'

Bridget endeavoured to absorb the hideous implications of Garrett's confession. His every action in this tale had been despicable. He had misled Mary and deceived Bridget by courting both women at the same time. He had fathered an illegitimate child and shirked all responsibility for the boy. He had cruelly abandoned Mary, an act which made her so desperate and wretched that in the end she took her own life. Bridget felt bile rising in her throat at the horrifying grief her husband had caused.

And yet, there was something in his voice, a waver which told her that perhaps he was not as pitiless as he seemed. Did he feel regret? Was Mary the woman he had spoken of – had he borne a sincere love for her, far stronger than anything he had ever felt for Bridget? But had he allowed himself to be ruled by society just as Bridget had been forced to do, against his own true desire?

That by no means excused his conduct. A woman was dead because of him. She had been a sister, a daughter, a mother, and now she was nothing but a corpse buried in cold ground.

Mirroring her thoughts, Cormac said, his demeanour deceptively controlled, 'Her death is on your hands. Drastic measures, you say. Were those measures suicide? Or murder?'

Garrett gaped. 'Are you asking me whether I killed her?'

'Hanging is an unusual method for a woman. Drowning is more common. Did you do it? Did you take steps to remove her as an inconvenience from your life?' His inflection rose ferociously towards the end, his restraint slipping again.

The look of horror on Garrett's face was more eloquent than any words he could have spoken, but he still stuttered, 'I would—*never*—she was—how dare you—I loved her!'

'Did you communicate with her at all on the estate?' Cormac demanded. 'Did you say anything to her that would have driven her to choose the path she did?'

'No.' Garrett's deep breath came through his mouth, his nose having become clogged with drying blood. 'Our only contact was when we passed each other on that road. At first, I was so fearful that she would reveal our connection, but after my temper cooled I found myself recollecting the strength of our feelings for each other. I did contemplate going to see her.' He slumped against the wall. 'And then that lady's maid brought the news of her death.'

292

Bridget could recall those incidents at Oakleigh so clearly. Garrett's anger with Brewer over a trifling rip in his glove. Ellen imparting Mary's tragic story through her tears. Bridget herself becoming distraught for Cormac at the loss of his sister while Garrett, she had thought, looked on coldly – when in actual fact he was concealing his own grief over the death of his lover.

Cormac crossed his arms. 'So you claim you were sincerely in love with her?'

'Yes, God help me, I was.'

'But you rejected her anyway.'

'It hadn't been my intention.' Garrett swiped a knuckle across his upper lip, smearing the blood. With a glance up at Bridget, he said, 'She was the reason I chose an Irish bride. I thought I could maintain our association in a limited way. My plan was to undertake an outward marriage with a lady who would tie me to Ireland, and continue to pay the baker to look the other way when I visited Mary in her room above the bakery. But the arrival of Patrick proved to be a rude awakening. I perceived that Mary would not be content to see me on the odd occasion when I happened to be in Dublin. The connection was too dangerous to sustain any longer, despite our mutual passion. I had to get far away from her, and decided to return to London for good. Of course, it was too late to back out of my engagement then.'

Bridget knew she ought not feel aggrieved. After all, she had long ago admitted to herself that she didn't love this man, and she was right now in the process of leaving him for another. And yet, his bald disclosure stung acutely. She had been selected from a throng of hopeful misses with the indifference of one picking a piece of fresh fish. Recalling her own genuine joy at the time, she felt like a fool. Injured tears sprang to her eyes.

'You goddamned swine,' said Cormac. 'Did you have no regard for anyone but yourself? You squandered the happiness of two women, not to mention two innocent children.'

'Children,' Garrett repeated. 'They have only been a blight on my existence. My first son forever out of reach because of his ignominious birth. My second son defeated by disease before he had hardly begun to live. And my "daughter"' – he could not keep the misery from his expression – 'a girl I knew was not mine but who resembled Mary so much that it pained me to even look at her. Had circumstances been different, she might have been our own child.'

Bridget's head swam. All along, she had assumed that Garrett detested Emily on account of her likeness to Cormac – whose only sibling to share his fair hair and blue eyes had been Mary. This revelation shed Garrett's attitude towards Emily in a new and unsettling light.

At the same time, another thought occurred to her. The night Garrett had bedded her in January, he had said he desired a son he could acknowledge. She had believed it to be a derogatory reference to Emily. Now she comprehended that he had meant Patrick.

'Children,' Garrett said again, 'have been my curse.'

Against her will, she felt a ripple of compassion for him. Cormac, however, succumbed to no such sentiment.

'I would beat you into a pulp if my daughter were not present,' he said with cold hostility. 'You are worse than the rats in the streets. It is you who should face the hangman's noose, not I. There is not the remotest possibility that I shall allow Bridget and Emily to remain within your sphere of influence. I am going to take them away with me today and you will never see them again. Do not even think of coming after us. If you do, I will expose you for the blackguard you are, even if it means condemning myself in the process. I know your secret and I can ruin you. Think hard about your reputation before you choose to follow us.'

He began to step away but, in the instant when his back was turning, Garrett leapt up and flailed at him. His fist connected squarely with Cormac's jaw. Incensed, Cormac retaliated with a blow to Garrett's stomach that knocked him back into the dresser. Lizzie squeaked in fright as the piece of furniture shook at the impact. Garrett wheezed for breath, winded, and yet he wore an insane smile as he steadied himself on the dresser.

'You believe you are in a position to make threats,' he panted, with the air of someone saving his trump card until last, 'but you are not. Did you think I would walk in here to confront you without a scheme in place? Have you not thought to wonder at the whereabouts of our ever-present butler? After Brewer informed me that you had entered the building, I sent both him and Thrussell to Raynesworth House. By this stage, Lord and Lady Bewley will be aware of the entire situation. I imagine they won't take too kindly to having been so deceived and will send constables to the river docks to intercept you. Perhaps they are even now giving the order.' He looked triumphant. 'You do not have a hope of setting foot aboard that ship.'

Cormac wasted no more time with words. He swung out at Garrett with such force to the side of his head that he knocked him out cold. Garrett slumped to the floor, ending in an awkward, half-sitting position against the dresser. Cormac did not spare him another glance as he ran back up the stairs to where Bridget and Emily stood frozen.

'We need to hurry,' he said. 'If Lord and Lady Bewley truly have dispatched constables to the docks, then we are now in a race to reach the river before them. We must get there with all possible speed.'

Bridget swallowed the dozen things she wanted to say after such an encounter and said, 'The carriage will get us there the fastest. Lizzie,' she called down to the maid. 'Ask Sawyer to bring the carriage around at once. I am afraid we cannot answer any questions you may have but please know that my husband has no reason to dismiss you. His anger is only directed at us and, with any luck, we shall be gone far beyond his reach by the time he wakes up. Now, I beg you, send for the carriage.'

Obedient as ever, Lizzie glanced at the unconscious form of her master and darted from the hall.

'We have to be quick,' Cormac reiterated and stretched out his arms to Emily.

She shrank away, trying to hide behind Bridget's skirts.

'I know you must be frightened by what you just saw, *a stór*,' he said in a soothing tone. 'I did not want to do what I did but he is a bad man and my temper got the better of me. I swear you have nothing to fear now. Do you remember I promised to look after you?'

She nodded, biting the tip of her tongue in Bridget's own characteristic gesture of anxiety.

'I still hold to that promise. You have no reason to be scared. But we are in a very great hurry now and we must make haste if we want to catch our ship before it sails away. Will you come with me?'

He reached out again and this time she stepped into his embrace. He lifted her up, squeezed her and then looked at Bridget. Alarm filled his taut features.

'Let's get out of here,' he said. 'Can you carry the valises?'

'Yes,' she said, picking them up. They descended the stairs and disappeared out the front door, departing from the house where she had denounced her mother, lost a child, endured years of misery, and had just learned that her unfaithful husband had been accountable for a needless death.

She was not sorry to leave.

# CHAPTER 34

Cormac's knuckles ached and he could feel a bruise developing on his jaw where Garrett had hit him. He rubbed the spot tenderly, irked that he had allowed himself to be caught off guard.

They were in the carriage, clattering through the streets of London as fast as the coachman dared. Cormac sat across from Bridget and Emily, who both had their hands clasped in their laps. Neither of them looked hopeful or excited anymore. Bridget's gaze was focused out the window and Emily was staring at the floor of the carriage. They were both doing their best to avoid eye contact with him.

He experienced a piercing stab at his heart as he imagined what they must be thinking of him right now. Where had the passionate lover and doting father gone? They had caught a glimpse of his darker side, the part of him that had been compelled to come to the forefront when he had worked for Cunningham. He had hoped to keep that dangerous man forever hidden from them but in the altercation with Garrett he had let his buried aggression take over. No wonder they could not look at him.

And yet, how could he have curbed his fury when confronted with the man who had destroyed his sister's life? Mary had been a vivacious girl whose greatest failing had been to fall for someone above her station. She had believed that love could transcend social class but Garrett had crushed her, throwing away her affection and leaving her to raise their child alone. Her spirit had been broken – Cormac had seen that in her muted manner following her return to Oakleigh – but perhaps in time it would have mended if she had not come face to face with her false lover on the estate. The shock of seeing him, after never expecting to lay eyes on him again, must have been enormous. His fists clenched at the thought of his sister ending her life on account of such a villain. Even now, he wanted to go back to Wyndham House and rip Garrett limb from limb.

But the fiend was inconsequential now; there was nothing he could do or say to bring Mary back or make amends for his reprehensible actions. Cormac would gain nothing from him except the satisfaction of his violent urges, which he must suppress if he did not want to risk scaring Bridget and Emily further. He wished desperately for either of them to look in his direction. If he could only say something that would remind them of the person he really was, of why they had been willing to run away with him in the first place, then maybe they would be able to forget the frightening scene they had just witnessed.

However, when he spoke over the noise of the rattling carriage, it was in a tone of brisk efficiency. 'We must remember to go by different names until we are safely on the ship and away from the docks. I will be Mr Jack Marsh. You, Bridget, shall be my wife, Molly, and you, Emily, shall be our daughter, Lizzie, just like the maid back at the house. We must not answer to our true names until we are out of harm's way. Do you both understand?'

They nodded. Emily continued to stare at the floor but Bridget cast him a quick glance before looking away again. Was she having second thoughts? Smothering the panic inside him, he said no more and silence resumed in the carriage.

At last, they reached the docks on the River Thames. He was relieved to see hundreds of dockworkers, sailors and passengers milling about; the crowd would make it easier for them to pass through unnoticed. The carriage had barely stopped moving before he had thrown open the door and jumped out, snagging his coat sleeve in his hurry. The air was full of the smells and sounds of the busy dock: the whiff of fish and the stink of the Thames, the shouts of dockworkers and the creak of moored ships.

Peter was sitting up front with Sawyer. He tossed down the two valises and Cormac caught them deftly.

'Thank you,' he said. 'I hope you will not get into trouble for doing this.'

The coachman winked. 'From what I heard, you gave the master a right blow to the head and he ain't likely to wake up for a while. I reckon he'll never know we was gone.'

'Look after the lady and the young miss,' said Peter, saluting. 'We're heartily fond of them. Her ladyship's the kindest woman I ever met, always looked out for my ailing mother. And there's nuffin but sweetness in the little one.'

'I will take very good care of them both,' promised Cormac. 'My thanks again.'

He returned to the door of the carriage and helped Bridget and Emily step out into the sunlight. The day was breezy but dry, good conditions for travelling on the water. Together, all three of them turned to stare at their vessel. Larger than the one on which he had stowed away, it soared above them, its rigging whipping in the breeze. Two gangways extended from it to the dock, one for wealthy passengers who were ushered aboard without scrutiny or delay, the other for the noticeably less affluent. A line of these folk stretched from the end of the lower class gangway across the dock and a ticket inspector stood at the top of the queue, scrutinising each passenger before permitting them to pass by.

Cormac had not purchased upper class tickets. That level of luxury was behind them now, and it would have been presumptuous to spend an excessive amount of the Bewleys' money. In addition, he had guessed it more likely that any pursuers would seek them in the more genteel section of the ship, given Bridget and Emily's status. Now, he doubted the wisdom of his decision and wondered how attentive the ticket inspector was to his duties.

Nervous, he guided Bridget and Emily to the end of the queue. He was pleased to note that a flicker of excitement had crossed Emily's features at the sight of the big ship. Perhaps her sense of adventure would eclipse all her qualms. Bridget held Emily's hand and stared straight ahead; her face was grave but she seemed worried rather than hostile.

The queue inched its way across the dock. He kept glancing over his shoulder but the noise and activity around them seemed no greater than what could be expected. The arrival of the constabulary would surely cause a commotion that would be conspicuous above the rest of the hubbub.

Would Lord and Lady Bewley accompany the constables, to see him arrested? He quailed at the prospect of facing the elderly couple. His final transgression against them had been to take enough money to assist his search for his family after they arrived in Ireland. He loathed himself for his dishonesty. But they were his second family, and he must prioritise his first.

When there was only a handful of people ahead of them, he withdrew the tickets from his pocket. A knot of anxiety was growing in his stomach. What if the constables were already here and merely waiting for them to reveal themselves to the ticket inspector? Perhaps they had given the man a description and he would raise the alarm at the sight of them. There would be no hope of escape in such a scenario and he would be heading for the gallows or, at best, a prison cell for the rest of his life.

Swallowing hard, he stepped forwards with Bridget and Emily. There was just one group left in front of them now, a mother with three or four children swarming around her and a baby crying in her arms. The inspector skimmed their tickets and hurried them through, looking like he wanted to be rid of the screaming child. Then he beckoned to Cormac, hand outstretched. Cormac set the valises on the ground, smoothed out the tickets and handed them over.

The man had a stubbly chin which he scratched absent-mindedly as he examined the tickets. 'Name?'

'Jack Marsh,' said Cormac, letting his Irish brogue become pronounced. No one with a cultured accent would be expected in this line of passengers. 'And this here's my wife, Molly.'

Bridget fixed a pleasant smile upon her face. The man nodded once at her and then looked back at Cormac.

'That's some shiner you got there,' he remarked, nodding at Cormac's jaw.

He didn't miss a beat, jabbing his booted toe into the side of one of the valises. 'Fell on me when I was taking it down off the top of the wardrobe,' he said with the air of someone used to being accident-prone. 'That'll learn me to move more quickly next time.'

The man gave a short laugh and handed back the tickets. 'On you go,' he said and stood back to let them pass.

Cormac picked up the valises, shepherded Bridget and Emily onto the gangway, and stepped onto it himself. When he looked back, the inspector had already turned away to scrutinise the next person's ticket. He had not even glanced at Emily.

They made their way down to the steerage area below decks. Berths lined the walls, most of them already occupied by other travellers. Cormac found an empty one and stowed the valises beneath it. The berth next to them had been taken by the woman with the innumerable children. Her baby had stopped crying and was drowsing in her arms.

'We made it,' said Bridget in disbelief.

'We did,' said Cormac but the knot in his stomach did not go away. He wouldn't feel easy until the ship had pulled away from the dock and they were out on open water.

'May I go up to look out over the dock?' Emily asked eagerly.

'Not just yet,' he said. 'Let's wait until the ship is moving.'

'Oh, please—' she began, but her plea was drowned out by the sudden sound of shouting above deck.

Cormac and Bridget exchanged looks of panic.

'Oh, no,' she moaned.

He knew he only had a few seconds in which to act. He caught hold of Emily's shoulders and made her look straight into his eyes.

'Listen to me, *a stór*,' he said swiftly. 'We are going to play a game but I need you to make sure you follow all the rules. You are going to sit over there with that family and pretend that the nice lady is your mother. You cannot answer to the name of Emily. You have to make believe that you are Lizzie, just for a little while longer. Your mother and I are going to find different berths and pretend to be other people too. You must act like you do not know us. This will only be for a short time and then we can be together again. Do you understand everything I've just told you?'

Her voice was faint as she said, 'Yes, Papa.'

He looked over at the woman with all the children. She was staring at him in shock; she had overheard everything he had said.

'Please,' he entreated. 'I am begging you, help me protect my family. Please allow my daughter to sit with your children.'

'I don't think—' she faltered.

'*Please*,' he said again. He flung an arm out to indicate Bridget. 'This is her mother. I swear we are both just trying to do what's best for our daughter.'

'It's true,' said Bridget with deep sincerity.

The woman hesitated before saying, 'So long as it won't get us into any trouble.'

'It won't,' he said and hoped to God he was speaking the truth. 'Thank you very much, I am so grateful.' He urged Emily to join the family at the next berth. 'Keep your bonnet on and your hair tucked into your cloak. Remember, the most important rule is that you are called Lizzie. Your mother and I are going to move away now but we will come back to you as soon as the game is over, I promise.'

He and Bridget both kissed Emily and walked away from her.

'They will be looking for a couple with a child,' he said. 'We must split up too, act like we are single travellers. I'll join those men in the corner. Will you go to the women over by the stairs?'

She nodded, the tip of her tongue caught between her teeth. They touched hands and separated. The steerage quarters were loosely divided into sections for men, women, and families. He reached the men's area and sat on a vacant berth, just as the disturbance above deck grew louder and three men appeared in the hatch at the top of the steerage stairs. Everyone fell silent. One of the men was the stubbly-chinned ticket inspector; the other two were uniformed constables. Cormac surreptitiously wiped his hands on the dirty floor and ran them through the hair that was visible below the edges of his cap. His fair hair would be a key element of his description; dulling it would make it harder for them to recognise him. He hoped Emily would be a good girl and keep her own hair hidden too.

The two constables descended the stairs and began marching along the family berths, peering at the passengers. Every so often, they paused and asked somebody a question but Cormac was too far away to hear the murmured responses. He could just make out Emily across the crowded space – she appeared to be holding a whispered conversation with the child next to her, but she stopped as the constables approached her berth. They were now near enough for him to distinguish what they were saying.

'These all your children?' one of them addressed the woman cradling the baby.

'Yes,' she answered.

The other constable squinted at the children. 'What're your names?' he said gruffly.

'Peggy.'

'Tommy.'

'Rosie.'

'Danny.'

'Lizzie.'

Cormac held his breath. The constable examined each child for a long moment and then, with a grunt, turned away.

The two men continued to walk along the berths but they seemed to be losing interest now, only bestowing cursory glances upon the rest of the passengers. They barely looked at Cormac as they passed by. It became obvious that their aim had been to inspect all the children in the steerage area – they did not expect to find the false Oliver Davenport without the kidnapped girl at his side. Having failed to locate their quarry, they climbed back up the stairs and retreated out the hatch with the ticket inspector.

Cormac didn't move; he would not allow himself to believe they were safe yet. Thankfully, neither Bridget nor Emily came to look for him. A hum of chatter rose up as the passengers discussed what had just happened. He waited but nobody else came down into the steerage area except for a few straggling travellers.

After many long minutes which seemed like hours, he felt the ship's steam engine rumble into life somewhere in the bowels of the vessel.

He started to hope.

Quite a bit more time passed, but at last there was the unmistakable sensation of movement and he knew that the ship was pulling away from the dock.

A grin split his face from ear to ear. It was as though a hand of iron had been clenching inside his chest and now it had released him. They were free.

He went to Bridget first; she threw her arms around him with a happy laugh. They returned to Emily, who was still sitting on the berth and playing a clapping game with the boy beside her. She ceased clapping at their appearance.

'Our game is over now, *a stór*,' Cormac said. 'Well done, you played it brilliantly.'

She looked up at them. 'I can be Emily again?'

'Yes, forever and ever,' said Bridget.

Emily jumped up and they enfolded themselves in a joyful, three-way hug. It was overwhelming to register the complete absence of tension. They were safely on their way and, Cormac was relieved to note, it seemed that all past transgressions were to be forgotten.

'Now may I go up to look out?' Emily appealed, hopping up and down in excitement.

'In just one moment.' Cormac turned to the mother who had helped save them from detection. She was observing their elation with great interest. 'I cannot thank you enough for what you have done for me and my family today. We are in your debt, Mrs...?'

'Nancy McLoughlin.' She contemplated his words and then waved them away. 'I don't know what I just involved myself in, but I can see the happiness the three of you share so I'm sure it was nuffin God'll punish me for. You ain't in anyone's debt.'

Both Cormac and Bridget expressed their sincere thanks once again. Then they left the woman to her brood of children and climbed the steerage stairs with Emily.

Up on the deck, the sun dazzled them after the dimness below and the breeze was fresh on their cheeks. The busy city of London lay on both sides of the river as they sailed down the middle of the Thames towards the open sea. Emily was in raptures at the sight and ran to the gunwale to stare all around her.

'Are we safe now?' Bridget asked.

'I believe so, yes,' said Cormac, his pulse still thumping with the euphoria of liberation.

'I heard the two constables muttering to each other before they went back up the stairs. They thought we must not have boarded the ship yet and were going back out to search the dock. What do you think they will do when they cannot find us?'

He gazed out across the water. 'After they eventually conclude that we are not hiding somewhere in London, I suppose there is always the outside possibility that they will choose to follow us to Ireland.'

Her forehead creased. 'And if so, should we not expect them to apprehend us? The most obvious place for us to go is exactly where we are going. What is there to stop a troop of constables from seizing us at Oakleigh?'

'I cannot rule out that scenario with absolute certainty, but I do believe that it is unlikely. A pursuit across the sea would put a substantial strain on their resources. In all probability, Lord and Lady Bewley will find the law enforcement less than willing to cooperate and the chase will peter out. Having said that, it would be a very different state of affairs if we were ever to return to England. I am positive that we, or I at any rate, can never set foot in this country again.'

'And Garrett?' she said tentatively.

A wave of emotion washed over Cormac as he grieved afresh for the sister he had lost. His rage rose again but he pushed it back down.

'Garrett is no longer a concern for us. When he wakes up and discovers that we have indeed escaped, he'll know he has been defeated. He will want to hide from society for a few days as the news spreads that his wife and child have left him. After that humiliation, I doubt whether he will dare to risk the further embarrassment of trying and failing to bring you back from Ireland as well.'

'Is that what you truly believe?'

'It is. And should I prove to be wrong, no matter. We shall deal with him if the situation arises. Until then, I advise you not to worry.'

He put his arm around her shoulders and kissed her on the temple. He hoped he had sufficiently eased her qualms, although he was not quite so unconcerned about the danger as he had led her to believe. It was very feasible that they might be followed to Ireland. But better for her to be free from that fear for now.

Without warning, she said, 'I would like to visit my mother when we go back to Oakleigh.'

He dropped his arm.

'I am aware that she is the very last person you would wish to see,' Bridget went on steadily. 'However, ever since you decided we should go back there, I have known that this is something I must do. I cannot say that I am ready to make amends, but she is ill and I want to see her, even just once. She is still my mother, after all.'

He looked down at her. Her dark brown eyes stared back. It was so hard for him to believe that she and Lady Courcey were the same flesh and blood. How had such a hardhearted, malicious woman produced a daughter capable of so much compassion? Lady Courcey could go to hell and rot there for all he cared; he had no desire to be in her presence ever again, except perhaps to witness her demise.

But Bridget's gaze was earnest; this was important to her.

He sighed. 'Very well.'

She squeezed his arm. 'We ought not dwell on it for now. Let us enjoy the beautiful day and rejoice in our release.'

They turned their attention back to Emily who was off in her own world enacting various scenarios on her mighty vessel. Alternating between a captain, a pirate and a shipwreck survivor, she sailed the unknown lands, fighting off mermaids and sharks and searching for buried treasure. Cormac felt a rush of affection for the little girl and knew how fortunate he was to be standing here at this moment with the woman he loved and the child he adored, rather than being marched away in shackles by the constables. Less than an hour ago, that prospect had been frighteningly close to becoming a reality, but their luck had held out and they were now free to be a family together. While Garrett lived, there was no chance that they could ever be married but, other than the official ceremony, they were as much a husband and wife now as it was possible to be. It would be nice, he thought, to have something to symbolise that union.

He glanced down at his coat sleeve, which was fraying a little at the end. He dimly recollected catching it on the door frame as he jumped out of the carriage in his earlier haste at the dock. Smiling to himself, he started pulling at the threads, working them out of the sleeve. Hoping Bridget would see the humour in what he was about to offer her, he twisted and knotted the threads together. Once he had fashioned a smooth circle, he took her left hand and slid the circle onto her ring finger. She stared at it in surprise and then beamed up at him.

'It is plain I have not much to offer you,' he said, 'but will you be mine?'

'I will,' she said. 'Now and forever.'

They kissed, as though they had just been pronounced man and wife at the altar. When he pulled away, he noticed that her brow was furrowed.

'What is the matter?' he asked.

'Nothing, really,' she said, lowering her gaze to the ring. 'I just have one last secret to impart. Since the day we were reacquainted in London, I have wondered whether to share it with you. Now I have resolved to do so. After this, you will know everything in my soul.'

He did not know whether to feel eager or wary. 'What is it?'

'I have not told you before because I always feel such intense regret when I think of it and I did not want to burden you with that feeling too. It was a case of bad luck and bad timing. Ten minutes might have made a lifetime of difference. But I suppose it is of no great consequence now.' She twisted the ring around her finger. Then she looked up and said, 'I ran after you. The day you were banished from Oakleigh, I told you I was going to stay with Garrett, but as soon as I realised I had made the wrong decision I ran all the way to your mother's cottage, desperately hoping you were still there. But I was too late, you were gone and I had no way of knowing where. So I had to go back to Garrett and you never knew I had chosen you after all.'

He closed his eyes, imagining what might have been. If he had stayed at the cottage just a little longer... If she had discovered her mother's betrayal just a little sooner... They would have spent these seven and a half years together rather than apart. He would have seen Emily growing up. They might have had more children. Neither of them would have had to suffer the pain and loss they had been forced to endure. There would have been other hardships, needless to say, but they would have faced them hand in hand as partners, as a family, not alone and not in fear. It was a wonderful image but it was something he had always believed to have been impossible for them then. And yet here was Bridget telling him that they had been tantalisingly close to achieving it, that it had been mere moments from their grasp. She was right, it was a burden to bear this knowledge, to know that those long years need not have unravelled the way they had.

He opened his eyes. She was biting the tip of her tongue in her own typical way.

'Should I have told you?' she asked, searching his face for his reaction.

He gave her a sad smile. 'Of course. It is right for me to know.'

'I have debated for a long time over whether to tell you. I know it has no bearing now but...'

'But it is important all the same,' he finished for her. 'It is a hard truth to acknowledge, that what we lost was almost at our fingertips.' He took her hand and rubbed his thumb over the thread ring, an intoxicating sense of jubilation coursing through his veins. 'But we got it back in the end. And that is what matters most.'

## What's Next

Thank you for reading! To nab some extra reading material, join the **Susie Murphy Readers' Club** on www.susiemurphywrites.com, where you will receive a collection of six free short stories. The first five are prequels to A Class Apart, while the sixth is a companion story to A Class Entwined. Do you remember the scene where Bridget was stunned to see Cormac appear at the party at Radcliffe House? The companion story tells that scene from Cormac's point of view! By joining the Susie Murphy Readers' Club, you will also be the first to get updates about A Matter of Class, including book release details and other bonus content.

Did you enjoy this book? If you did, please help other readers discover Bridget and Cormac's story by leaving an honest review about A Class Entwined on Amazon and/or Goodreads. A short review will make a huge difference in spreading the word about A Matter of Class.

The next novel in the series is A Class Forsaken, available now.

# Acknowledgements

My sincere thanks to Averill Buchanan for her terrific editorial feedback, and to Andrew Brown at Design for Writers for producing another gorgeous cover. Between them both, I knew my book was in very safe hands.

One of the most special things about writing and publishing is joining a community of people who are so kind and generous when it comes to everything about books. I can't say thank you enough to each and every person who has spread the word about A Class Apart or A Class Entwined, be it in big or little ways. I am especially grateful to the following for helping to give my novels a push out into the world: Hazel Gaynor, Pam Lecky, Ashley O'Melia, John Butler, Deirdre O'Toole, Eoin Hoctor, Fran Curry, Anne O'Grady, Shane Cahill, Yvette Poufong, Laura Whitmore, Vanessa O'Loughlin, Mary Tod, Heather Webb, The Book Trail, Anne Mendez, Linda Green, Claire Bridle, Valerie Whitford, Lisa Redmond, Stacie Tyson, Suzanne Leopold, Kathleen Kelly, Jenny Q, Diana G. Tierney, Lauralee Jacks, Margaret Cook. You are all legends.

My deepest gratitude goes to my husband, family and friends for their enthusiastic encouragement. I am incredibly lucky to be surrounded by such wonderful support.

Lastly, thank YOU for reading. It's such an amazing feeling to have actual readers, and I appreciate every single response, whether it's writing a review, interacting online, or sending me a message. I'm so happy that you are following Bridget and Cormac's journey and I already can't wait to show you what happens next...!

## Get in Touch

www.susiemurphywrites.com
www.facebook.com/susiemurphywrites
www.twitter.com/susiemwrites
www.instagram.com/susiemurphywrites
www.tiktok.com/@susiemurphywrites